Changeling Press. LLC

ChangelingPress.com

Taken by the Maine Coon/
Taken by the Huldra Duet
Paranormal Women's Fiction
Megan Slayer

Taken by the Maine Coon/
Taken by the Huldra Duet
Paranormal Women's Fiction
Megan Slayer

ISBN: 978-1-60521-951-6

Publisher:
Changeling Press LLC
315 N. Centre St.
Martinsburg, WV 25404
ChangelingPress.com

Printed in the U.S.A.

Editor: Jean Cooper
Cover Artist: Bryan Keller

The individual stories in this anthology have been previously released in E-Book format.

Table of Contents

Taken by the Maine Coon (Taken 9)
A Paranormal Women's Fiction Novel
Megan Slayer

A big cat and a woman without magic could just be the right combination.

Meela Durning swears she doesn't belong in Eerie. She's not magical. Never has been, but she's the child of paranormals. When she's forced to return to Eerie to sort out the problems from her past, she finds a big, fluffy cat. The animal lover in her has to make sure the feline gets home. He could be missing. Someone has to want him, right?

Aslan Maine has known from the moment he met Meela that she was destined to be his. He's seen her in his dreams. When she picks him up to return him to his rightful home, he can't hide his secret any longer. He's no ordinary cat!

She can't believe her eyes when the fluffball she rescued shifts into the sexiest man she's ever seen. When he offers her forever, she's got to decide if she deserves to be alone or to have a future with the handsome shifter.

If she can survive her past, she can have him. Right?

Chapter One

"Christ, I'm tired." Meela Durning stretched and cracked her back. She shook her head, then closed her laptop. She hadn't spoken to anyone in particular. There wasn't anyone there to hear her. Just as well. When she'd had someone there to listen, he hadn't listened. Hadn't wanted to be there, either.

She'd grown used to being alone.

Tonight, she didn't want to be by herself. It wasn't like she could poof a man into existence. She'd wanted to try that for ages, but with no magical abilities, a spell was out of the question. She supposed she could summon one, but that only worked in her dreams, and she knew it had nothing to do with magic. Just her overly active imagination.

She shrugged, then stretched her legs before standing. The man of her dreams might only be in said dreams, but that didn't matter. He couldn't let her down that way. Didn't have faults. He wanted to be there. Wanted to please her. Wanted to be with her.

Unlike her ex -- the rotten troll.

She sighed and pushed in her chair. She didn't even have a fish. She'd wanted a cat, but the building manager didn't permit animals that had fur. Ridiculous rules.

She checked that the apartment door was locked, then picked up her phone before switching off the lights. She padded into the bedroom. Once she tossed the phone onto the bed, she made her way into the bathroom. She stripped out of her shirt, and bra, then her jeans and panties, returning to the bedroom long enough to don her sleep shirt. She brushed her teeth, but her thoughts turned to the man of her dreams.

She paused, mid-brushing. *Man of her dreams.*

That sounded so silly. The only time he'd ever appeared physically, she'd been asleep.

A vision of him formed in her mind. Tall, muscled, but not huge... thick dark-blond hair with just a bit of shag to it. Enough to remind her of a superhero, with his hair blowing in the breeze. Twinkling green eyes, a wicked smile that hinted at mischief, but he'd been a gentleman. A dusting of hair from his navel to below the belt.

She'd never seen his cock, but she'd felt it. Heat washed over her. She swore she'd felt his hands on her body, the way he'd touched her and kissed every inch of her. He took care of her. Treated her like a treasure. Like she had worth.

She knew damn well she had value. It'd taken her years to figure that out, but now that she knew, she wasn't about to let anyone tell her otherwise. She refused to be a doormat again.

Meela finished in the bathroom and switched off the light before crawling between the sheets. Something in her bed vibrated. For a moment, she thought she'd left a toy from the night before. When a rectangle lit up beneath the blankets, she remembered - - her phone. She must've lost it under the blankets when she climbed into bed. She retrieved the irksome device and checked the notifications.

An email. Now what? She swiped to retrieve the message. *Overdrawn.*

"You have to be kidding me," she muttered. She swiped to her banking app. Sure enough, the money she'd expected to be deposited there... wasn't. Her ex-husband hadn't bothered to pay alimony. Again.

She scrubbed one hand across her forehead, then checked her texts. The asshole hadn't messaged her. Hadn't bothered to let her know he'd be a bigger asshole by not paying. She did the math in her head. This was the sixth month in a row he hadn't bothered to deposit the money. The fucker.

She switched back to her banking app and shifted money from her savings to the checking to cover her bills. Once satisfied everything would be paid out of her wages from the software company, she brought up the chat box to her lawyer.

Eerie, Ohio, wasn't exactly her favorite place to go. She didn't belong there. She had paranormal blood, but no magic. Couldn't conjure, summon, wake the dead... wasn't a shifter, vampire, necromancer, faerie... Nothing about her was extraordinary. She'd simply been the child of a conjurer and a celebrity psychic. All she had was her bloodline.

But if she wanted to meet with her lawyer, she'd have to go back to the place of her birth. She'd have to head back to Eerie. Would have to talk to Norm Slone, divorce lawyer gnome. His name had a distinctive ring to it. No one forgot him. Thankfully, he could be a junkyard dog in the courtroom, too.

She opened the chat box and sent him a message.

Need to meet with you. Tiernan isn't paying alimony. Sixth month in a row. Tired of being shafted. Help?

She hit SEND, then darkened the phone and tossed it onto the side table. If Norm Slone had time for her, he'd let her know in the morning. Besides, she didn't want to give her ex any extra space in her mind. He owned too much as it was. Some days, he lived there rent free. Those were the days she second-guessed divorcing him. She'd loved the troll once, hadn't she? Thought they could make a future together, right? A woman with no magic and a troll could make things work, in theory. The more she considered her past, the faster she remembered the reason she'd left Tiernan. He'd only married her under the assumption she'd inherit money from her parents.

Wrong.

After the wedding, when he found out she was penniless, he'd walked out. He claimed he wasn't interested in her any longer. He had to work late. He'd made friends with other people. Their lives were going in different directions. Other days, he simply didn't speak to her.

He'd packed his belongings up in the middle of the night and walked out.

Her head ached. She'd lost a dozen years of her life to him. Years she could've been happy. Could've been single but making the best of her situation. Instead, she'd tried her damnedest to keep the marriage together. Tried to make herself loveable to him again.

What a waste. He wasn't going to love her then or now... or ever. She had to stop living in the past and thinking about what wasn't going to happen in order to focus on the future -- whatever future she had.

She switched off the light and snuggled in her blankets. She might not be living with anyone, but then again, she didn't have to share the bed. Didn't have to argue with anyone. Didn't have to explain herself. But the loneliness overwhelmed her at times.

She closed her eyes and allowed herself to forget the day, forget her situation for a little while. Forget her Ex. Time to dream. She loved her dreams. Her mysterious stranger showed up when she closed her eyes.

Would he come to her tonight?

Meela drifted, her body languid and her mind free. She wasn't sure where she was. Lost in the endless gray of her thoughts.

"There you are."

She knew that voice. *Him.* She turned, searching for him. *"Where are you?"*

"Here." He strode up to her, seeming to come out of the fog. *"I've been waiting for you."*

"Have you?" She tried to keep her excitement at bay. *"You don't need to wait for me."*

"Why not?" He grasped her hand. *"I look forward to our time together. It's renewal. It's a chance to find my heart."*

He spoke such kind words, she almost believed him. She allowed him to tug her into his arms and sway. They danced to a song she couldn't hear, but the rhythm surged through her body. She grasped his shoulders, holding on as he swept her against his chest.

"You don't have to come to me," she said. She wasn't sure why she'd let that thought slip. Should've kept it to herself.

"Why wouldn't I come to you? I'm entranced by you." He splayed his hand across her back. He tucked her to his hips and continued to sway. He danced her in circles, as if they were in the midst of a waltz.

"You're entrancing…" She swore her entire being blushed and burned. *"I'm not magical."*

"What's that got to do with anything?" he asked and led her to a window.

There were windows in her dreams? In her mind? She breathed in the sweet scent of flowers and sighed. *"I don't know."*

"You know." He turned her away from him and pressed his chest to her back. He eased his arms around her. He caressed her belly and kissed her neck. His breath tickled her skin and skittered along her soul.

"Do I?" She wanted to stay here forever. *"Don't*

hurt me."

"*Can't. It's not in me to harm you.*" He brushed his lips along her neck, then nuzzled her earlobe. "*I want to build you up. Make you fly.*"

"*You do?*" She had to stop asking questions. She leaned into him and basked in his heat. She wanted to think about this moment but pushed that notion aside. Why did she have to ponder everything? Why couldn't she simply enjoy being held?

She'd never been good at letting go.

"*I don't come to you because I have to. Don't do it because I'm placating you. I come to you because I need to. You're a drug to me,*" he murmured against her throat. "*You force me to be better than myself.*"

She turned in his arms to face him. "*I do?*" So much for not asking questions.

"*You do.*" He kissed her hard, stealing her breath.

She eased her arms around his neck and held on tight. She didn't want to be held lightly. Why? She'd rather have him pin her to the wall and make her scream. She sucked on his tongue as he opened to her. He slid his hands under her backside and lifted her to his chest, forcing her to wrap her legs around his waist.

She gasped and panted, breaking the kiss for a moment. "*Yes.*"

"*Yeah?*" He pinned her to the window frame and shoved her dress out of the way.

She hadn't even realized she was wearing a dress until he moved it. She hooked her ankles together and held on the best she could. "*Make love to me.*" It was too fast, but she didn't care. He made her feel something. Like she was someone. Like she could do anything. Like someone gave a fuck about her.

"*Always.*" He kissed her again. This time, he moved with a bit more tenderness. "*My girl.*"

She wasn't sure how much of the dream she should believe, but right now, that didn't matter. She'd take all of it as gospel. She dug her nails into his shoulders. He tasted like wine and sin. Did sin have an actual taste? It must've -- because that was how she'd have described his kiss.

"*I want to be inside you.*" He shoved her dress out of the way again and entered her in one swift thrust.

The sheer velocity of his movement stole her breath again. She loved the way he took control of the act. He fit inside her, like he was made for her. The burn from his push encouraged her. She shifted her hips to adjust to him. Something within her vibrated and snapped.

Meela unleashed her desire for him as well as her need to be loved. She rode him, meeting him thrust for thrust. The sounds swirling around her seemed to blur into nothing. Like everything centered on him. She gasped and whimpered as he increased the tempo of his lovemaking.

"*Yes, babe. Do it. Let go with me,*" he said. "*Come with me.*"

She didn't need the coaxing. He had her right on the edge already. That's how he managed to get to her every time. He knew how to touch her, speed up the intensity of being with him and how to make her crazy for him. Was it magic?

This was something deeper than she could understand. Something metaphysical? She wasn't sure. All she did know was that she didn't want to miss it. He could go as fast as he liked because she needed every second of this time with him. If she never had to let go again, she could live with that.

He pushed harder into her as his movements turned jerky. He cried out. Hearing him come apart finally nudged her over the edge. She groaned and clamped her pussy around his shaft. The orgasm started in her belly, then spiraled to her limbs before hurtling back to her cunt. She swore stars exploded behind her eyelids and the rest of the world melted away. Every cell in her body screamed for him. When she opened her eyes, she rested her forehead on his and panted as he came apart.

"Jesus fuck." He practically smashed her between his hips and the window frame. A shudder rocked through him. *"You turn my brain to mush."*

"Good thing the feeling's mutual." She chuckled and clung to him, glad he could keep her upright.

"Yeah?" He kissed her again. *"Went too fast."*

"It did."

"It'll last longer next time."

He always said that, yet every encounter flew by at warp speed. She stared into his eyes. She loved looking at them, so green and deep. Like looking into his soul. He certainly saw straight to hers.

"Don't go," she whispered. *"Stay with me tonight."*

"I'm always with you." He pulled out and helped her to her feet. *"Doesn't feel like it, but I am."*

She shook her head, but he silenced her with a kiss. When he broke the connection, he nuzzled her cheek. *"We'll be together more often very soon."*

"How do you know that?" She wanted to believe him, but it seemed so fantastical. *"You always go when I wake. You're here to take what you want and leave before I'm ready."*

"I know, but that's not the truth." He kept one arm around her waist and brushed her cheek with the pad of his thumb as he cupped her jaw. *"I can't explain it to you right now. I don't have time, but I will soon enough. You'll know and when we come together, it'll be forever."*

She stared at him. Heat slid over her cheeks. She wanted to answer him, but the words clogged in her throat. He seemed to know how to bring her to the highest flights during sex, then slash her spirits in the next instant.

"Don't cry, my beloved. It won't be long," he said. *"Have patience."*

It wasn't like him to speak to her this way. The other times they'd come together, it'd been all about sex and the feral actions of making love. This time, he'd added emotions and a future to the discussion.

Why did it hurt so much? Because she feared this would be the last time she saw him. The last time she'd be held and kissed. The last time she'd get her heart broken.

"I'm coming for you. I can't handle the space between us any longer. I'm looking for you and when we find each other, it'll be right. We'll know." He kissed her. *"Follow your heart. Mine's calling for yours."*

She reached for him as the fog claimed him. A scream caught in her throat, but again, no sound came out. Tears burned on her cheeks. God damn it. She'd find him. She'd search the world over for him if that's what it took.

But where in the hell was he?

Fuck if she knew.

Chapter Two

Meela tossed her phone and bag onto the passenger seat of her car. She'd learned to live sparsely after having to leave her little house in Eerie. She'd taken herself on a vacation right after the divorce finally went through, to get her head screwed on straight, but when she'd returned home the place had been ransacked. Her jewelry had been stolen, her clothes all over the lawn, and her belongings torn. Most everything she'd owned had been destroyed.

She hadn't been sure it was Tiernan, but she had an idea. Since then, she'd learned to live on the lighter side and not have too many belongings. The less to lose, the better.

Meela ensured she had her phone charger, her purse, little safe and the nest egg she'd saved. Once satisfied, she locked the car doors, then drove off. She'd come back to the apartment, but if something happened to her, then there wasn't much to go through. Not that she had anyone to worry about her.

She pulled away from the curb and drove through town to the outskirts. Her thoughts wandered to the night before as she merged onto the freeway. Her dream man filled her mind. She wanted to relive their time together over and over. To feel him holding her. To kiss him. For it to be real.

Too bad it never would be. She wasn't going to find him. He might have said he'd find her, but she knew better. After Tiernan, she didn't expect good fortunes. Life had a certain way of kicking the blocks out from under her.

She drove the hundred or so miles from Lexington to Eerie. The closer she got to town, the more her skin tingled. She hated coming home. She'd never felt like she belonged there. Maybe it was because Tiernan was still there. She wasn't sure.

She barely noticed the miles, until she registered the sign. Anyone who wasn't paranormal and didn't have paranormal blood in their veins wasn't going to see the sign. Call it a quirk of Eerie, but only those privy to the magic could experience the town properly. Those who couldn't see it simply drove along the road, passing the town by.

But she could see it. She'd grown up there. Her family used to live there. She'd once believed she'd spend her future and end up dying in that little house.

So much for belief.

She slowed to the lower speed limit and noticed an orange cat in the weeds on the side of the road. Was he moving? When the cat pounced, she relaxed a bit. At least the little thing wasn't dead. Though the more she looked at it, the animal wasn't little. He was the biggest damn housecat she'd ever seen.

Funny, she'd always wanted a cat, but hadn't bothered to adopt one for fear Tiernan would do something terrible to it.

Some day.

She kept driving and headed to the cabins at the edge of the woods. The trolls didn't venture into the woods, and she could be alone. If she was going to live in town for a few weeks, then she needed control over her lodgings.

When she reached the gravel path leading back to the cabins, she sucked in a ragged breath. What if Tiernan was tailing her? He could be. She'd have to take her chances.

She stopped at the main cabin and paid the fee for three weeks, then accepted the pass for the door. As she walked back to the car, her heart lodged in her throat. The last time she'd lived in Eerie, she'd lived in a sweet little development. That was the world she'd known. The place she'd loved. There were memories in this town -- good and bad.

She'd thought she'd found love in Eerie. She'd fallen for someone, but it'd been one-sided love. Then there was the thrill of marriage, only to find out her partner didn't care.

She winced at the thought of the fights. The arguments. The thrown fists.

She tamped down the strangled cry bubbling in her throat. The house had been trashed and ended up sold. Her dreams were discarded, and she'd vowed never to come back. But here she was.

She drove back to her allotted cabin, then deposited some of her belongings on the couch before locking the building back up. The thought of leaving anything of value simply bothered her. She returned to her car, then drove away from the cabin.

If she hurried, she'd make her appointment. Good old Norm Slone had finally answered her. So kind of him, really. She snorted as she pulled onto the main road. He'd cleared his calendar, he claimed, just for her.

She skirted past her old housing development and noticed another orange cat. Could be a brother of the first one. Could be the same cat. Then again, could be a totally different animal. What caught her attention was the cat's size. She'd never seen one so big. Had to be larger than a dog. Were cats supposed to be that big? Or that fluffy? He reminded her of a small lion. If she wasn't mistaken, he or she sure looked like a Maine Coon. But who would let what had to be an expensive animal loose like this?

She rolled her eyes. For all she knew, the cat was

a female, yet she'd referred to it as a boy. Still, she wanted to meet this animal up close. Was it ferocious? Sweet? Finicky?

She'd never know.

A few moments later, she parked in front of the law office. Although he wasn't her favorite paranormal, she trusted Norm Slone. He had shifter guards outside of the office and prowling the grounds at all times. They weren't even visible most of the time, but they knew damn well what was going on.

But who would be foolish enough to argue with Norm Slone? No one with any brains. He wasn't a gnome to be trifled with, because he carried himself with confidence.

She grabbed her bag and locked the car before going into the office. As the door creaked, she stepped out of the way when it closed. "Hi," she said, wondering where the receptionist had gone.

"Norm Slone, divorce lawyer gnome," a booming voice said from around the corner. "Not taking any new clients." Norm shuffled into the waiting area and adjusted his jacket over his paunchy belly.

"I have an appointment," she said and held tightly to her bag.

"Meela. Good to see you." He tucked his tie behind his jacket as he wrestled the buttons closed. He wobbled up to her. He might be formidable in the courtroom, but he was almost a caricature in person. His jacket barely contained his belly. He stood only four feet tall, but smoked cigars and badly needed a shave.

He stuck out his hand and she shook hands with him. "Hello," she managed. "Did you forget the appointment?"

"No, but I got busy working on a few court filings. One of my paralegals quit to get married. I told her it was a silly idea, and that she'd be back in a few months when he ran out on her, but she held firm." Norm shrugged, then gestured to the adjacent room. "Come on back. Kiley? Where are you?"

A blonde faerie wearing a flowing chartreuse dress appeared from what seemed like out of nowhere. "Sorry. I had to powder my nose."

"Right." Norm snorted. "The front office is yours. Don't let me down."

"Yes, Mr. Slone." Kiley settled behind her desk and tucked her wings away. "Good luck."

"Thanks," Meela said and inched back to the inner office after Norm.

"So he's being a rat?" Norm asked. "Won't pay, huh?"

"Unfortunately, you're correct." She moved one of the chairs to put more space between her and the gnome. Norm could be a good man, but he could also be slime. If the mood struck, he could be pushy and grabby. He tended to make improper comments, could be gruff and standoffish. Despite that, he got the job done. Anyone going against him in the courtroom knew better than to argue with him because they'd be shouted down. He'd make rude comments, but he also knew how to verbally spar with an opponent to the point the opponent apologized to him.

He'd managed to work out a great settlement for her and even got her alimony far above what she'd expected. Now she had to hope he'd come through again.

"I got your message and did some digging," Norm said and collapsed onto his chair. The furniture groaned under his girth. He flipped through pages on his desk, then adjusted his glasses. "I've got your bank records and see that he's not going through the courts. He's not paying a damn thing."

"No, he's not." She folded her hands on her lap. "What are we going to do about it?"

"I've got some ideas." He moved the laptop aside. "First, dragging him into court isn't going to do anything."

"He'll evade." Still, she was afraid this would happen.

"And breaking his legs isn't legal."

"No." But the thought had crossed her mind.

"He knows he's not paying and doesn't seem to give a rat's ass." Norm glanced up at her. "Is there more?"

"Besides the fact he's six months behind in the alimony?" she asked. "I can't be sure it's not him, but I swear he's the one who broke into my apartment and trashed my stuff. My car is destroyed."

"Brake lines?" Norm asked, then resumed tapping on the laptop.

"That and sugar in the gas tank."

"Why can't anyone be original these days?" Norm shook his head. "Fool."

She wouldn't disagree. "He showed up at my work. He told my boss I'd been rude to him on multiple occasions and got me fired."

"Because?"

"I was fired because I wasn't giving Tiernan proper service even though I'd never served him. He claims I'd lost his order for a sofa and had the wrong armchair delivered to his house. I don't know where he lives because I didn't take the order, but I do know he's already engaged. He didn't wait to hook up with a woman named Tilly. His soulmate." She relaxed her hands, not realizing until now she'd had a white-knuckle grip on the handle of her bag.

"Do you have video footage? A viewing bubble? Anything we can use to show the courts he's the one doing the dirty deeds?" Norm asked. "Or is it all a gut feeling?"

"I don't have footage, but my former boss picked him out. He was my witness." She knew she didn't have much of a case against him -- not where the physical damage was concerned.

"I thought that might be the case. I'll get some of my people on him. If he tries more shit, he'll have to go through me." Norm tapped the handful of pages together. "But we can prove he's not paying. We're going through the courts because it's how this needs to be done, but I'm getting my team on him, too. We're going to see where his money is going and find out why he feels he shouldn't pay."

"Because he hates me." She sagged in her chair. "He'd rather I die than get another penny of his money."

"Then the dipstick should've thought of that before he got married."

"Yeah." She sighed. "He thought I had money. I told him the truth and my father was blunt with him, but he didn't listen. He swore we'd lied to him. The money was somewhere, and he'd get it once we got married."

Norm stared at her. "We've had this conversation before, and I'll say it again. Love is bullshit. I don't know how you ever fell for him."

"I thought he liked me," she confessed, ashamed by her naiveté. She wasn't exactly the kind of girl who attracted attention from the males in her classes or social settings.

"You're a cute girl."

"Woman," she corrected.

"Woman," he repeated. "You're cute. Any man would be foolish not to give you attention, but guys are dim. I know. I'm a guy."

"You also don't believe in love." She'd heard that line from him a million times.

"I don't, but that doesn't mean everyone else should agree with me." He folded his arms. "You do realize I've been married three times."

She hadn't known that. "Oh."

"Three times I thought I'd found the one. Three times I was wrong." He leaned back in his seat. "Doesn't mean I won't chase women. I don't like being lonely any more than anyone else. But I'm smart enough to know there's the chase and there's the catch. I don't want to catch. Just do a little running."

She wasn't sure why he'd told her that.

"I've got my people on his ass right now. If he tries anything, they'll know and intervene. Also got my people on his records. Give me forty-eight hours and we'll know where he's spending his time and his cash. If we have to, we'll get his wages garnished. He fucked with the wrong people."

Now that's what she wanted to hear.

"I won't argue with you if you happen to find yourself a bodyguard," he said. "I don't have anyone free, but I'd suggest you locate a warm body that's willing to keep an eye on you."

"Where am I going to find someone I can trust?" she snapped. "I'll be fine." She doubted that, but she had little choice.

"It's Eerie. Anything is possible," Norm said. "I've got your case well under way."

"And how much is the retainer this time?" She'd

already shelled out over four grand for his services.

"No charge. I hate bullies like him and it's my pleasure to piss him off." Norm grinned. "I told you, he fucked with the wrong person."

"You did." She nodded, then debated what to do.

"I'll keep you in the loop. Rest, try to relax and let me handle this." Norm stood. He stuck out his hand again. "You're welcome to stay here."

If he said he'd always had a thing for her, she'd bolt. "I don't want to be a burden." She shook hands with him, then pulled away. She didn't need to give him the wrong idea.

"You wouldn't be." He grinned.

"You're my lawyer. Nothing else. I'm sorry, but I don't date my lawyer." She grasped her bag. "I should be going."

"Understood. I'll do my best for you." Norm sank back onto his chair and grunted.

She turned on her heel. She'd been dismissed and appreciated the gesture. The faster she could get out of the office, the better. He'd do his best for her, no doubt, but he didn't have to be slimy in the meantime.

She left the building and made her way to her car. An orange cat sprawled on the hood. The cat licked its paw, then stared at her.

"What are you doing here?" She unlocked the door and plunked her bag on the front seat before shutting the door again. "You should go home."

He continued to stare at her.

"Someone must be looking for you, big boy." She held her hand out, giving him a chance to sniff her. "I guess you could be a big girl. Either way, you're the largest cat I've ever seen."

She petted the cat, marveling at the softness of his or her fur. The animal didn't appear to have a collar or any other markings to prove it had an owner. Good gravy, this cat was huge for a pet. House cats didn't run this large unless they were indeed Maine Coons.

The cat also didn't seem interested in leaving the hood. He rolled onto his back, then flipped onto his other side before licking his paw. His tail thwacked on the hood and he stared at her. When she reached for him, he head butted her hand, allowing her to pet him again.

She tucked her keys into her pocket. "Why don't you come with me? I can't leave you here, but I can't stick around much longer. I'll put up flyers, and we'll see if we can find your owner. First, I'll get you something to eat."

Although looking at him, she doubted this cat needed food. The owner sure had fed the critter well. She scooped the cat into her arms and her senses tingled. She carried him over to the driver's side, awkwardly opening the door. For being such a large animal, the cat didn't squirm or fight.

She managed to get the cat onto the front seat, then hurried into the car. She slammed the door. "I hope you don't mind spending the night in a cabin."

She drove away, wondering what kind of person let their pet roam this way. The cat could've been run over, attacked or something worse. For a while, it'd be okay. For a while, the cat was safe.

She'd done a good thing.

Chapter Three

Aslan didn't mind her scooping him up or the way she'd plunked him onto the front seat. He wasn't about to complain. Living on the streets wasn't fun. If he could be in the company of a pretty girl, then even better.

Besides, he had to be with her. He'd had to find her. She was the reason he existed. The one he was meant to protect.

He curled up on the front seat as she drove. As the vehicle moved, he licked his paw, then turned over, mashing his head into the seat. He wasn't sure where they were going and didn't care. As long as he was with her, he'd be fine. He could do his job.

Soon, he'd be able to explain to her so many things. He might even have the chance to be with her.

She parked and dropped her keys onto her lap. "I don't know." She reached over and scratched behind his ears. "You're too cute to be loose. Why hasn't anyone claimed you?"

He knew exactly why -- he'd been waiting for her.

"You should have an owner." She continued to stroke his fur. "Someone probably misses you."

If they did, he didn't know about it. He'd been a wanderer all his life. Not that she knew that.

He stared at her. He'd seen her so many times in his dreams. Kissed, touched, made love to her and memorized every second of their time together. Now that he'd met her in person, he couldn't let her go.

Soon, he'd have to let her in on his secret. Just not yet.

"You're a big one." She scratched him again, then moved his leg. "And you're a boy. Good. I felt terrible not knowing. I wanted to call you a him, but it'd be terrible if you were a girl."

Her observation and means for checking amused him. He'd never had anyone make sure he was... a him. But then he'd seen the same behavior in pet owners, so it wasn't odd. Just funny.

"So what's a big, fluffy, slightly dirty old boy like you doing out on your own?" She shifted in her seat to face him. "You've got pretty eyes."

So did she. He wanted to keep staring at her. Being in the warm car, with the person he'd been searching for, made him sleepy. He snuggled in the seat and tried not to ignore her.

"I'll bet you're worn out. I'd say you're hungry, but you've got a bit of a paunch. Could be something worse, though," she said. "Better get you to a vet. I'll have to figure out where to go, because I don't know any veterinarians out here."

He didn't mind. Before they got to that point, he'd reveal his secret. If he told her right now, she'd freak out. Besides, he wasn't sure he wanted to be naked in her car. Not with the chance of being seen so high.

She settled back behind the wheel and engaged the engine. "I should make up some posters or something to help get you home. Bet your owner would like to know you're not on the street."

He supposed so, but since he was his own man, he had to answer to himself.

"You're not the kind of cat anyone would miss. I almost thought you were a mountain lion." She laughed and drove away from the law office.

The sooner they left Norm Slone's place, the better. He didn't dislike Norm, but some of the characters who hung around the office weren't anyone he wanted in his life. He'd dealt with too many people during his lifetime to want to mix with ruffians.

Then again, to some, he was the uncouth character.

He watched her as she drove, marveling at her poise. He wanted to know her story but wanted to hear it from her own lips. Wanted to know what made her tick and how she felt. Mostly, he wanted to hold her. Everything he'd learned about her so far made his heart beat faster.

She pulled off the main road and onto the gravel one. He didn't have to look out the window to know where they were. He smelled the lake water, the crispy leaves and the earthiness in the air.

The cabins. Smart choice. If she wanted to stay out of sight and heal, then this was the best place to be.

She parked, then switched off the engine, and he stretched, then stood, swishing his tail. She'd probably hate him for letting her think he was only a cat for this long, but he had to find the right time to tell her his secret. If he shifted in front of her, into a naked man, she might not appreciate it. She might even hate him for withholding this long. Or hate him for showing up in her dreams.

Fuck. He had to tread lightly. The last thing he wanted to do was scare her off. He knew down to his core that she was the one he'd been sent to protect. His person. His other half. Now if he could get her to see it.

"I'm in the cabins." She snorted. "I don't know why I'm telling you this. I doubt you understand me and if you do, you probably don't care." She shook her head and stopped talking.

He wanted to tell her he didn't mind her talking. Hell, he liked listening to her. Her fears and concerns didn't scare him, either. He wanted to help her.

"Come here. I'll carry you inside. Don't want any of the wild animals to snatch you before your owner learns you're here."

She scooped him into her arms, then tucked him to her chest. He wasn't about to run from her. Why would he? He'd longed to be in this position for so long. Soon, he'd hold her in his human form. He'd feel those hands on his chest and be able to listen to her cry out as he tasted her.

"You're like a gigantic ragdoll of a Maine Coon," she said and hefted him into the cabin. "Or a stuffed animal." She plunked him onto the sofa, then turned on her heel. She ducked outside long enough to retrieve her bag before rushing into the cabin and slamming the door.

He needed to be honest with her soon.

"Okay." She left her purse and keys on the small table. "So… I need my laptop. I should make some ads for social media to let people know I found you. Should get the posts up and expect messages. Someone has to be looking for you."

If she took a breath, he'd interject, but she was on a roll. He sat on the sofa and listened to her.

"But I don't want to put my information out there. Tiernan probably already knows where I am." She sat on the floor in front of the couch, sitting face-to-face with him. "I don't know if you care what I'm talking about, but it's nice to have someone to talk to. I hate what he's done."

He listened as she scratched him behind the ears again and stroked his back. She'd put him to sleep this way. If nothing else, he'd be relaxed. He sprawled on his side and swished his tail.

"You're so calm. I bet your owner is so sad." She trailed her fingers over his back. "Why is it people have to be cruel? I don't think your owner is cruel, but why do people have to be that way? He knew I wasn't rich. He knew I didn't have money, but he had to be a jerk. I kept begging him… I thought he loved me, but I didn't have the cash he wanted. I begged him to let me go if he thought he was going to get a payday. He had my heart in his hands and crushed it because the money -- which didn't exist -- was more important than me."

His heart ached. He had the feeling she needed to get these words out, though.

"I thought he loved me," she said as tears ran down her cheeks. "He never loved me. It was all a lie. I knew in my gut it was a lie, but I bought it because I was so desperate to be loved."

Something crashed against the cabin, and she whimpered. She curled against the couch, ducking her head. Another object thunked against the wall, then glass flew through the air. A rock rolled across the floor. Lights flashed and another rock went sailing into the cabin.

He'd had enough. Aslan embraced the magic within him and the cat receded. He stretched as his limbs extended. His fur disappeared and his ears shortened. He groaned. The shift wasn't painful, but he'd been compacted up for so long, he needed to move.

"Oh my fuck." She skittered across the rug, scrambling away from him. "What in the hell?" Her eyes widened. Her mouth formed an O and she paled.

He didn't give a shit he was naked. He grabbed the blanket from the sofa and covered himself from the hips down, then rushed to the door. "Whoever is tossing shit at my cabin better stop. I'm armed," he shouted. "I'm a trained sharpshooter."

An engine gunned and tires chattered as a vehicle sped away.

He glanced out the window, taking note of the car and license plate. A red compact version with a plate featuring all numbers. He committed the information to memory, then faced her.

"Who or what the fuck are you?" She collided with the sofa. "Don't hurt me."

"Slow down." He knelt on the floor and held up his hands. "I won't do anything to hurt you. It's me. Aslan."

She narrowed her eyes, then scrambled to her feet. "Get the fuck out. Where's the cat?"

"I'm the cat." He remained crouched on the floor. "Meela, I'm the cat who was just here. I'm a Maine Coon shifter. Please. I didn't mean to scare you."

She kept space between them. "I can't trust you."

"I know you can't." He rested on his backside, keeping the blanket over his nudity. "I wanted to tell you."

"You did?" She managed to stand and shook her head again. "I -- you -- this is nuts."

"Will you give me a chance to talk?"

"You? I told you all those things. I said so much... I can't trust you." She coughed and tears streamed down her cheeks. "God, I have the worst fucking luck. I would find the one damn cat that's not a cat, but a man." She held up her hands and trembled.

"Please let me talk." He didn't move from his position on the rug. "If you let me explain, I can."

"You'll tell me lies to get what you want." She pushed herself into the corner. "I got rocks in my windows and was terrorized again, but you're wanting to talk to me. Jesus H. Christ."

He understood her concern, but she had to listen,

even if only for a few moments. "I know who did that."

"One of your cronies? Your girlfriend?" She covered her face with both hands. "I'm tired of this."

"I know you are." He wished he could take her pain away. Wanted to make the past melt into nothing so she could start over.

"Why won't he leave me alone?" She sobbed and coughed again. "Go away."

"I won't." He finally stood and held up his hands. "I won't let that bastard do this to you."

"Stop," she pleaded. "Leave me alone."

"I can't." He inched across the floor, slowly bridging the gap between them. He hadn't touched her, but he wanted to. "I know he's tried to hurt you. I know he's determined to do you a whole lot of wrong. I'm not him. You need to give me a chance to talk."

She tensed and stared at him, but didn't push him away.

"You know me. I'm the cat you saw when you came to town. I'm the cat you'd see when you were here before. We've run into each other before. Remember when you fed me? I'd stop at your little house, and you'd leave food for me." He held out his hand. "I wasn't starving, but you made sure I had something."

She blinked but said nothing.

"I've seen you in your dreams, too." He slid her hand into his. "I'm Aslan. Remember? Every time I came to you, every time I touched you, it's all seared in my memory."

"You?"

"Me." He rubbed the inside of her palm. "I'm sorry. I didn't want to tell you this way. I wanted to give you time, but he took that time from us."

"He did?" she whispered. "How do you know?"

"I know that car. He must've followed you. Red car? License plate that's all numbers?" He inched closer to her. "He terrorized you, and he hasn't stopped yet."

"No," she murmured. Her shoulders slumped and she averted her gaze. "I'm a mess."

"You're allowed to be a mess." He bridged the gap between them and tucked her to his chest. "You're allowed to be mad at me. To hate me. I don't care. I won't push you to accept me until, and only if, you're ready. It's scary to welcome someone in. Scary to put your heart out there. I can't promise everything will be perfect, but I can promise I won't do anything in my power that will hurt you."

She balled her hands against his chest. "You don't have any owner, do you?"

"No." He curled his fingers under her chest. "All your worry was truly for nothing. No one's waiting for me. No owner or anything else. But I liked that you cared enough to find my home. I appreciate that you were worried."

"I'm still angry with you."

"You should be." He'd been dishonest with her -- for a good reason, but still.

"Did you follow me out of here?" she asked. "Out of Eerie?"

"No."

"Are you bound to Eerie?"

"Sort of," he replied. "I can't leave the city limits until I'm united with my person." It was an archaic rule, but one he had to abide by.

"What if you never find her?"

"Then I keep looking." But he knew he'd found her. The moment he looked into Meela's eyes, he knew.

He wouldn't have been able to travel to her through her dreams if she hadn't been his one.

"I'm still mad at you," she repeated. "But you're taller in person than I thought."

He tried not to laugh, but her comment amused him. "I am, huh? Too tall?"

She flicked her gaze over him. "No."

"Good." He slipped his arms around her. He had a lot of work to do to get her to relax and trust him, but he was up for the challenge. "We need to get the police and the Princess involved. A crime occurred here, and neither entity wants anyone to not feel safe."

"Fine." She shivered in his embrace. "Don't have to call the Princess."

"Why not?" He tipped his head to meet her gaze. "Why don't you want me to?"

"She can't do anything. He's a troll. He won't listen to her or anyone else." She half-shrugged and tensed all over again. "He ignores the courts, and isn't afraid of Norm."

"Norm isn't my favorite guy."

"He's slime, but he gets the job done."

"True." He fought the urge to tighten his grasp on her. "Either way, we have to get the authorities involved. He can't keep doing this. One way or another, he has to be stopped."

"And you're going to do that?" She sighed. "He's terrorized me since the day I married him. I used to think he was a wonderful man. A troll, but still wonderful. Then he changed. It was like the second he verified I wasn't bringing him a dowry and that wedding ring burned into his finger, he became a different man."

"The man he really was, but had restrained to fool you into liking him?" he asked.

"Maybe." She bowed her head. "I was young and foolish."

"You were dying to be loved. There's no crime in that."

"No? Then why do I feel used and thrown away?" she asked. "A means to an end. If he didn't want me, he should've left a long time ago."

"I'm guessing he wasn't strong enough to do that." He debated how to reach the police. "Do you have magic?"

"No." She laughed, without any cheer in her voice. "That's another way he felt I was terrible. I'm paranormal, but without any abilities."

"Abilities aren't all they're cracked up to be. Do you have your phone?"

"Yeah." She nodded to her bag. "If he's not somehow tapped it."

"Fucker." He groaned, then let go of her long enough to retrieve the device. "He knows where you are and already tried to scare you. I wouldn't put it past him to track you."

"Got a better idea where I should go?"

"I do." He dialed the number for the police. He'd hoped she'd ask that question so he could get her the hell out of there to somewhere safer. There was only one choice possible. Even if her ex tried to track her, the magic would keep him out. Shifter magic could be wonderful, and could also be fucking dangerous. "My place."

Chapter Four

Meela stared at Aslan. Of course he'd say his place. She didn't trust him an inch, yet he wanted her to go home with him. Seeing him in the flesh and getting to touch him pleased her. He was more than she'd even imagined from her dreams. But she didn't trust him. How could she? One minute he was a cat and the next he was a naked man in front of her.

"I don't know if that's wise," she said. "Won't the cops want us to be here?"

"They do, but they won't want us to stay. Not when it's a crime scene." He pressed the phone to his ear. "Okay." He held the device out and set it to the speaker setting.

"This is the Royal Guards. What's the nature of your emergency?" the woman on the other end of the line asked.

"There's been an attack on one of the cabins. My name is Aslan, and I'm charged with protecting Meela Durning. Her ex-husband, Tiernan Durning, has been attacking her."

"Aslan, you haven't checked in with the captain in quite a while. Good to hear from you. Finally decided to surface?" she asked.

"Is this how the Royal Guards always talk?" Meela asked. "And why does she know you?" So many questions, but she deserved answers.

"I'll tell you in a moment." He turned his attention back to the phone. "I had a job to do, and I've been doing it. I'm currently protecting her, but her ex got the jump on us. We're fine, but rocks were thrown through the windows and should be investigated. We're in cabin…"

"Four," Meela said. "The one closest to the

clubhouse." She'd thought it'd be the safest. So much for that.

"We have Guards on the way. They should be there within the next couple minutes," the woman said. "Aslan, you have a job to do, but that doesn't mean you can't check in. You need to be touching base with us more frequently."

"I know. I will." He held onto the phone, then jerked. "I see the lights. They're here." He swiped to disconnect the call.

"We'll give statements?" Meela asked. She hated to admit to herself that hearing him talk to someone else rankled her. Why? She didn't have any ties to Aslan. They weren't together. Still, jealousy rose in her mind. She didn't want to share the beautiful man who held her and had shifted from cat form into a human.

"Yes." As if on cue, an officer, with a phone pressed to her ear, walked into the cabin. "I'm Officer Carouthers. It's good to meet you. I'd wondered when someone would snatch this character up." She elbowed Aslan.

"You make it seem like I'm a cad." Aslan shook his head. "I'll go with Dickson if you want and give my statement. She'll probably feel more comfortable talking to you."

"You read my mind." Carouthers nodded to him. "Out there."

Meela sighed. It was like she wasn't even there. She still hadn't wrapped her mind around the fact Aslan had changed from a cat into a man. She'd picked him up. She'd carried him into the cabin. Talked to him. The more she looked at him, the more she wondered if he was really the one who'd come to her in her dreams.

Dear God. If he'd been her mystery man... she'd

opened herself up so much to him. She'd been brazen with him. Her stomach clenched. She'd started falling in love with him -- when she'd thought he was a figment of her imagination.

He'd said he'd find her. They'd find each other. Was this what he meant?

"Ma'am?" Carouthers touched her arm. "I bet you're in shock. I'm Carly Carouthers with the Royal Guards. I should've introduced myself earlier, and I'm sorry. Why don't you tell me what happened?" She produced a bubble on her hand.

"Is that...?" She hadn't seen a communicator bubble in so long. "Wow."

"You're para?"

"I am." She sighed again. The weight of the day and now evening washed over her. "Sorry. I'm the child of a conjurer and celebrity psychic. You've heard of Clyde Essence?"

"The old psychic? He wasn't bad." Carouthers nodded. "Was your mother Edna?"

"The very same. She's where I get my paranormal blood. I don't know if Dad ever was any good at what he did. To me, he was a better guesser and good at reading people, more than having any psychic ability." She laced her hands together to keep them from shaking. "I don't have any magic. Just have lucky blood."

"I'm sure there's something magical about you. Everyone here has something. You might not have found it yet, and that's not bad. It'll take time." Carouthers rolled the bubble in her fingers. "So what happened here tonight?"

She recounted her story about coming to Eerie and talking to Norm, adding in the bits about seeing Aslan before she knew who he was. "We were here, and he was in his cat form. I'd talked to him about my life and was trying to figure out how to get him back to his owner when something thumped against the cabin. It wasn't seconds later when another object collided with the cabin, then rocks came through the windows." She pointed to the rocks. "We didn't touch them. I scrambled away from the windows and tried to hide."

"Is that when he shifted?"

"I guess. It was so fast." Truth be told, she wasn't even sure. "I barely saw it. He was a cat, then he wasn't."

"And you're sure he wasn't the one who broke the window?"

"Positive." She nodded to the glass on the floor. "I don't know him well, but he wouldn't do this."

"Understood." Carouthers widened her stance. "Is there anything else you'd like to add?"

"I didn't look out the window. I was too busy hiding, but he got the license plate numbers and saw the car." She shook her head. "I came here to get my life sorted out and to start over. I'm tired of being harassed by my ex-husband."

"Who is that?" Carouthers narrowed her eyes. "We need that information."

"Tiernan Durning. The king of the trolls." She curled into herself. "I don't have conclusive proof, but he's been following me. I'm sure he's got something loaded on my phone. My apartment has been broken into a few times. Stuff was broken in my apartment. He trashed my car. I was in a rental when I got here. That one out there is a rental."

"Here in Eerie?" Carouthers asked. "Why haven't you notified us before now?"

"Not here. I ran away from Eerie because I thought I'd be safer. I wasn't." She wanted to get the hell out of the cabin. "I don't want anything to do with him, which is why I divorced him, but he doesn't want me alive."

"You have proof?"

"He shouted it in court." She'd never forget him standing up and declaring he'd rather have her dead than pay her.

"I see." Carouthers shook her head. "Anything else?"

"I stood in the corner with Aslan, wanting them to get the hell away from me and wishing I'd gone somewhere else."

"Them?"

"If Tiernan is lurking anywhere, he never travels without Pee Wee. Yes, his best friend, another troll who is almost an inch taller than him, is named Pee Wee." She shivered. Pee Wee had come along with them on their honeymoon. He'd been the irritating presence never really leaving them alone.

"I've made a note of that." Carouthers popped the bubble. "And everything you've told me is part of the Guard record. We will follow up on this. Whoever assaulted you and your property will be apprehended. If you don't hear from me about this incident, you will hear from the Princess. She's very hands-on with this sort of thing and won't stand for this behavior."

"Whoa." She hadn't expected the Princess would care. "Really?"

"She is. She's got a handle on what goes on in this town and I know when she finds out what he's been doing -- if she doesn't already know -- then she'll put a stop to it," Carouthers said. "No one has the right to be a bully."

"Carly?" The other officer poked his head into the cabin. "We're going to secure the location."

"Sure." She turned her attention back to Meela. "Do you have somewhere to go? I'm sure we can get you lodgings at the castle or hotel. Has Aslan offered you a place?"

"Where would we go? Somewhere in the woods? Wherever he hunkers down?" she asked. Her patience shattered and tears slid down her cheeks again. The stress of the situation was too much. She'd run away and hidden for so long. Every time he found her. "I'm sorry."

"It's fine. I get that you're stressed," Carouthers said. "But you're shortchanging him. He's a good man and shifter. If he came to you, there's a reason. Shifters are peculiar creatures. They don't gravitate to many and tend to be loners, unless they've found a purpose. You might be his purpose." She held up her hand, almost as if to silence the question or charges she assumed Meela would lob. "I get it. He seems like he's rough around the edges and he's charismatic, but again, if he's here for you, it might be to protect you. That might be his purpose. Don't shut him out. Give it all a chance, as much as you're giving us the chance to solve this, and you might be surprised. In fact, I'm sure you will. We won't stop until we get to the bottom of this, and he's just as tenacious."

"Sure." She didn't have much to lose. "Do you want my phone? To check if there's a tracker on it? Or anything else?"

"Yes. We'll ensure you get it back." Carouthers accepted the device. "In the meantime, use this for correspondence. If you're unsure how to use it, just ask Aslan." She offered Meela a small rectangular object that looked nothing like a phone.

Before Meela could ask any questions, the other officer arrived in the cabin. "I've got a portal for you to go where you need to go. Aslan's ready to leave. We'll have the cabin secured until the investigation is over, but rest assured, you'll know what's happening every step of the way."

Most police departments didn't offer that kind of attention. Then again, this wasn't any force. This was the Royal Guards.

"Expect a visit from the Princess, as well. She'll want to know exactly what's going on," Dickson said. "Now, Aslan would like to see you. As soon as you decide where you'd like to go, please let me know and I'll have the portal ready for you."

"Thanks." She swore she was numb. Her nightmares were coming back. She'd never be able to outrun them. Would Aslan be able to protect her? She wanted to believe so, but she still had serious doubts.

Dickson nodded to her. "Your belongings are safe."

"Sure." The numbness flooded her body. She'd been violated again. Tiernan was back to his old tricks. He'd been awful once they were married and hadn't changed since.

"Hey." Aslan inched into the room. "Will you please come with me? I want to get you out of here and to somewhere safe. I promise with my life I'll keep you safe."

She flicked her gaze to him. "How can I trust you? How can I trust anyone? Everyone who said they loved me fucked me up." He didn't know her full truth and that bothered her, but right now wasn't the time to explain it to him.

"I know and I'm sorry." He inched up to her. He'd switched from the blanket to a pair of sweats and a sweatshirt. His feet were bare. "I don't live in a hovel or even the wilds of the woods. I have a home, a nice one, and I want to share it with you. You'll have your own room and can rest, but I guarantee the Princess will not permit me to leave you alone."

She fought the urge to roll her eyes. No one would give her space unless she allowed Aslan to whisk her out of there. Fine. She'd go, but she wasn't about to let him into her bed. Good God. Why was she even thinking about having sex? Because as much as she wanted him to go far from her, she needed to curl herself around him and have some normalcy.

"Come with me?" Aslan held out his hand. "Please?"

"Fine." She took his hand, feigning some irritation. Holding his hand did relax her.

He nodded and smiled. "This way."

Dickson opened a portal, allowing them passage directly from the cabin to a living room. She stepped through, following Aslan. When she looked back, the portal had closed. Like it was never there.

"Christ." Aslan bowed his head. "This wasn't how I envisioned this night going."

"No?" She let go of him and sank onto the arm of the closest chair. "It's not what I wanted to do, either. I'd planned on taking care of a cat, crying a little, hiding a lot, and trying desperately to decompress." She'd hoped for so much and had so little to show for it.

"I'm sure." He rested his hands on his hips. "I'd like to show you to your room and offer something to eat."

She wanted to say something snarky, but her fury evaporated. "Thanks."

"You want to be so combative." He offered his hand again. "You want to argue with me. Shout, scream and probably lash out. Don't you?"

She nodded. "Guilty." She grasped his fingers. "I just wanted to rest, you know?"

"I do." He caressed the back of her hand with the pad of his thumb. "I get it, and I want to help you. You're not used to being helped."

"No." She met his gaze. "I want to be mad at you, but I don't know who to be angry with any longer."

"And then here I come, dragging you somewhere you don't know, claiming to protect you and giving you little choice," he said. "Guess I'm not much better than him."

"I wouldn't say that." The weight of the day crashed through her again. "Would you mind if I rest? I don't know if I want a visit in my dreams -- if that's you. But I don't want to be alone." She wasn't sure why she'd confessed that, but she had.

"This way." He grasped both of her hands and showed her down the hallway. "I'm on the other side of the wall."

"Don't." She kept hold of him. "I don't want to be alone. I don't want to have sex, but I don't want you to go." A sob strangled in her throat.

"I won't leave you." He gestured to the bed. "I was going to give you a chance to change. I'll get you a shirt if you'd like to sleep in it."

"Oh." She hadn't thought of that. "Thanks."

"Let me get one." He disappeared long enough to clunk something in the other room. When he returned, he held a large blue shirt. "I hope this is okay."

"It'll be fine." She'd never had a man be so kind. She accepted the garment and sank onto the bed. "You don't have to go. I'm so tired of hiding and being afraid."

"You don't have to with me." He turned his back on her and rummaged through a bureau.

"No?" She undressed, then abandoned her clothes on the floor before shrugging into the shirt he'd given her. The shirt smelled good. Smelled like him. Not earthy and animalistic. More like a soft cologne. The scent comforted her. She crawled between the sheets, then stretched out. The bedding had the same comforting aroma. She'd be asleep in seconds if she wasn't careful. "Aslan?"

He glanced over his shoulder, then faced her. "Yes, sweetheart?"

Sweetheart. It might be a bit early to be referred to that way, but she liked the way the term of endearment rolled off his tongue. "Stay with me?"

"I'm not going anywhere." He stretched out beside her but remained on top of the covers. "Rest."

Soon.

Chapter Five

Aslan faced her and wished he could take her pain away. The look on her face sent an ache to the center of his being. He had no idea what all she'd been through and wasn't about to ask, but damn. His heart bled for her.

"I'm sorry," she whispered.

"For what?" he asked. "You have nothing to apologize for. I'm the one who shifted in front of you, didn't tell you right away what I could do. I should've been more forthcoming with you."

"No." She pressed her index finger to his lips. "There wasn't a good time to tell me those things. Not after what happened."

"You might be right." But that didn't take away his guilt.

She snuggled up to him and sighed. "I didn't know I wasn't special. Dad was the biggest charlatan. A huckster. He couldn't see the future. He just knew how to read a room and a person that well. Mom, she was the magical one. She lit up a room when she entered. She had a sparkle to her. That's why he loved her. She made him better."

"She sounds like a lovely person." He wished he could've met her mother.

"Dad played the role of celebrity, but we were never rich. Weren't even comfortable." She eased her arm from under the blanket and twined her fingers with his. "He did help a few people, but he worked hard to maintain that celebrity image. Project what you want to be, he'd say."

Aslan nodded and caressed her hand. He'd never get tired of touching her. Her skin soothed him. The glitter in her eyes spoke to something in his soul. His cat liked her, or he wouldn't have been able to shift in front of her. Hell, the cat approved of her. If he hadn't, he wouldn't have made himself visible so frequently. The cat wasn't a people pleaser. The cat preferred to stay to himself.

Then she entered his life, and both sides of him wanted her around for always.

"Dad made such a big deal about us having money that when I was old enough to start attracting a mate, Tiernan practically smashed down the door," she said. "I was nineteen, hadn't dated, and was too damn shy. I had no experience with males. I was invisible to boys at school because I wasn't magical."

"You were the oddball?" he asked. If he'd have known her back then, he would've dated her. Money didn't make any difference to him. It was her smile, those eyes and her sparkling personality that attracted him. "Why did you say 'attracting a mate'?"

"That was Dad's terminology. He swore there was a mate out there for me. Not a husband or partner, but a *mate*, and I had to attract him." She rolled her eyes. "I was brainwashed."

"You believed your parents. That's not totally brainwashing." *Loyalty maybe.*

"Whatever it was, between that and my shyness, I bought into what Tiernan told me. He was brooding, a little scary, a bit of a bad boy -- what little I knew -- and I thought he cared about me. When he first started coming around, he was kind to me. He listened. Dad and Mother swore he was a catch, and I should be grateful." She tensed. "But a tiny voice in the back of my head knew there was something wrong. I should've listened to that voice."

"You were young." He brushed a lock of hair from her face. "Don't beat yourself up for your naiveté."

"No?" she asked. "You have no idea how close to the truth you are."

"How so?" He shouldn't have posed that question, but the words tumbled out before he could take them back.

"He wasn't interested in planning the nuptials, which was fine because it was a small affair, but the second we signed the paperwork, he changed. I was told when I was a little girl that when your mate shows up, it'll be electric. It'll be bigger and stronger than you can imagine, but it'll feel like a bond."

"It wasn't with him?"

"No." She smiled, but the expression faded within seconds. "I thought he liked me, but I never felt loved. I believed it could become love, but it wasn't that head-over-heels, can't-live-without-him kind of attraction. It was more utilitarian. An illusion we were expected to maintain. Worse than that, he plainly told me I wasn't his mate. I was his wife."

His heart broke for her all over again. "He had someone on the side?"

"A few someones. Trolls are supposed to be solitary, but he's always had someone waiting for him," she said. "I was the one with the documents, but they were the ones with his heart."

"Tiernan doesn't have one."

"No, he doesn't." Sadness filled her eyes. "He'd lay hands on me. Throw things at me. He said things I won't repeat. I doubt he ever really loved me."

"Any person who puts their hands on anyone in anger needs to be punished." He gritted his teeth. He didn't know every circumstance around the relationship, but he really disliked Tiernan. "I take that back. What he did was reprehensible. You didn't deserve that, no matter how much he might have changed his feelings for you. He was cruel."

"He was." A tear slid across the bridge of her nose, then beneath her left eye before plopping onto the pillow. "I swore when I ran away and divorced him that I'd never allow myself to be hurt like that again."

"Good. You deserve to be happy." If he could do that, then he would to his deepest ability.

"I just want him to stop. I never wanted to be cheated on or hurt. After we divorced, I thought he'd leave me alone, but he won't. He wants me to feel pain." She shook her head. "I don't understand it."

"He wants you to feel pain for the perceived slight he suffered and for the attack on his ego. You didn't do anything wrong." Aslan caressed her cheek. "A person who truly loves you won't lay hands on you in anger. Won't scream at you, call you names or speak ill of you. They'll be honest. They'll be bare. They'll offer their heart and expect yours in return. They'll be loyal and sweet."

"You're sure of this?"

"I don't know what his plan is, but he was never going to be kind to you. Trolls are notorious bastards, but that doesn't give him the right to be terrible. You still standing and you still living are what's pissing him off. You didn't shrink or fade and he can't handle that, so he's showing his ass. Hold your head up. You're a wonderful person, and sweet as can be. I'm quite fond of you." He'd spoken some of the words in his heart and he had no regrets. He wanted time to develop his feelings, but still. He had nothing to take back.

"I know." She held onto his hand tighter. "Somewhere in my being, I knew he'd never be truly kind to me, but it's why I don't trust anyone. That's why I gravitated to your cat. You wouldn't talk back, but could turn on me, but if you did, then I wasn't out much. I'd chase you and try to take care, but cats are fickle."

"They can be." His was on occasion, but always with a reason. "You can't paint everyone with the same brush."

"No?" She sighed and closed her eyes. "You came in, took me from my situation and are holding me hostage. What else would you call it?"

"You're not a hostage." The fact she said that pained him. "I wanted to keep you safe."

"I know." She murmured the words, then dropped off to sleep.

He remained with her, listening to the cadence of her breathing. He knew some of what she'd been through, and it broke his heart. No one deserved to be treated that way.

If it took every breath in his body, he'd show her not everyone was out to cause her pain.

"Aslan?"

He sat up and raked his fingers through his hair. He knew that voice.

The Princess.

"Yes, my Queen." He left the bed, careful not to disturb Meela. "Just a moment." He shouldn't keep the Princess waiting, but he had to tread lightly. Meela had been through enough and he didn't want to add to her distress. He hurried to the doorway to the mirror in the hall.

The Princess's image shimmered in the polished glass. She smiled and clasped her hands together. Her blonde hair caught the light, and her eyes seemed brighter. She wasn't officially the Queen, but she was *his* queen. She'd brought so much stability to Eerie. She'd figured out how to harness the power of the cyclops and brought a love out in him the creature might not have thought possible. She commanded respect, but ruled with a careful touch. Aslan respected the hell out of her.

"My Princess." He bowed his head. "Thank you for your visit."

"You called me 'Queen.' Aslan, I'm no queen. Just a woman trying to keep this raucous town from falling apart," she said. "Look at me."

He did as she'd commanded. "Sorry."

"Don't apologize. You do that too much," she said. "I've been made aware of the situation with Meela. She sleeps?"

"For now." He leaned on the doorframe, then glanced back at Meela. She hadn't moved. Either she knew how to be that still, which wouldn't surprise him, or she was still asleep.

"She's been through so much," the Princess said. "She'll require a lot from you. Patience, tenderness, love."

"I'm sure."

"She's concerned she has no magic, isn't she?"

"Very much. Her father --"

"Her father was a charlatan, but he did have paranormal blood. He could read minds, but the severity of what he read overwhelmed him. He turned his work into an act and made a fool of himself in order to run from the turmoil. He heard everyone's thoughts and knew their desires. No one needs that much insight, but he had it," the Princess said. "And her mother was a conjurer. She helped her husband to keep his mind and body sorted out, but even his madness was too much for her to handle. He kept his problems from his daughter to protect her."

Fuck. One person could only handle so much. It sure seemed like life heaped onto her in truckloads. "No wonder."

"'No wonder' what?" the Princess asked. "She's scared? Tired?"

"No wonder she wants to hide from everyone and protect herself. No wonder she's depressed. She gave in to Tiernan because she probably thought she didn't deserve better. She was primed to be abused."

"Unfortunately, yes. She didn't know there was more. Her parents made a strong example, one she couldn't get out from under."

"What do I do to help her? She can't live that life." He wanted to see her smile. A real one, not the forced version she'd used. He craved the woman he'd made love to in his dreams. In her dreams. A thought occurred to him. "You said she's got magic. Is that how we managed to connect before we physically came into each other's orbit? Through the magic of dreams?"

"I know her magic, but I can't tell you. She has to find it for herself. What I can tell you is your meeting on the higher plane is part of that magic." The Princess smiled. "Now, about why I came here. I have eyes on Tiernan. I'd prefer she doesn't go back to the cabin, but it is safe. If you can keep her with you, even if it's to show her around town again, then do it. He wants her dead because he's afraid of her magic. He's afraid that when she realizes what she can do, she'll destroy him."

"Will she?"

"She could."

He wanted to ask more questions but didn't. If he was meant to know the answers, Meela would tell him. Hell, they'd only known each other for a couple hours. They hadn't had time for a date, to hold each other or even truly kiss.

"You need to be strong for her. She's been hurt and abused, and she'll want to lash out. Be kind to her." The Princess exhaled and leveled her gaze at Aslan. "Your cat called to her. Your human side is entranced. Embrace the love of your mate, even if it takes a while for her to come around."

"My..." He must've heard her wrong. His mate? Already? He barely believed her, but if anyone knew the truth, it was the Princess. She had an uncanny ability, no doubt magic, to know what was best for her people.

Before he could ask any other questions, the Princess disappeared.

He shook his head. She had lots of abilities, but coming and going as she pleased had to rank among the top. But she was a Princess. She should be able to do as she wanted.

He glanced back at Meela. She continued to sleep. She'd balled her hands and curled into herself. The tension on her face, despite being so still, bothered him. He could only imagine what she dreamed about.

He checked to make sure the house was locked up. No one, save for a powerful magical being like the Princess, would be able to get to them. He pressed his hand to the tablet pad to ensure everything was secure, then made his way back to the bedroom.

He'd left her alone for much too long. Still, he needed a shower and to change his clothes. The police sweatsuit was nice, but he'd rather wear his own stuff. He closed the door to the hallway before hurrying to the master bathroom. She'd have his bedroom for the duration. He'd switch his bathroom essentials to the spare bathroom in the morning.

He switched on the water. While the shower

heated, he stole a couple glances at Meela. The sooner he cleaned himself up, the faster he could be back beside her.

Steam billowed from the stall as he stepped into the vast space. The hot water stung his skin. The water also pissed off the cat. The animal didn't want to be wet. But he hated the sweaty scent after a shift. He stood under the rain showerhead and let the hot water wash over him. His muscles ached.

He cleansed himself, then washed his hair before rinsing. Once he turned off the water, he dried off. He'd worked hard to ensure he had a good life. Saved his money up so he could do what he wanted, not be dependent on someone else for his livelihood.

Now he wanted to share the benefits of his hard work with Meela. Would she allow it? He couldn't be sure.

He dressed in a T-shirt and running shorts, then crawled into bed with her. He stayed on top of the covers.

"You came back." She opened her eyes a fraction of an inch. "You smell good, too. Like soap."

"I wanted to be clean for you." He caressed her hip. "Everything okay?"

"Yeah." She snuggled against him. "I had a dream you'd left. Didn't want me any longer."

"Never." He could promise *that* wouldn't happen. If the Princess was right and Meela was his mate, if the cat was true in his decision to choose her as his person, then leaving wasn't part of the equation.

"Hold me?" She rolled onto her other side and pressed her back to his belly. "He wants to kill me."

He slid his arm around her and nuzzled her hair. The very thought someone would want her dead pissed him off. He didn't have to ask who she meant to know the truth. Tiernan wouldn't stop until he did the worst.

Let him. He'd have to go through Aslan first. And the cat wouldn't put up with anyone's shit.

Fuck Tiernan. Fuck him straight to hell.

Chapter Six

Meela huddled into Aslan. She couldn't explain her fears, but she certainly felt them. Darkness seemed to envelop her. A chill swept around her, despite Aslan holding her. She fought the urge to run. She could feel Tiernan trying to find her. She could almost hear him screaming at her.

Had to be residual anxiety from his past behavior. She'd have to shake that fear. Her future life mattered more than her past.

She trembled and tucked in tighter to Aslan. She feared the men in her life. Would she be afraid of Aslan eventually, too? God, she hoped not.

A vision of Tiernan's hulking form filled her mind. Anger blazed in his dark eyes and the creases in his brow deepened. His lips curled in anger. He shook his fist at her as he thundered toward her. *"You'll never get away from me,"* Tiernan said. *"Never ever get away. You're mine."*

She shuddered. His voice and presence were only in her memories, but that didn't diminish her terror. He'd managed to invade her mind. Managed to scare her all over again.

"You thought you'd get my money. Thought you'd get to keep my name. You lied to me." Tiernan reached for her. His gigantic hands clenched. *"You're never getting away from me."*

"No." She thrashed and kicked, anything to get away from him. The more she moved, the more her fear grew. He seemed to get closer. Jesus Christ, his threats were true. She'd never get away from Tiernan. Never be able to have a life of her own. "Get the fuck off me. I'm not property."

"Meela."

"No." She punched, connecting with something. Tiernan's hands on her? She wasn't sure. She kicked again. "Get the fuck away from me."

"Meela."

She knew that voice and it wasn't Tiernan. She gasped and fought through the blankets. "Fuck."

"Meela."

She blinked as she surfaced from the nightmare. Aslan caressed her arm. "Sweetheart, wake up. No one will hurt you."

She snapped to attention and rolled onto her other side to face him. She opened her mouth to speak, but no sound came out. She knew what he'd said and she trusted him, but she couldn't break free from her fear. Her heart hammered and her chest ached. She tensed all over.

"Meela, my brave, beautiful girl, you're safe. I promise you're safe." Aslan lightly held her hands. "My cat and I won't let anyone hurt you. We'll give our life for you."

She stared at him to process his words. What he'd said made sense. Why couldn't she accept it? Her conditioning refused to allow it. She closed her eyes and rested her forehead on his mouth. "Sorry," she whispered.

"You don't have to be sorry." He kissed her head, and his breath warmed her skin. "You were having a nightmare."

"One that's lasted for too long." She sucked in a ragged breath, then leaned back to look him in the eye. "I don't tell many people about my past, but last night, it all came tumbling out. Don't look at me with pity."

"Who pities you?" He brushed her hair off her face. "You've been through a lot, but you're still standing. That's the thing. You're still here. You might be hiding from him right now, but you're not quitting. He wants you to give up. To run away for good or worse and you're not going to do that. You're stronger than he expected."

She didn't feel strong. More like out of options and doing her best to keep body and mind together.

"I know, sweetheart. It's difficult, but you're not backing down." He brushed his nose along hers. "Don't be so hard on yourself."

"Yeah. I'll try." She tamped down her hesitation. One of these days she'd have to believe in herself a little more. Why did it seem so easy, but a gigantic mountain to climb? Just one foot in front of the other. "Have you been here all night?"

"I have. Don't want you to be alone, but I had to get cleaned up," he said. "And the Princess visited."

She snapped her attention to him. "What?"

"She did." He nodded. "Did you not want her here?"

"I didn't think she knew I existed." She'd tried so hard to stay out of sight.

"She knows everyone who's in the town. That's her job." He crinkled his brow. "I wanted to take you to see her and properly meet her this afternoon."

"I..." Properly... Holy shit. "I don't have anything to wear to attend court." She should be dressed in something good enough for the occasion. She barely had a couple changes of clothes. The notion of dressing for court, royal or otherwise, hadn't crossed her mind.

"You'll be fine. She wants to meet you and isn't expecting you to be in a gown. I won't be in a suit." He offered a smile. "Just be yourself. She's impressed with you and wants to speak to you about your protection. You deserve to breathe and get through this next part of your journey here in Eerie."

Her... She sat up and raked her fingers through her hair. Everything he said made sense, once again. She'd been through the wringer, but she'd let Tiernan win. She'd kept her distance and allowed him to screw her. No more.

She had no idea what the future with Aslan involved, but she'd been on her own for over seven years. The stretch of loneliness had to end. She didn't have to marry him, but she could enjoy more than his company. Wasn't that the life? Do what she wanted and worry about her heart later?

Her pesky heart wanted to get to know Aslan on a deeper level. Not just in bed in her dreams, not only in real life -- although she wanted that from the moment she'd seen him -- and not as merely a friend.

But it was too soon. She wasn't in love. Hell, she wasn't even sure what love looked like any longer, but she cared about him. His attraction to her seemed real, too. Why not explore it? She could keep her heart behind the wall for a while and enjoy him. Experience life a while.

Let Tiernan get fucked.

Besides, the Princess wanted to meet her. Wanted to help her. No one, save for Norm Slone, divorce lawyer gnome, had bothered before now. Not her parents, who'd abandoned her for the chance at fame outside of Eerie. Making money and having a following was more important than their only daughter.

Fine. They'd abandoned her and she could live with it.

Tiernan had screwed her over. Whatever. It wasn't a new thing, but she wasn't going to stand back while it happened.

Aslan had fallen into her lap. She refused to push him away.

It was time for her to accept the good things and make a few more happen for herself. She had a life that needed to be lived.

A resolve she hadn't known she possessed slid through her and settled in her brain. "You're right."

"Right about what?" Aslan sat up with her and folded his legs beneath himself. "I'm listening."

"I don't know what the future holds for me, but if the Princess wants to meet me, then fine. If I'm supposed to be in your orbit, then good. I've let Tiernan win for so long. It's time he paid for being a dick." She met his gaze. He'd given her clothes, a place to stay, and she swore he'd said something about protecting his mate. Was she that mate? Or had she dreamed the words? She could've.

"Then what do you want to do?"

She had to think. There were so many things. "How about a date? A chance to be normal, young and free. To do what everyone else does. You and I spend time out together. Yeah?"

"You're not afraid?" he asked. He nodded. "I'm very interested. You intrigue me and I want nothing from you other than to spend that time together."

He said the right things over and over. "I'm scared. I'll probably be scared of him for the rest of my life, but I can't let that fear run my life."

"You're right." He grinned. "What can I do to help you?"

She didn't have to think very long on this. "I would like you to stand beside me. Can you do that?"

"Of course." He slid his gaze over her, then winked. "You've intrigued me since we first met."

"We've made love and you still find me

intriguing?" She allowed herself to laugh. The break in tension helped. She liked the throaty sound of his laughter. She glanced at his mouth and the primal urge to kiss him swept over her. She'd kissed him so many times in her dreams. Why not in real life?

"What are you thinking?" he asked. "And yes, I do find you intriguing. Dreams are good and I cherished every moment of our time together then, but this is now. You still fascinate me. I want to get closer. I want what we did in dreams to be real."

"So do I." She bridged the gap between them and crushed her mouth onto his. The second she tasted him, she swore she'd come home. He tasted like sin and earth. Like the missing piece she hadn't known she'd lost.

He gathered her in his arms as she straddled his lap.

She wrapped her legs around him, basking in his heat. She threaded her fingers into his hair. The soft strands pleased her. Like touching pure silk. She bumped noses with him, then opened her mouth and nibbled on his bottom lip.

A growl rose in his throat. The sound vibrated from him to her chest. Her nipples beaded. Her pussy clenched and she grinded on him. Heat enveloped her. He sucked on her tongue. While he tasted her, he caressed her back down to her ass. His touches sent shockwaves through her system. She whimpered and smashed into him. She rubbed her chest on his, like she had to imprint his scent on her body. He cupped her jaw in one hand and squeezed her ass with the other.

The desire in his touch spurred her on. She slid her hands under his shirt, touching his bare chest. She swore her fingers burned. Still, she needed more.

He broke the kiss. "Yes." Aslan leaned back long

enough to remove his shirt, then embraced her again. "Touch me however you want. I'm in your hands."

She'd never been told that before. She caressed the planes of his chest, learning him. His flat nipples beaded under her touch. Another groan vibrated in him. He arched into her, and she plucked one of the tight beads.

"Fuck," he bit out. "More."

She loved his responsiveness. More, she loved being directed. She needed a patient lover, one who took the time to learn what she liked and could push her forward.

He rested his forehead against hers and panted. His eyes were tinged with yellow among the green. "Fuck. I want to touch you, too."

"Yeah?" she asked and nodded. She wriggled, then yanked the hem over her head. For once, she wasn't worried about her hair being in the right place or if the few extra pounds in her belly were visible. She wanted to be free. To let completely loose and enjoy lovemaking. To fuck.

He cupped her breast, caressing the sensitive skin in his fingers. "You have gorgeous boobs."

"Yeah?" She wouldn't have said that. Why was she even thinking hard enough to ask it?

"You do." He kissed his way along her jaw to her throat. "You both made and haunted my dreams. I couldn't wait to find you."

"For real?" She leaned back, offering her chest to him. Her bra straps slipped down her shoulders.

"Christ." He reached around her and unhooked the lingerie, exposing her upper body.

Instead of shying away from him, she moaned and tipped her head back. As he sucked on her nipple, she whimpered. She threaded her fingers in his hair again. Words escaped her. Her body tingled all over and she couldn't think straight.

She rocked on his lap. The world and her troubles seemed to melt away around her.

"I want to be inside you," he said against her breast. "Need to."

She wouldn't argue. She scooted off his lap and stretched out on the bed before wriggling out of her panties. Being nude tended to freak her out. She'd been under such scrutiny until she met Aslan in her dreams. Then he seemed to worship her. He was beautiful. When he looked at her now, she felt the same way. Cherished.

He stood long enough to drop his shorts, then crawled between her legs. His cock bobbed and rubbed against the sensitive skin of her inner thigh. She reached for him, but he simply laced his fingers with hers.

"No, sweetheart. Don't rush this. We've rushed too much." He situated his dick between the folds of her pussy and grinded on her. The liquid of her excitement slickened his way.

She wanted him to slide right into her. She wrapped her legs around his hips in silent encouragement.

"Soon." He braced himself on one hand and his knees. He curled over her and sucked on her breast again.

The sensations of his heat on her clit, the desire to be fucked, the way he raked his teeth over her nipple and his humming turned her senses inside out. Rational thought left her brain. She writhed and panted.

"God," she managed. "Fuck." Everything within her seemed to vibrate. Power like she'd never known radiated through her veins. She tipped her head back and gulped for air.

"Cry out for me." He let go of her breast, then arranged her hips. He entered her in one swift thrust.

She gasped at the fullness. Being with him in her dreams was delicious, but this was even better. Her pussy burned from being stretched. She wouldn't change a moment of their time together. The burn added to her delight.

She cried out and met him thrust for thrust. The sound of skin on skin echoed in the room. Fire lit in his eyes. His hair slipped over his forehead and tickled her skin. She stared at his face, memorizing the lines at the corners of his eyes, the flecks of green and yellow in his irises, the way he blushed as he made love and the corded muscle of his upper chest. She clung to him. Each thrust pushed her closer to coming apart.

"My God, I love this." He moved faster, pumping into her.

She loved the tenderly rough treatment. She clawed at his shoulders. "More."

"Always." He ratcheted up his speed until his movements turned clunky and feral. "So close."

So was she. She hung on tightly and moaned. She barely recognized her own voice.

"More." He nodded and continued to thrust. "Come with me. Tumble right over the edge."

She had no idea how he managed to sound so sexy and coherent. But his coaxing sent her blindly into orgasm. Her body tingled all over. Her nerve endings buzzed, and she swore she floated. The world evaporated around them. He was the only thing that mattered. Her troubles and worries were nothing. All she saw was him.

He pushed into her a few more times as he

growled and gritted his teeth. He surged into her, ramming his cock into her pussy. His seed spilled deep in her body. "Fuck."

She loved that they were both moved to one-word sentences. They'd affected each other so deeply. She'd never be the same. Making love to him in her dreams was good and being with him now was better. She couldn't wait for the next time they made love.

He collapsed on her, but instead of crushing her, he braced himself on his forearms and knees. His cock slipped from her pussy. He panted. His breath warmed her skin. "You blew my mind." He eased out from between her legs and flopped onto his back beside her on the bed.

"Uh-huh." She wanted to say something more intelligent, but the afterglow of the climax was too strong. She closed her eyes.

"Can't speak?" He slipped his arm across her belly. He nuzzled her cheek. "Got me scrambled."

"A little." Her body buzzed. She rolled onto her side and faced him. She wanted to bask in the afterglow of the orgasm, but words filled her mind.

"What's wrong, sweetheart?" He drew circles around her navel. "Talk to me when you're ready."

"I'm probably not the best person to get involved with because I'm broken in more places than I want to admit. I'm not innocent and I've been hurt. I'm not sure I want to be involved in a deep relationship, but this thing we've started is something I want to explore. I can't guarantee we're going to stay together or even make it. My heart's been too battered for me to know."

"Understood." He stayed beside her and tangled up closer.

"You don't have to convince me to fall for you or work extra hard to show me life is good. It'll happen if it's supposed to. Just be beside me. I've never had a fling in my life and maybe that's all we're supposed to be. We could be meant for more. Then again, you could decide you don't want me."

He sighed, but the tenderness remained in his eyes.

"Be patient with me. I'm trying to figure a lot out and while I am, I want you in my life." Truth be told, she'd started falling for him when she'd met him in her dreams. Was it love now? Not hardly. She didn't know him. He could be the kind of person who left socks all over the floor or tracked mud in. Could be the type of man who screamed and shouted.

Or he could be the love of her life, if she just allowed the feelings to fully develop.

"I don't back down easily and I'm not the one to get pushed around. I'm faithful and loyal. I won't shape myself into the person you need because I can only be the man I am. If I'm enough, great. If I'm not, then I'll still be your protector. I've seen through your dreams what you're afraid of and don't blame you for being scared. He's a monster. But if you give me the chance, I'll show you not all men are assholes."

Again, he said the things that mattered. She let his words wash over her, but she knew to her core he was right.

"Can you give me that chance?" Aslan asked. "Just a chance?"

She waited a beat, then nodded. "I can." If she had to be honest, she'd lost a piece of her heart to him already. She needed time to figure things out and fall harder for him, but something stirred within her. Something strong she couldn't ignore.

Right now, she needed time to fight back against her ex and to heal.

Chapter Seven

Aslan exhaled and a piece of him relaxed. She'd at least given him the opportunity to prove himself. Good. That's all he wanted. Christ. If she only knew how much he needed to belong. He kissed her again. He'd never get enough of touching, nibbling, and kissing her.

She leaned into him and sighed. "What time do we go meet the Princess?"

Shit. He'd forgotten all about that. "Doesn't matter, but it's probably best we get going soon."

"I'd like to have a shower." She smiled, albeit weakly. "Maybe the chance to raid your closet for a shirt."

"Of course." He hadn't thought about something better for her to wear. "I have a few things you might like, but yes, I'll..." Why did offering the bathroom to her seem so strange? Because he hadn't had a girlfriend in so long. He'd never had someone live with him. He'd screw this up.

"You can direct me to the bathroom. I can handle myself." She smiled. This time the genuine emotion came out. "I'm okay."

"I know you are, and I know you can." He grasped her hand. "I'm not worried *about* you. I'm worried *for* you and for what he might do to you."

"You are?" She narrowed her eyes but smiled. "I want to dismiss you, but I appreciate the concern."

"I don't know what all he's capable of, but I do know desperate people do stupid things to stop being desperate." He squeezed her fingers. "I'm scared he'll try to hurt you."

"He has already." She sighed. "He has no idea what he's in for. I'm not the same woman he cheated on. Not the same one he left. Not the same one he's pushed around for these years or the woman who hid from him."

"That's wonderful."

"Yeah?" She laughed and the sound was music to his ears.

"I'm proud of you."

"So am I." She brushed her nose along his. "I found something in me because I found someone who wasn't going to give up on me. More than that, I realized I don't want him to win. I'm tired. I don't want to be tired any longer. I want to live my life."

"Then start right now."

"I already did." She kissed him. "But I'm pretty sure I smell gamey. I don't want to meet someone important this way."

"I know." He left the bed and offered his hand. "Come here. The bathroom is this way."

"Thank you." She bumped shoulders with him. "I need a minute, but next time, I want you to join me."

"Yeah?" He couldn't wait. "It's an open shower stall. Rain showerhead. Just gotta stand under it and the buttons are on the wall. If you need help or something goes haywire, let me know."

"You know I will." She splayed her hand on his chest, then rubbed his nipple with her thumb. "I should've known when I saw that big old cat I was in for a wild ride, but I'd never be alone."

"Wish you hadn't met him?" The cat liked her too much to back down. That's why the animal had rubbed all over her. The cat needed to have his scent on her, so every other shifter knew damn well she was his person. She'd been chosen. If she asked him to walk away and give her space, he would, but he'd keep watching from afar. He also hoped like hell that wouldn't happen.

"Hadn't met you? I don't wish that. I'm glad I found that scruffy-looking cat and decided I needed to take him home to find his owner. I had no idea I'd be the owner, but I'm glad I didn't pass him or you by." She flicked his nipple again. "I don't feel worthy of a shifter or worthy of a sweet man, but I wouldn't change a thing about meeting you."

"I feel the same way." He patted her hip. "I'll get some shirts out for you, but why don't we plan on going for a ride after? I'll take you out and we could get ice cream or something. Yeah?"

She grinned and, overall, seemed to brighten. "A date?"

"Yes." He kissed her cheek. "Very much a date."

"I'm honored you asked me and yes, I'd love to go with you today." When she smiled, the light filled her eyes and she almost seemed to glow.

"Get cleaned up, sweetheart. I'll be here. Towels are on the rack and don't worry about getting water on the floor. It cleans up and won't hurt anything." He kissed her, then left her to her devices in the bathroom.

As he stepped into the bedroom, his phone buzzed. Odd. He hadn't set it to vibrate. He couldn't remember the last time he'd done that. He picked up the phone before swiping the screen. The icons flashed on the status bar. Texts and voicemails.

What the hell?

He retrieved the texts and scrolled through the list. His heart lodged in his throat. The number wasn't one he knew. Whoever it was had sent over fifty texts. He read the various lines and shook his head. The sender had some serious anger issues.

The minute he saw Meela's name, he froze. Fuck. These had to be from Tiernan.

Get her out of your house.
Get rid of her.
You won't like what's going to happen.
She's a whore.
A slut.
She cheats.
She lies.
She'll fuck you over and make you pay.
She made me pay.
She ruined my life.

What kind of man wrote that sort of stuff? A man with a fucked-up head. Part of him wanted to delete every one of the messages, but the rest of him opted to save them. He'd show these to the Princess and let her handle him. Should he tell Meela?

Fuck. How in the name of fuck had Tiernan gotten his number? He hadn't published it. He only gave the digits to people he trusted.

Someone he knew must've decided to offer up the information. That pissed him off. He kept his life on the down-low. He might not have mixed with the best people, but he didn't share his personal life with them. The more he kept to himself, the better.

One girlfriend claimed he was too much of a lone wolf for his own good.

Sure he was -- except his cat hated being referred to as a wolf.

So far, being on his own served him well. Then he'd met Meela and his outlook changed. He didn't want to be alone.

He also didn't want this shit with Tiernan.

The phone buzzed again, but this time with a call. Same number. He declined the call and waited for the icon for his voicemail to light up. The damn voicemail box should've been full by now. The icon blinked. He tapped his code to unlock the messages. Might as well listen to one.

He braced himself for whatever Tiernan would say.

"I know you're there. I saw you go home. Pick up and answer me, you fucking worthless cat. You're a fucking waste if you stay with her. She'll bring you down. She's trying to get me to pay years after she left me. She cheated on me and I'm paying her. Fucking don't believe it. She's a fucking mess, and you'll be a bigger one if you don't talk to me. Bitch."

He silenced the phone, then pinched the bridge of his nose. Holy fucking... This was unbelievable.

"What's wrong?" Meela joined him in the bedroom. "You're pale."

"What?" He growled, irritated with the turn of events. "You said he knows how to find people, right?"

"Who?" She rounded him. "He got to you?"

"He's connected, but he hasn't gotten to me." He held the phone out to her. "He called me. You can see the texts and listen to the voicemails, but I don't think you should. I won't hide them from you, but he's upset."

"I'm sure he is." She held tight to the towel around her body. "How'd he get your number?"

"I was going to ask you that." He met her gaze. "You said he tracks you. Be honest with me -- not because I'm angry. Because I want to be able to tell the Princess everything. Does he have magic that helps him locate you?" The more the Princess knew, the better she could handle the situation, and this was her town. He trusted her. Trusted both the Princess and her husband Diesel.

"If he's got magic, then I don't know about it. He's got a lot of troll friends and they're not stupid.

They're savvy and they know how to find information on people. I have no doubt he, or one of his minions, saw us together. I'm sure he's watching me. I don't know how they got your number, but it wouldn't shock me."

"Okay." He enveloped her in his arms and held her. He breathed in the scent of her hair and memorized the way she felt in his embrace. He wasn't sure how to protect her, but he did know how to get to the Princess.

"What?" She rested her forehead on his and tensed. "You're concerned? Want me to go?"

"Why would I want that?" He'd just gotten through to her. "I don't quit this easily."

"Maybe you don't, but a lot of people would. I have a lot of baggage and it's a lot to handle. I wouldn't blame you if you decided to run."

"No." He kept her in his arms. "You need someone who will stand up with you. Not someone who's going to buzz out when the going gets tough. Besides, my cat won't let me leave you. His senses tingled when we saw you. He loved the way you held him. You weren't afraid of the big fluffball. Weren't scared that this gigantic cat would eat you. A lot of others have been afraid."

"You're a big cat, yeah."

"Do you know others have run from me? Others have told me when they met the cat that they can't be with me? I'm too scary?" He shook his head and let go. "I honestly thought when I shifted in front of you and you were freaked out that it'd be the end before we'd had a chance to start." The possibility chilled him to the bone. Still did.

"You did startle me. One minute there's a cat, then the next there's a hot guy."

He chuckled. "Hot? You think I'm hot?"

"Yeah." She stuck her fingers in the waistband of his shorts and tugged him closer. "I don't just sleep with anyone. I'm attracted to you."

"Are you?" He nuzzled her cheek. "That's good. I'm attracted to you, too."

She blushed from her hairline to her chest. "What are you going to do about it?"

"I'm going to have you get dressed, get myself dressed, and get to the Princess." He doubted Tiernan and his goons were listening in, but he'd put nothing past them. Magic was a strange thing and could be manifested in many ways. So could technology. If someone wanted to listen in, there had to be a way. If they wanted to find him, then they could do that when he met with the Princess.

"I like the way you think." She kissed him. "I also like that you're being strong."

"Of course." He gestured to the shirt. "Your jeans will work, but this button-down over your tank should be fine. You can roll the sleeves up and tuck it in or something." He wasn't good at fashion. He barely knew what to wear himself. Plaids and stripes... what did or didn't look good together. Not his forte.

"Sure." She let the towel drop, then turned her back on him. She donned her panties, then her jeans before untwisting her bra. She shrugged into the lingerie. When she moved her hair out of the way, he rushed up to her.

"Let me help you." He hooked the clasps together. He kissed her bare shoulder. He noticed the dark spot on the back of her neck. He hadn't seen it before. Then again, he hadn't been looking at her hairline. "You've got a tattoo."

"No, it's a birthmark." She let her hair fall. "I've

never seen it."

"Want to?" He picked up his phone, then hesitated. "I'll show you later."

She frowned at him and tipped her head. She mouthed the word *why*.

He couldn't tell her right now. He simply shook his head. When they got to the Princess, then he'd show her. Something about the mark bothered him, but not in a bad way. The Princess could explain what the mark meant. It wasn't something that had occurred naturally when she was born. He knew that because he'd seen plenty of those. This was something else.

She narrowed her eyes but continued to get dressed. A few moments later, she'd donned the tank and shirt. When she rolled the sleeves up, he swore she was a model.

"Wow." He didn't have time to delight in her body right now, but he sure as hell wanted to. She was electric.

She blushed again. "We should… I don't know what we should do."

He did. It was time to go. He rushed through getting dressed, then abandoned his phone by the bed. The device wouldn't help him now. Not when magic would.

He pointed to a door at the back of the bedroom. "Here." He twisted the knob. When the door opened, a blinding light filled the room.

She started to speak, then silenced herself. She grasped his hand. When she nodded, she gave him courage. They were going to do this. Going to move forward.

He ushered her through the portal, straight into the castle. He hadn't made this move often. Normally, he walked or took his motorcycle. Today, though, was different. She might be safe in his house, but they needed a little more help.

He stood in the foyer, a known public space, then shut the portal. This might be a public space, but it was still behind the castle walls and still within protection of the Princess's guards.

Once the light extinguished, Meela exhaled and collapsed into him. "Oh, my God."

"Yeah." The whole thing was a bit overwhelming... and he hadn't even gotten her near the throne room.

"I didn't know you could do that."

"Get you out of trouble?"

"That, sure, but also have that kind of magic." She held onto his arm. "I thought only witches and mages had that kind of power. Are you extra magical? Or just that endowed?"

He snorted and bit back a laugh. She wasn't trying to be suggestive, but she'd done it anyway. "I have some abilities in my back pocket."

"I'm glad." She squeezed his fingers. "Why did you silence me back at the house?"

"I can't be certain, but I believe he was listening. I'm not sure how he infiltrated there, but I'm guessing he's somehow tracked your phone so he knows you're in town. He doesn't know where, but he knows you're here. He's got magic that's not usually imbued to a troll. Normally, they're not that smart, so does he have help? From whom? He knows too much. I get they're destructive and dangerous, but this is beyond that, which makes me think he's got inside information."

"How?"

"That's what we'll find out here with the Princess." He had to trust she'd have the answers. She was their biggest hope to get to the bottom of the truth.

Chapter Eight

Meela held tight to Aslan. She'd never set foot on the castle grounds -- until now. She hadn't needed to venture onto the property. Not when her father had been a huckster and her mother didn't like that sort of attention. She, like her mother, wanted to stay far away from the spotlight.

Going to the castle and around the property involved being seen. Right now, though, she was a bit invisible, which was good. Did the Princess even know they were there? Maybe not.

"Do we need to tell her we're here?" she asked. "Did she know we're coming over?"

"I haven't made a formal request, no." Aslan drummed his fingers on his hip. "I should tell someone."

"I'm guessing they have eyes everywhere and can see us." It stood to reason the most important being in Eerie would have the best security. "She probably knows."

"Still." He let go long enough to tap a pad on the wall. "It's old school and involves a code, but it works. Type the numbers, the code goes to the main board and the cyclops knows we're here."

"With a magical backup." Eerie was nothing but magic. She tensed as a thought occurred to her. The question had been digging away at her since he'd mentioned it. "Why'd you ask about my birthmark? People have noticed it -- my schoolmates, the kids who teased me, Tiernan who deemed it the mark of the devil... We don't have devils in Eerie. Do we?"

"We've got everything else," he muttered. "I'm sorry. You asked me a question and you deserve an answer."

Yet she felt dismissed by him. Like he hadn't been listening to the gravity of what she'd said. "I did. What's with you? Does that mark freak you out?"

"No." He snapped his attention to her. "God, no. But I don't want to give you the wrong information. I don't mind your mark. I think it's unique and makes you who you are. That's nothing to be ashamed of. Nothing to hide."

"Oh." Her irritation hadn't dampened. "I'm not a freak?"

"No." He offered her a small smile. "Far from it."

"Then what am I?"

"I'd like the Princess to let you know for sure, but I believe it's the mark of the phoenix."

"You're joking. I don't catch fire." She wasn't a phoenix. "I don't do anything. Don't have magic or anything." If she'd have had some sort of magic, she'd have known. She would've done something with it. Nope. She simply had a strange mark on the back of her neck.

"Then ask the Princess," he said. "I didn't expect you to believe me."

"It's too much." Good God.

"Why?"

"I've been ridiculed my entire life. When I found someone I thought might care, he turned out to be a waste. He lied to me, and I made it into something bigger than it ever was. I never pinned my hopes on a happily-ever-after, but I deserved better than him. If I have any magic, I should've seen his bullshit coming and run. I didn't." She'd veered off topic, but the fury she'd pent up had finally dissipated a little. "Sorry."

"You don't need to be sorry. You're frustrated and I get it."

"I also don't have to take it out on you."

"No, but I'm strong enough to handle it." He held her hand. "I've been through my share of shit. My mother was a full breed Maine Coon. Dad was a shifter, and his cat fell in love with Mom. They had a litter, my litter, but only two of us made it. She died birthing us and most of the kittens were underdeveloped. My sister lived for a few days, but she was too tiny. Sucked, but what's worse is that the pain of losing them all nearly killed my father. He lost a lot of himself because he felt guilty for the destruction. He drifted, and I ended up alone. It's not easy to be a kitten on the loose with no guidance. Now imagine being a shifter with no restrictions. I was chased in my cat form, harassed in my human form, and not wanted in either place."

"That's awful."

"It is. I learned to live in the shadows, taking scraps until I was old enough to make my own way properly. I made sure I got education, used it to play the financial markets, and built myself a nest egg. That's why I'm comfortable, but it's lonely. Women I'd meet didn't want a shifter. They wanted the cash. I've been attacked with a broom, nearly shaved, chased, bitten by dogs, in too many close scrapes with cars and never quite found my place."

"Until now?" she asked. "You're happy now?"

"I am with you, because we're both survivors and we're better off together. We understand each other."

"Maybe, but it doesn't make it hurt less." She withdrew from him. "I'm used to being ignored and pushed aside. To be honest, I don't mind being forgotten."

"Maybe you do, but I'm not him. I won't treat you like he did."

"No?" She had to calm down.

"No. What's wrong? I mentioned the mark and you're all upset. You've got a look in your eyes like you want to run from here. What's going on?" He held out both hands. "I'm in this with you."

She tried to take comfort in that, but it was almost impossible. "What if my mark is something bad? If it's not a phoenix or whatever, but something terrible? I could be the spawn of Satan or something. I could deserve this bad treatment. You don't know."

"I do know you don't because you're not the spawn of Hell." He continued to reach for her, but didn't grab. "You're asking for any answer to explain this and there is one, but we need the Princess."

"Where is she?" she snapped, not caring who heard her. She'd been left waiting a long time. A heartbeat later, she realized what she'd said and regretted her insolence. "Oh, my God. I'm sorry. Holy shit. I'm losing it."

"You might be, but so what? You've been through a lot. It's okay. I'm not sure where she is, but she'll be here. She's good people. Reliable."

Defeat overwhelmed her. "I know." She didn't deserve a meeting with the Princess. How could she when she didn't know this woman?

"Talk to me."

She capitulated. There was no point in holding out longer. "I'm scared. No one's ever brought up the mark being anything besides bad. I'd forgotten about it -- pushed it from my mind, really -- and moved on. It's a mark, it's there, I can't see it, but it burns every so often and I ignore it. Plain and simple. Now you've seen it, you have thoughts and I don't know what to say, other than I want it gone."

"I know what you could say." A woman walked

into the room. She smiled and offered her hand. She was dressed in a simple pair of jeans, burgundy tunic blouse, and flats. Her minimal makeup enhanced her looks and almost gave her a sparkle. "How about I help you?"

"Whoa." Meela froze. She'd never seen someone so understated and elegant in her life.

"I'm sorry I kept you waiting. Seems like every day there's another disaster. I'm Piper and yes, I'm the Princess. I'm in charge of Eerie. Hello, Aslan. And you must be Meela. I've heard a lot about you. It's good to get to finally meet you."

"You're..." No way. Piper looked more like the girls she'd worked with at the restaurant. Not like a Princess. Words escaped her as she shook hands with Piper.

"Hello, Your Highness," Aslan said, then bowed. "Good to see you again."

"And in the flesh." Piper smiled. "Diesel will be joining us in a moment. We had a gnome uprising at East Side and he's in the middle of sorting it out. He's better with stopping potential acts of violence -- way more than I am. I want to talk it out and he's more likely to glare quietly but get people to stop being silly. So, I hear you'd like an answer to your mark question, and we have an issue with a troll."

"Yes." Aslan nudged Meela. "You can talk. She won't bite. Promise."

She knew that, but she was in the presence of a Princess. She had to have decorum -- more than she'd had so far. She exhaled to center herself. "I'm Meela."

That was the dumbest thing she could've said. Piper had used her name. Of course, she knew who she was.

"I know." Piper gestured to Aslan. "I see Diesel's

here. Why don't you talk with him and give us a minute? He's got some questions about the *Locust Groove Club*. I've heard you're in the know about that place."

Meela jolted from her frozen state. *Locust Groove Club*? The strip club? And he knew about it? What was Aslan doing there? She had no right to be angry with him for having desires. For all she knew, he'd helped build the club or he knew the manager... or he'd dated one of the dancers. She didn't like the notion he might have been to the club recently.

Jealousy was truly a shithead.

"Yes, Your Highness," Aslan said. He bowed again, then turned his attention to Meela. "I'll be right back."

"Sure," Meela mumbled.

"Well." Piper waited until Aslan joined Diesel by the door. "I tell him every time to call me by my name. I hate that *Your Royal Highness* stuff. She shook her head, then motioned to a sofa. "Have a seat."

"Thanks." She joined Piper on the couch and rested her hands on her lap. "So."

"So."

"I'm in trouble." She had to be. The Princess would cast her out for being a problem. Maybe for her mark. For something anyway.

"You are?" Piper tucked her legs under her. "How so?"

"You don't know?"

"I have an idea, but I'd like to hear it from you. You've got a unique take on this, and it deserves to be heard." Piper laced her fingers together on her lap. "I'm listening."

"I was a sheltered young woman who married the wrong man... er, troll. He thought he'd get money from my family, but he didn't. We don't have any. But he thought we did, and he was terrible to me because he felt he'd been lied to. We divorced and he was forced to pay me alimony. He doesn't want to pay anyone, and he's threatened me." She leaned against the back of the sofa for stability. She poured out the rest of her story, all the times she'd been assaulted or abused, how she'd been stalked, and her things destroyed. "Now I'm here. I came to see my lawyer, Norm Slone --"

"The divorce lawyer gnome?" Piper sighed. "He was in the thick of the uprising. He wanted better living conditions for the gnomes."

"That's not terrible." She didn't know what sort of housing the gnomes lived in. "Bigger trees? Or mushrooms?"

"They have houses, but they're not paid well because... some of the magical beings discount them for being short or small. Don't ever tease Norm about his height. He'll go nuclear," Piper said. "I've seen it."

"So have I." She stared at Piper. "Aslan's been trying to help me, but it's a mess. I'm scared I'll be attacked. It appears Tiernan got to both my phone and Aslan's. I don't know what will make him stop."

"I've got some ideas." Piper nodded once. "First, let's see your mark."

"Do I have to show you?" She didn't want anyone else to see it. Albeit with reluctance, she turned and lifted her hair. "Okay."

"Ah." Piper touched the mark, caressing the edge. "Remarkable."

"Don't make fun." She let her hair fall around her shoulders, then faced Piper. "It's bad, right? I'm the devil's child or something?"

"No," Piper said. "Have you ever seen it?"

"No and I don't want to."

Piper held up her hand and a bubble formed on her palm. "Look."

An image formed in the crystal-clear shape. The back of Meela's neck. God damn it, she'd have to look at the mark after all. "I don't want to see it. I don't like it."

"Why not? Sweetie, it's the mark of the phoenix -- a bird with open wings." Piper rolled the image bubble in her fingers. "It's quite pretty."

She wouldn't have said pretty. Sure, she saw the image of the bird, almost bluish in nature, or a light purple like a fading bruise, but it wasn't anything cute. "Why do I have that?" She forced her gaze from the image. "So I have it. So what? Is it evil?"

"Who told you that?" Piper asked. "Tiernan? Aslan? It's not like him to say that."

"Not Aslan." Her nerves frayed. The more she contemplated the mark on her neck, the more it bothered her... almost like handling a time bomb because it could implode her life. "Is it bad?"

"No."

"You sound so sure and unbothered." Unlike her. She couldn't stand the thing. It freaked her out. And where was Aslan? Why hadn't he come back?

"First, the mark isn't evil. It's a phoenix, which means that you, like the bird, may be destroyed or feel as if you were, but you come back stronger. You do, don't you? You've had some times lately where you've felt utterly defeated, but you're still standing. I can see you."

"It's more like surviving." She'd been through her share of garbage.

"You're a fighter. You might feel like you've given up, but you haven't. Not really," Piper said.

"You can't entirely quit on yourself."

She hated to agree, but it was the truth. Every time she hit a wall, she put her head down and kept trying. She hadn't had much choice. Either she had to continue on or be bulldozed.

"You have an iron will you disregard because you're afraid -- to be like your parents, to fail. You're concerned that you won't measure up or that you'll get what you want, only to find out it wasn't what you thought... There are a hundred other reasons." Piper leveled her gaze at her. "Am I wrong?"

"Yes, you're wrong. I don't measure up." She was grasping, but also unsure of what to say. Besides, the Princess had to see what she meant. Simply had to.

"Sorry, but wrong." Piper shook her head, and a small smile curled on her lips. "Think about a time recently, like I asked before, that you could've backed down, but didn't. You've got one in mind, don't you?"

She might. Standing up for herself and deciding not to let Tiernan walk on her was one moment. "Okay."

"You didn't back down and you felt a power surge in you, didn't you?"

"A little." It was more like a tingling, but whatever. "So?" She really had to stop being so snotty, but she refused to admit she was worthy.

"Did the mark burn?"

"No." She had to think about it. "Well, a little. Sort of?" What a terrible answer...

"You do realize that was your power."

"No." She refused to believe it. "Can't be."

Piper stared at her and her brows rose, but she said nothing.

Meela processed what she'd been told and tried to consider every reason why Piper was wrong. Except that didn't feel right. Piper wasn't wrong, and she knew that to her core. But if this was her power, then how did that have anything to do with Tiernan? "He hates me, so why does he want me dead? He can't use a power that's on a mark on my body."

"Aslan?"

"Tiernan."

"Tiernan, yes."

"Why? It's not transferable -- is it?" She supposed it could be. "It's not actual magic."

"There are many kinds of magic, my dear. Some you can see, some you feel, some you know is there, but it's more like an idea, some that can move from one being to another and some that doesn't seem to do much. Shifters are the kind who can be seen. Witches cast spells that you feel. Mages and psychics have magic that can't be seen or felt but can be believed. There are those who have paranormal blood and a magic in them simply because they're something mortals haven't seen. Then there's the magic of immortality." Piper toyed with her ring. "Tiernan wants your magic for himself. He could've had it if he'd kept control of you."

"He was too greedy for that." Tiernan wanted fame, fortune, and status. She couldn't give him any of those.

"Your magic is confidence, but you're afraid to harness it. That's what he wanted. If you're confident, then you see he's full of bullshit."

She stared at the Princess. Everything she'd said made sense, but it also seemed ridiculous. "You mean, he needs my confidence? That I don't have?"

"Yes." Piper laughed. "Honey, you've been forced to shove that confidence so far down. Think about it this way. He's threatened to kill you, yes?"

"That, destroyed my stuff, messed up my car, wished me dead... you fill in the rest."

"Right. Now, back to thinking. He owes you money, right?"

"Alimony." She shrugged. Only for a few more years, but still.

"Okay, when you were scared of him, he had power. He could do whatever he wanted, and he knew you'd back down because of that fear. But now, you're not as afraid. You've got my help, Aslan, the court and the royal court. If he has any sense, he'll see he's up against so many people who aren't interested in his pompous troll ass. He's a troll and scary. So what? But when you show you're not afraid, that strips his power and he resorts to spiraling. It doesn't seem like that's much of a power, but it's huge."

"So stop backing down and he'll get angrier, but eventually, he'll run out of steam and stop being an asshole?"

"That and once you embrace that confidence, you'll realize you've had power all along. You've got the power to remake yourself, despite all that destruction. Honey, do you get it?" Piper asked.

"No." She didn't. Well, not entirely. She understood what she had to do with Tiernan -- not let him see her sweat.

"You're an immortal." Piper's smile widened. "The phoenix that can come back, despite the odds. If he could have a few drops of your blood, he might have that immortality. How would he get it? By, yes, causing you bodily harm, but also you giving it to him because he'd torn you down so much. That's why you don't quit. You know, somewhere in your cellular structure, that you're not giving up. Now do you get it?"

She let the words wash over her. The longer she stared at Piper and considered what she'd been told, the more she sagged in her seat. "Holy shit."

"I know, right? Immortal."

"Yeah." It didn't seem possible.

"Now, what are you going to do?" Piper asked. "You know."

"Live my life."

"You will and are. You've got a sweet man who is smitten with you and wants to be good to you."

"Aslan?" She balled her hands to hide the trembling. "I barely know him."

"So? You have plenty of time. It's not like you have to decide right now how you feel, but I will tell you the magic of mating doesn't lie. If it's chosen for you, then you have to comply. Doesn't mean you have to comply right away. It means you take time and get to know him. Get to understand. Get to find the ways he whimpers, moans, and gets his ire up. The good, the bad, the romantic."

She spied Aslan and her heart raced. She longed to throw herself into his arms. She'd never felt that way before. Did she understand mating magic? No, but if it was possible, then she wanted it with him.

"Okay?" Piper asked.

"Okay." She might not be sure of much, but she was sure she wanted to try.

Chapter Nine

Both Aslan and his cat couldn't wait to get back to Meela. His skin itched and he hated his lack of attention to Diesel, but his innate need to protect her overwhelmed him.

"You're going to get your head stuck that way permanently," Diesel said. "I get it. You're head over heels for her and you're not happy being here versus there."

Aslan tensed. He hated being so transparent. "Maybe."

"Don't bullshit a bullshitter." Diesel folded his arms. "Don't lie to yourself, either."

"I don't." He faced Diesel. "That gnome issue… who was involved?"

"Funny you've asked that." Diesel adjusted his hat, then bowed his head. "The gnomes want recognition and respect."

"Then earn it." He didn't see the issue. "What do they want respect and recognition for?"

"Dealing with the trolls. Apparently, some of the trolls have been causing trouble and the gnomes have fought them off. I've seen the clashes and have had to stop them, but this is getting out of control." Diesel shifted his hips, switching his weight from his left to his right foot. "The thing is, Meela's lawyer is the one heading up the arguments."

"Why?" He didn't understand. "Is he trying to argue with the trolls for a reason?"

"Big one. He's got a vested interest in Meela." Diesel crooked his brow, but his eye was obscured behind his dark glasses. "He knows about her mark and her parents. Her father had a psychic ability that's extremely sensitive. He played it off as bullshit, but he knew what he was doing. Her mother wasn't just a conjurer. She amplified his magic. That's why they worked together so well. But they're dead."

The cyclops excelled in being blunt. "They're dead?" Did she know?

"For two years. It's believed the trolls killed them."

He swore the wind had been knocked out of him. "Did anyone tell Meela?"

"She knows they're gone, but she doesn't know about the trolls," Diesel said. "I personally intercepted discussion between a few of the characters involved. She doesn't realize how long Tiernan's been gunning for her."

"Gunning?" His stomach churned.

Diesel nodded. "Look, you've been called to her, right?"

"Yes, but I don't see what that has to do with this situation. I'll protect her with my life." Something didn't add up.

"I know you will." Diesel shifted his weight again. "Tiernan's directing the other trolls to attack her. That's who's been harming her stuff. He doesn't have his hands directly in it, but he's the ringleader."

"So what's it got to do with her or her parents? He just hates her?" He needed a few more answers.

"He wants her powers and since he couldn't get them, he wants to destroy her. She has the ability to bring him to his knees through her confidence and sheer will."

"What? Come on." This was all bullshit. "You're normally so blunt. What's going on?"

"She's immortal."

The two words blew his mind. Immortal? Everything started to make so much more sense. She hadn't survived attempts on her life that he knew of, but she'd been through so much.

"Now do you get it?"

He nodded slowly. The wind rushed out of him anew, but he managed to stay upright. "He wants her blood so he can be immortal."

"Indeed."

"An immortal troll..." Brute force, dumb luck, and immortal. No one would be safe. "If he gets upset with anyone, they're fair game."

"Uh-huh."

"So it's not about the money he owes her or even the divorce. He thought she'd just give herself up to him and let him do... what?" Aslan asked. "And did you know that I'd be connected here?"

"Piper knew you were meant to be with Meela, but it took her a while to get you two in the same space. That's why you were directed to prowl yesterday. As for Norm, he knew she'd be coming back because of the money aspect. He's doing whatever he can to get rid of Tiernan on his own," Diesel said. "It won't work. Tiernan's hell-bent on destroying anyone who goes against him. Norm has no chance."

"But he's trying in court and on his own?" Foolish, but worthy of respect. "So what do we do?"

"Norm's still fighting the good fight in court and somehow on the streets. There are other trolls trying to rise up with Tiernan, but they don't really know why. You and Meela need to go about your business. That sounds foolish, I know, but you need to," Diesel said. "Live your life and have fun, if it's possible."

He stared at Diesel. The man didn't say much. The fact they'd had this conversation, with Diesel speaking at length, wasn't lost on him. He nodded and let the words mull around in his brain. "The more she simply exists and isn't afraid of him, the more power he cedes. If he's not explaining to the other trolls what's going on, then they'll lose interest. Eventually, either Norm will end up in court or dead, but somehow there will be an answer." He didn't want Norm to end up killed over money. "This is fucked up, and all because Tiernan wants to be immortal."

"When you can be immortal and wreak havoc for eternity, I guess that's a goal?" Diesel shook his head. "They're done and you need to go to her. Meela needs some time to regroup, but she also needs to be normal - - as normal as you can be in this town."

"Understood." He could do this if she'd allow him. "I'll take care of her."

"She's going to give you a run for your money. She's a fighter."

"I know." That's what he liked about her. "Doesn't bother me."

"Just know what you're up against." Diesel snorted. "Go to your girl."

"I will." He abandoned Diesel on the other side of the room and rushed up to Meela. He didn't want to look too eager, but he did look forward to holding her again.

"Hi." Meela's smile appeared forced. She rubbed her arms and fidgeted. "You're done?"

"I am, are you?" He slipped his gaze to the Princess. "Your Highness."

"I told you, call me Piper." Piper shook her head but laughed. "Did Diesel talk your ear off?"

"He did." He rubbed Meela's back. He wanted to say something, but he wasn't sure what words might ease her mind.

"When you get him to talk, he's chatty. It's getting him to talk that's the issue." Piper leaned into

Diesel. "You were talkative?"

"Had to be." Diesel shifted his hat low on his brow, obscuring his eye. He said nothing else, not that it bothered Aslan. His cat wasn't much for chatter, either.

"So," Meela said. "Live my life?"

"You should," Piper replied. "Here's the thing. You've got a lot to live for, but you've also got one hell of a spell around you. Not just mine, but one from your father, too. Your parents knew you were special, but they were too overwhelmed with their situation to help you when Tiernan showed up. That's *why* you were surrounded with the spell. You're immortal, sure, but that's an extra layer. Mine will be one, too. Now you've got the help of Aslan, who won't leave your side, Norm, the fool gnome, the gnome fighters, Diesel, and me. That's a lot in your favor."

"It is." Meela leaned into Aslan. "I want to get out of here. I should see Norm, but I'd like something to eat, too."

"You bet." He'd do whatever she wanted.

"Oh." Piper held up her hand. "If there's an issue, we're watching you. Not because I don't trust you, but because I don't trust Tiernan. If he makes a move, I'll know, and it won't be pretty for him. You may not see those around you keeping you safe, but they're there."

"I appreciate it." Meela slipped her hand into Aslan's back pocket.

"Let's go. I know a few places to eat and there's a whole town to explore." Aslan kept her close. "It's different when you're here in a good mood."

"I bet it is." She finally smiled and seemed to relax. "Thank you, Piper. Diesel. I appreciate it." She nodded, then walked with Aslan to the door.

"Thanks, Princess. Cyclops. We won't let you down." Aslan twisted the knob, then waited for Meela to enter the hallway first.

Once the door closed, Meela whimpered. "I don't know what to think."

"Does it matter?" Aslan laced his fingers with hers. "I don't mean that in a flip way. Don't worry about what's going on. You've got one job -- to live your life. Do it."

"I should." Meela flipped a lock of her hair off her forehead. "Do you know where we could go to get some ice cream? I haven't had Eerie ice cream in so long."

"Complete with magical sprinkles and candy charms?" He nodded once. "I have an idea. Ever been to *Cat in the Cream*?"

Her eyes lit up. "Not in years. It's still open?"

"It is." And he knew how to get there quickly. "Shall we?" He offered his arm. When she accepted, he led her down the corridor to the main gates of the castle.

"The sun's so bright." She blinked and shielded her eyes with her free hand. "Smells good, though."

He'd caught the scent of the castle and the air in Eerie plenty of times, but now he appreciated it a bit more. There was a sweetness surrounding them. "Almost feels like comfort. Like being in a warm blanket on a chilly day. Or cake."

"Definitely cake." She bumped shoulders with him. "I'd cuddle up in a blanket with you or your cat."

"He does like you." He strolled right down the main street of Eerie with the prettiest woman on his arm. His chest puffed out, and he embraced a pride he'd never felt before. When in his cat form, he preferred to blend into his surroundings. It made life easier. If he couldn't be seen, then he could move around without getting hurt or caught. But right now? He wanted everyone to see him. Not because of Meela. Because he was finally happy.

"You're beaming like a fool." She grinned. "You like ambrosia ice cream that much? Or is there a sweet little kitty there waiting for you?"

"I've got the sweetest kitty right beside me." He kissed her cheek. "I'm not exactly a ladies' man."

"No?" She laughed and the sound pleased him.

"Nope. Women seemed to be turned off by a guy who shifts into a cat."

"Are you serious? I love that you do."

She'd said *love*. He shouldn't read so much into it, but he couldn't help himself. He wanted someone to love him the way he'd started falling for her.

"You're stunned." She nodded, the move exaggerated. "But hear me out. I can touch all over you when you're like this and please us both. Let's be honest. It's rather nice to enjoy each other's body. But then when the cat comes out, I've got the best job, which is taking care of him. Cuddling him. Burying my face in his fur. Feeling him purr and listening to his chirp. I'm a cat lady from way back, but I haven't been able to have a cat, so I'm all for this."

"Just to be my owner?" he asked and opened the door to the creamery. "I require more than an owner. I want a lover and a partner."

"Who says I can't be those, too?" She poked his belly as she slipped past him into the building. "I might want to be all of those things."

He sure hoped so. He followed her up to the counter.

Sassy, one of the cashiers, whooped. "He lives."

He swore he blushed all over. His ears burned.

"You live?" Meela grasped his hand. "Were you about to die?"

He inched up to the counter, ready to argue with Sassy, but she spoke first. "Oh, my God. We thought you'd been killed. It's a mess. The gnomes and trolls are at war with each other. We heard you'd been caught up in it. Someone said they saw you'd been killed. Another person thought you'd been taken prisoner." Sassy rubbed her brow, then rushed around the counter. "If anyone can get out of a jam, it's you."

She made him sound better than he was. He fumbled. "I'm fine. I'd like you to meet Meela."

"Meela?" Sassy's eyes widened. "So you're the famed woman?" She tipped her head, then swept her gaze up and down Meela.

"Is there an issue?" Meela asked. "I can leave."

"No." Sassy's eyes widened again and she stepped back. "I see why everyone thought Aslan was dead. It all makes sense."

"It does?" Aslan wanted to hide. He hated being the center of attention. He hadn't minded walking up and down the road with Meela, but this wasn't his idea of fun.

"She's beautiful, As. And I can see in your eyes that you care about her." Sassy turned her attention to Meela. "You're in good hands, honey. He's the best."

Meela shifted her gaze between Aslan and Sassy. "I know."

At least one of them did. Aslan and his cat both wanted to get the hell out of there. The attention was too much.

"Let's get you some ice cream. My treat." Sassy waved her arm. "Sprinkles and candies included."

He shrugged, not sure what to say. He'd have to do a lot of explaining, but he also wanted to ask about the battles. After food. Meela needed some normalcy.

Meela ordered her ice cream, then waited for Aslan to place his order. When Sassy handed over both cones, Meela nodded once. "Thank you. This looks delicious. I told Aslan I haven't been here since I was a little girl."

"I remember." Sassy's grin softened. "Your parents were kind people. They never seemed to mind shifters, gnomes, those with a shaky grasp on their magic, even the minotaur and chupacabras weren't shunned. That's a big thing. And little Meela was right there, trying to help. I bet you don't remember that."

Meela toyed with her cone, flicking at the paper with her thumbnail. "I don't."

"You will. Let the town wash over you." Sassy winked. "Aslan, bring her around and don't be a stranger yourself. We like seeing you both here. You're always welcome."

"Thank you." Aslan held the door for Meela. "Just a moment." He left her by the door, but within her view.

Sassy tipped her head again. "What's wrong?"

"You said you'd heard I'd died or been caught. What's going on?" he asked. "Tell me what you know."

Meela joined him and nodded. "I'd like to know, too. I don't want you to be in danger."

"We're not in danger," Sassy said. "So, there's a troll who thinks he should run this town. He's making life difficult for everyone who gets in his way. No one knows what's pissed him off. Just that he's upset. He's killed half a dozen gnomes. Norm Slone's pissed. The gnomes haven't done anything to deserve it other than exist. I heard the troll killed a handful of cat shifters and destroyed a rental house. I don't know what's gotten into him, but the destruction is ridiculous. I thought you were one of the shifters killed, but you're here, so that's good. Terrible for them, though."

Meela covered her mouth with her free hand and a tear slid down her cheek. "This is nuts."

"Do you know what's pissed him off?" Sassy asked. "No one knows why."

"He's angry with me." Meela fiddled with her cone. "I should get a cup for this. It's going to melt."

"Sure." Sassy retrieved two dishes. "Here. What do you mean he's mad at you?"

Meela stuck her cone into the dish. She recounted the story and shrugged a couple times. "It's a mess."

Aslan hated for the conversation to go this way. "He's a son of a bitch, wanting something that's not his, and he's angry because he can't have it."

"So he's making everyone pay for his perceived misfortune?" Sassy clicked her tongue. "I knew it had to be something that ignorant. Trolls. They could mean well, but they're trouble."

"It's misguided anger, even if he is entitled to it." Aslan dropped his cone into the second dish. He accepted a spoon from Sassy. "I don't know what it'll take to stop him."

"I do." Meela dug into her ice cream. She ate a spoonful and groaned. "I forgot how good this is."

"I'm glad you enjoy it." Sassy grinned. "I don't know what you're going to do, but I trust you both. Aslan's good with tactics, and you seem to know what you want, Meela. Gives me hope this will end soon and without too much more bloodshed."

He didn't have quite as much faith in himself as Sassy did, but he refused to show it.

"I can't say how fast it'll be over, but it won't last forever." Meela held up her dish. "Thank you for this.

When we're done, we'll be back and we'll pay. I love a good deal, but I'm not above paying for something, especially when I love it."

"I look forward to it." Sassy waved. "Come back soon."

Aslan nodded to bid her farewell, then followed Meela out of the shop. "What did you have in mind?"

Meela gestured to one of the tables. "First, we feast. We can't waste this delicious ice cream."

"No, we can't." He couldn't eat, though. "Talk while we feast?"

"Okay." She folded her legs under her and faced him. "This is what I want to do."

"I'm listening." He wasn't sure what she had in mind, but he wasn't about to argue. He sensed a resolve in her that hadn't been there before. Almost like that same fire that'd sparked after they'd made love was back and stronger. He hoped he was part of the reason for that blaze.

She'd created an electricity in him he couldn't deny. He'd follow her anywhere. Give up his life for her. Keep her safe at all costs.

She had his heart. Even so fast. He'd found his mate. He'd do everything he could for her.

Everything.

Chapter Ten

Meela ate her ice cream. The cool cream slid down her throat and the candies added a bit of pop. She hadn't delighted in such a treat in so long. Part of her longed to remember those days with her parents. If Sassy swore she'd been there, then she probably had. Meela just wished she remembered it. So many things from her past were missing. Had she ignored her childhood because of the embarrassment of her parents? That seemed odd. She remembered other bits, like traveling and various hotels. The speaking engagements and crowds. But not the creamery.

"You're deep in thought." Aslan finished his ice cream first. "Are you okay?"

"I'm a little sad, but you'll think it's silly."

"I won't."

She trusted him. He probably wouldn't find her musings goofy. His smile, full of sincerity, gave her courage. "I wish I remembered being here when I was small. I don't. There are so many memories that are gone because I blocked them out. That makes me sad. Why are those memories gone?"

"The mind is a fickle thing. It keeps certain memories and tosses others. I don't know why." He put his dish down. "Maybe once this is all over, you'll find the memories and can put things all back together."

"You think so?"

"When you can heal, you will. You haven't been given much of a chance to do that. You've been running, hiding, and scared for a long time. Now you can rest. Heal." Aslan caressed her thigh. "You're strong."

"I know." She placed her dish with his. They'd

have to take the dishes back into the shop soon, but she had to tell him a few things first. "I thought I wasn't. Thought I was going to fade away. I'd let him run my life. Now that I've had a taste of what I can do and have seen what's out there in the world, I don't want to be directed. Don't want to be controlled."

"You shouldn't be."

"You won't try? To control me?"

"Never."

That reassured her. "You'd be a partner?"

"In whatever mischief you can find." His eyes sparkled. "I'm a cat. I'm naturally curious and up for an adventure."

She scooted closer to him and grasped his hand. "I'm game for an adventure. First, we have to deal with my troll, which could be good and could be shit. Are you interested?"

He leaned in. "I'm listening. What do you have in mind? On either account?"

She screwed up every ounce of her courage. If she wanted something, she needed to tell him. "Piper says I'm being watched, yes? Then she'll know when we have to face Tiernan. I'm tired of running from him, so let's end this. I don't think he's got the guts to kill me. He wants the fear. Wants me to cave. Fuck him. I'm not caving."

"You shouldn't." He held her hand, caressing her knuckles. "I'm in this with you."

"You barely know me." She hadn't said it out of anger. More like bewilderment.

"Maybe not, but we'll have a long time afterward to do just that. I can't explain what I feel, but there's a connection between us. Diesel said you and I were meant to find each other. I'm not arguing. I like you. Might even be falling for you." Aslan sighed. A smile curled on his lips. "Jesus. I haven't said such things to anyone else. Never tried to. You bring out a protectiveness in me. I want to help you, touch you, make love to you. Grow old together -- inasmuch as you can."

She slipped her hand over his cheek and cupped his jaw. "Is it crazy that I feel it, too?" She'd been drawn to him. Completely unexplainable, but true. Besides that, he'd said he'd started falling in love with her. Maybe she was naive, but she liked that. She wanted someone to fall for her, to love her for her quirks and join her in her adventures while she joined him on his.

"Nope. Not crazy at all." He scooted her onto his lap. He held her and rested his forehead against hers. "I'm game."

"Me, too." She stared into his eyes and saw not only the man, but the cat and their pure heart. "What I want to do, before we stop his ass and make him pay for the atrocities he's created..."

"Yeah?" He caressed her backside.

His touch emboldened her. "With Piper and the full power of the royals behind us."

"Sounds about right." His breath tickled her skin. "Then what?"

"Before that, I want to make love to you." She threaded her arms around his neck. "They said we should have a life and live it, but I'd rather stop him first."

"And we make love after?"

"No." She kissed him hard, needing his touch and to taste him. She bumped noses with him, but she didn't care. This connection mattered. When he broke the kiss, she panted. "I need to make love to you. Need to feel you moving in me. Need your arms around me."

"We can go back to the house." He patted her ass. "I'll get us there."

"No." She placed her finger over his mouth. "Right now. I know where we can go. Not far from here, but it's private enough." Truth be told, the act of making love outside, with the distinct possibility they'd get caught, turned her on. Hell, she was wet for him after simply sitting on his lap. She wanted him to ravish her, make her bite her lip to keep from crying out, and to make her shudder around him.

Was that too much to ask?

No.

"You do?" His eyes lit with fire and his lips curled in a smile. "I'm game."

"Still?"

"Always."

She managed to stand, but her knees wobbled -- out of desire, excitement and electricity. When he offered his hand, she grasped his fingers.

"We should take the dishes in." Aslan hesitated.

"I see Sassy. She'll get them. Come on." She tugged him, encouraging him to move. She had plenty of ideas where they could go, but not enough time. She'd been all over this town, and knew nooks and crannies probably only the Princess knew about. A thought occurred to her. Piper, if she was truly keeping an eye on them, would be able to see what they were doing. For once, she wished she had a cloaking spell. But then again, if she used it, with her luck Tiernan would find her and she'd end up dead. No one would see her. Maybe it was better that she could be seen.

Getting caught certainly did add to the excitement of the moment.

Her senses buzzed as she dragged a more-than-willing Aslan to the woods. She'd seen a couple of cabins there and clusters of large rocks. Down by the creek would be a good place, too.

"We don't have to rush." Aslan scooped her into his arms. "But we don't have to go that slowly, either." He hurried into the woods.

She slipped her arms around his neck. "I bet you know all the good places."

"I might." He practically ran along the path through the trees.

She barely saw where they were going. Instead, she held on for dear life and laughed along the way. She marveled at how he seemed unbothered at carrying her. Wasn't she heavy?

"Aslan." She buried her face against his shoulder. The sunlight warmed her cheeks and the mark on her neck burned. For once, she didn't mind. It had to be a sign she was doing the right thing. Following her heart.

He carried her to a clearing, then to an outcropping of boulders. The niche was perfect for a tryst. The cool air, the scent of pine... and they could hear anyone coming to interrupt them.

He placed her on her feet. "Good?"

"Better than good." She crushed him between her body and the rock, kissing him. When he opened to her, she sucked on his tongue. At the same time, she reached between their bodies and popped the buttons on his jeans. She had the denim open in no time.

He broke the kiss and moaned. "Gonna make me come before I get inside you."

"So we'll go two rounds." She kissed him again and tasted him. The sheer force of being with him overwhelmed her. Her brain swam.

He opened the front of her shirt, then shoved the

undershirt up over her breasts. She clawed at him as he pushed her bra up out of the way, exposing her boobs. The sheer excitement of the moment washed over her. She loved being this free.

"Want you inside me." She fumbled with her own jeans, finally popping the button. She'd never been this free with anyone. With his help, she managed to shove her jeans down one leg and freed her foot from the cumbersome material.

Aslan turned them around, bracing her on the rock as he draped her legs around his waist.

The sound of the birds, the bits of sunshine dappling the grass and the slight breeze didn't matter. She held onto his shoulders and panted as he pushed into her in one thrust. The tight fit spurred her on. Like he was made for her. She wriggled her hips in a silent invitation for him to move.

"Need you."

"Need you, too." She used the leverage of her body on the rock as well as the excitement brewing between them to invite him to thrust.

"Can't hold back." He began to move, pistoning into her in seconds.

Meela basked in the thrill of being free with him. For the first time in she couldn't remember how long, nothing bothered her. The devil was at her heels, her world could fall apart at any second, but she could handle it because she had this moment.

"Tight, sweetheart." He panted as he sped up his rhythm. The sound of skin on skin, their moans, and the crunch of leaves under Aslan's feet were so loud.

"Feels good." She tightened her legs around his waist. She met him thrust for thrust, matching his cadence.

A fresh wave of delight rippled through her.

They could be caught, could be fined or even jailed. Did that matter? No. Being with Aslan was too much fun. Too perfect. She'd never done anything so mischievous in her life. She stayed within the lines and followed the rules. No waves made and no trouble. Why? Having some good fun and making some mild trouble wasn't so bad.

"Making my knees weak." Aslan tipped his head back and moaned. "How do you do this to me?"

She wasn't sure, but she liked it. She bounced on his cock, loving the way he felt inside her. The fit was tight, but perfect. He touched her in places she hadn't known existed -- like her heart. Her nipples beaded and sensitized as they brushed against his shirt. She longed for him to grasp one of her breasts as he pushed into her. Next time.

The coil in her belly that had tightened with each thrust wound so tight she couldn't think straight. Too much more and she'd combust. The mark on her neck heated but didn't hurt. Almost like a warm blanket on her body.

She dug her nails into his arms. "Aslan."

"Right. Here." He grunted, and his moves turned feral. He smashed her into the rock. "I can't…"

Neither could she. She wasn't even sure what he meant, but she couldn't. She lost herself in the growing orgasm. The coil, unable to be tightened any further, sprang. The climax slammed through her body, starting in her brain, then down to her limbs, through her pussy, before exploding in her chest.

Aslan pushed harder. His cries filled the air as he gritted his teeth. He buried his face against her neck and thrust into her to the hilt. His cock throbbed as he came. A shiver ran through his body. He said something, but she had no idea what.

She lolled in his arms, riding the waves of bliss. She'd come before, but this was unlike any of those times. This was heady, but also like she'd melted. Like every one of her limbs was jelly. Impossible. She held onto him and closed her eyes.

This moment not only made her happy. It changed her. She'd finally experienced overwhelming desire and being loved. Being needed. Being wanted. She'd never be the same.

Did she want to be? No. She preferred this breathlessness.

She panted. "This was so crazy."

"You know we could've been caught." He rested his head on her shoulder.

"Yeah, we should've been." She laughed and held onto him. "I don't care."

"I don't care either, unless I get a knife in my back because they snuck up on us." Aslan sobered. "It's quick, but I'm fond of you already. I will give my life for you."

"And your cat?" She didn't want to get too excited, but she'd longed to hear those words for what seemed like an eternity.

"He agrees."

"When this is all over, I want to see him. He gave me a reason to feel needed. Then he brought you to me." She was so glad she'd seen him on the side of the road. He'd truly saved her. She owed Aslan and the cat her life.

"You've got both of us." Aslan slipped out of her and placed her on her feet. "Did you hear that?" He stuffed his cock back in his pants. He tipped his head and froze.

Her mark tingled. No, this time it full-on burned. She righted her bra, then buttoned her shirt. He tugged her jeans up. Something rattled in the woods. She'd heard it. Definitely. "We need to move."

"We do." He turned, then stopped and held up his hand. "Come on. This way."

She trusted that he knew the quickest way through the woods and well enough to be undetectable. She followed closely behind him and held onto his shirt. Her mark felt like it was on fire. Was this her chance to prove herself and that she could be rebuilt? She hoped so. She wasn't ready to back down again. No, she was tired of it, really.

At the edge of the woods, she spied Tiernan. "Oh shit."

"You thought you could get away from me?" Tiernan blocked their path. "Thought you could hook up with the fuzzball and be free? Yeah, no."

"No?" What an odd thing for him to say, since he'd been the first one to leave.

"No." Tiernan strode up to her. "I used to wonder where we went wrong and why we ended."

"I'm not your puppet, that's why. I stopped giving in to you." She folded her arms. "You wanted money, and I wasn't able to give what I didn't have. Never have had it." She'd never been this bold before and she rather liked it.

"Your old man lied," Tiernan snapped.

"He did that." She stood her ground. When she glanced through her peripheral vision, she noticed Aslan beside her. "But you knew that, Tiernan."

"No one lies to me." Tiernan's lip curled in a sneer.

"Except a liar." She stepped toward him. "But you knew that, too."

"I knew he'd lied so I'd marry you and get you out of his house."

She didn't doubt her father would've said something like that. Her father liked to play games. "But he knew something, and so did you. Something you both should've told me."

"And what's that?" Tiernan asked. He whipped the axe from his belt and slapped the handle in his hand. The clicking and slapping were so loud!

Was he trying to be scary? It wasn't working. She held firm, refusing to be intimidated any longer. "He told me trolls are fickle and narcissistic. They're out for themselves. They only want to do what makes them happy. They're greedy and selfish. They're rotten and mean, too," she said. "But most of all, they lie."

"We can't," Tiernan said. "Isn't in our DNA."

"Your DNA. You make yourself sound like you're intelligent." She stepped up to him. "If you are, then why are you trying to kill me?"

"Just wanted to scare you."

"Do you want to go with that answer or try for the truth?" She wasn't sure where Aslan was at the moment. She hoped he'd gone to get help. "You know."

"Your daddy said you had money, and you didn't. So what's there to lie about? You know the truth now," Tiernan said.

"I did know that truth. Knew that you didn't really love me. Never." She flexed her hands. Something surged within her. "I knew you didn't want good things for me. You wanted to see me hurt."

"No." He shrugged. "Just needed to get you in line."

"Why?" She needed him to say it. Needed him to speak the words, not just dance around it. He knew the truth.

"You needed to be broken." Tiernan glared at

her. "And your boy toy left. I told you, you weren't going to amount to anything. You should be broken."

"When you couldn't get to me, you broke into my apartment. You stopped paying the money you owed me. You killed gnomes to make your point." Her voice strained. "Destroyed my car -- the one I bought on my own? To get me in line? Even I know better than that." She clicked her tongue.

"You do?"

"And I don't need Aslan here to help me." She trusted Aslan would, but also that he'd get the right people to assist them as well. "I can handle it."

"Why?"

"You know why." She still needed him to say it. "You know."

"Your daddy's unstable magic won't help you and his money was a joke. You're on your own," Tiernan said with a snort.

"Never." She placed her hand on the axe. "You know why you wanted me and why it'll never work."

"You're the devil." He glared at her anew. "Devil woman."

She rolled her eyes. "That mark has nothing to do with the devil and you know that, too."

He scoffed. "You don't think it has to do with immortality, do you? It's not true."

"No?" But he'd brought up immortality. She hadn't. She ran her finger over the blade, drawing a drop of blood from the cut. "Prove it doesn't matter."

His eyes glazed. He licked his lips. He flexed his hands on the axe and stared only at her finger. At the bright red blood.

"For a man who doesn't care, you're paying a lot of attention to my blood. Funny, that." She eased her hand back and licked her finger. "You know as well as

I do why you want me. I can give you what no one else can." The mark on her neck blazed. A power she'd never known she possessed surged through her.

"You could give me power beyond my wildest dreams." He whipped the axe through the air, holding the tool high. "Bleed for me."

"No." She flexed her fingers. The power in her hands radiated to the axe. The implement flew from his grasp. She moved her hands slightly and directed the axe without her direct touch, holding it to his throat. "You picked the wrong girl to mess with. You thought you'd get me in line. Make me work for you. Not a chance. I didn't know my power before, but I do now. You can't stand confidence. Can't handle courage. Don't want a woman who won't listen to commands. If you want those things, then I'm not your girl."

"We were fated," Tiernan said. A bead of sweat slid down his temple. "You can't kill your mate."

"No one says I will." She pushed the blade closer to his throat. "But as you're not my mate, it doesn't matter."

"No, but he is." Tiernan continued to sweat, but he nodded behind her. "Your puss won't like dying. Skin him if she tries anything. Skin him anyway. I want her to tremble."

He could be bluffing. Then again, he could be trying something stupid and dangerous. Right now, she didn't have time to argue.

The Princess said she'd always help. She'd always be watching. It wasn't the time to look back because she couldn't break her gaze with Tiernan, but she could move faster.

I'll be fine. I land on my feet, Aslan said in her mind. *The one holding me is one of Piper's guards cloaked in a spell. Do what you must.*

She could accept that. Meela yanked the blade down hard across Tiernan's throat. "That's for lying to me. For lying, using, destroying, and cheating. It's also for teaching me to build myself up." She forced the blade down, rending his head from his shoulders. His head rolled to the grass, staining it with blood. "You messed with the wrong girl, fucker. I'm not going to be pushed around."

The axe fell to the ground and the energy sapped from her body. Her knees buckled. She'd faced the devil and won. Her head swam. Why did she feel nauseous? Darkness swallowed her and she fell. To where? She wasn't sure, but not to the grassy woodland floor.

Where was Aslan? What had happened?

She'd figure it out after she landed.

Later.

Chapter Eleven

Aslan yanked himself free from the fake troll and rushed to Meela. He'd tried to tell her he'd be okay, but this wasn't right. She shouldn't have collapsed. "Meela."

The trolls not affiliated with the Princess scattered. Without their leader, they had no reason to stay. Why wasn't anyone trying to help Meela? Aslan screamed. "Where are you?"

"Right here." Piper knelt beside him. "She used a lot of her power and energy. I'm proud of her, but she's drained herself. You need to be patient. She'll be okay once she recharges."

"Yeah." Tears and worry thickened in his voice. "I couldn't save her."

"She didn't want you to save her. She needed you to do exactly what you did." Piper opened a portal directly to Aslan's room. "Take care of her. She needs your strength and freedom."

He wasn't sure what was going on. "Yeah," he said, almost as an afterthought. His vision blurred with tears. "I know."

"She'll change a little. Phoenixes do, but it's making her stronger. It's saving her."

"How? Will she remember me?" He scooped Meela into his arms and carried her through the portal to his room. "What if she forgets me?"

"She'll remember." Piper placed her hand on Meela's forehead. "She gave of herself to save herself and you. That's the greatest kind of love. She also sacrificed herself. The power she used will take time to come back, but it will. I doubt she even knew she had that kind of ability."

He knew she didn't. Meela hadn't believed

herself to be worthy or even magical. "What do I do?" Anything asked of him, he knew that much.

"You stay with her. Protect her. When she comes around, you love her. She's your mate, understand? That's not something to take lightly."

The weight of her words rushed over him. "Absolutely."

"When she's ready, you bring her to me. The rest will be revealed then."

"Like what?" He, like the Princess, was so demanding. He needed to stop being such a pain in the ass.

"You'll see, but you'll be happy." Piper closed the portal and disappeared.

What would happen to Tiernan and the mess? He should've helped to clean it up. Right now, he couldn't think of that. He needed to focus on Meela. He had to save her.

He sat by the bed. Her stillness bothered him. It looked like she was dead, but she was truly only sleeping. He had to trust Piper, but the waiting would kill him.

God, this was difficult.

He clasped his hands together and bowed his head. He wasn't a religious man and wasn't good at praying, but he did believe in a higher power. Some sort of big magic was in the world. Had to be, right? How else would everyone in Eerie and the town itself actually exist? They wouldn't have magic otherwise.

"I don't know who is listening, but if you are, help me. I'm begging. I can't lose her. I get it, I get it. I just met her. How do I know if the mating thing is true, especially this fast? I don't know, but something in me is pretty sure. Like, the missing piece I've been looking for was found when I looked into her eyes. Like my world makes sense." He shook his head.

"We have our lives to figure this out. But I'm not one to choose on a whim. My cat knew. The cat chose her as his person. If the cat knows, then I do, too. But what do I do? Kiss her to bring her around? That's creepy. She hasn't consented to me doing that. But God or whatever is out there, please help me. I'm serious." He refused to allow the hopelessness to overwhelm him, but how could he not?

"What do I do? Sit and wait? I will, but it's so difficult. I want to do something. I can wait for years but give me an idea how long it'll be. Years? Please? I don't ask for much. Never have. But I need help. Guide me. I've fallen in love with her." He chuckled without mirth, mostly because he wasn't sure what else to do. "The cat has fallen for the bird and we're in over our collective head."

"Do you mean it?"

He hadn't realized he'd closed his eyes. "Meela?" He snapped his attention to her. He blinked back tears. "Sweetheart, talk to me." His hands trembled as he reached for her fingers.

She tipped her head to look at him from under heavy-lidded eyes. "Did you mean it?"

"Mean what?" He couldn't think straight. Not when it appeared she'd come back to him.

"That you love me." She closed her eyes, and her breath evened but was shallow. "Do you really feel that way?"

He couldn't lie to her. "I do." He brushed her hair from her face. "All the way, my powerful, dangerous, beautiful woman. You amaze me." He continued to stroke her skin, not wanting to stop touching her.

"Good." She half-smiled. "I feel that way, too."

His spirits soared and his heart filled with love for her. She'd made him the happiest man in the world. He wasn't sure what to do next.

"What?" she murmured. "You look odd."

"I'm all messed up," he confessed. He continued to touch her face. "I thought I'd lost you. You were so brave and magnificent."

"Was I?"

"You were." He caressed her forehead. "I'm supposed to get you to the Princess once you wake."

"Why?"

"She said something about all being revealed. I don't know." He half-shrugged. "But she was serious."

"Let her." She reached for him. "I don't want to go anywhere. I want you to come here and lie with me. Keep me warm."

He wasn't about to tell her no. He crawled onto the bed with her and under the blanket. As he tucked up tight to her, she rolled slightly into him.

"I don't want to think about anything. Don't want to go anywhere. I just want to be right here with you." She splayed her hand on his chest. "I've had to fight for so much. To be seen, to be loved, to be held… to survive. I don't want to fight any longer. Don't want to have to be courageous or strong. I'd like to simply exist."

"Then that's what we'll do." The Princess had told him to get Meela to her, but she hadn't said right away. They had some time to sort things out. Time to find their peace and fall deeper in love. Things would be okay.

Within a few moments, her breathing deepened and her head rolled heavily onto his chest.

He sighed. They were safe. No one wanted to kill them. No one wanted to harm her. She could live. He closed his eyes and joined her in slumber. He'd expected to dream, but instead, he simply drifted off. Nothingness.

He couldn't remember the last time he hadn't dreamed. Every time he'd allowed himself to dream, he'd met up with Meela. He hadn't known her name, but he'd known her. He'd figured out she belonged to him and he to her. Those dreams buoyed him. They'd helped him to move forward. To keep searching for her. Once he'd found her, he hadn't wanted to let go. Now he wouldn't have to.

He wasn't sure how long they'd slept when he woke. He stretched, then glanced over at her. Something caught his attention. Her hair wasn't blonde any longer, but red. Not ruddy and natural, but flame red. Her skin seemed to shimmer. She'd parted her lips and sighed. She looked so sweet and angelic.

"My girl," he murmured. He remembered what she'd asked him -- if he could shift for her so she could cuddle him. Once again, he wasn't about to prevent her from having what she wanted. He allowed his cat to come forward and shifted from his man form into the feline. His cat stretched, flexed his toes and claws, then shook before curling up in the crook of her body.

He snuggled against her, loving her warmth. He'd never been loved on and petted in his cat form. More like shooed away and chased. She'd been the first human he'd let get that close. He didn't dislike other humans, but it'd never felt right to be around them for long.

Everything felt right with her.

He listened to the cadence of her heartbeat. The rhythm of her breathing. Her sweetness and softness entranced him. He purred, happy to be beside her.

"You're vibrating." She opened her eyes. "I

didn't think you'd shift for me. Charming boy. May I kiss your head?" She pressed kisses to the top of his head.

He wasn't sure he'd like being touched this way at first. The more she nuzzled him and snuggled him, he relaxed. He'd been told to be loved was to be changed. Now he knew it was completely true. His grumpy street cat settled with her. The grunge seemed to fall away, and he melted for her.

"You're an adorable boy." She kissed the top of his head again. "Why does petting you calm me? Like holding a big, fuzzy baby."

He wasn't sure he appreciated being called a baby.

"I love you, big guy." She nuzzled his fur. "Too much."

He loved her right back.

As her breathing evened again and she fell asleep, he remained in his feline form. There was no point in shifting. He wanted to be tangled up with her this way for a little longer. She appreciated him -- both sides -- and both sides were happy. That wasn't easy to come by.

He settled against her chest and allowed himself to sleep. He needed the rest. Seeing a troll die, a woman find strength deep within herself and a phoenix come into her own was draining. He could've lost her, but hadn't.

Now, he'd found his mate. Despite the rough spots, it was the best day ever.

* * *

Meela rolled over. She could've sworn the big, fluffy cat beside her was Aslan. She hadn't imagined him, had she? Dreams filled her mind. Was he going to visit her? In his feline state? Or shift? Didn't matter.

She'd had one hell of a day. She knew what she'd done. She'd slain her private devil. Still, it didn't feel real. Tiernan had been a pox on her life for so long. She wished she'd have known earlier that she had the power to win out against him. She would've fought back sooner.

But she wouldn't have met Aslan.

She opened her eyes. Was he still there?

The orange cat thunked his tail next to her. His eyes were closed, and he looked so serene. She ruffled his fur. He was real, and right here beside her. Perfect. Now she had the man of her dreams, a cat to love... and her freedom. She had her mate.

Her mate. It was unbelievable. She never thought she'd find him because she hadn't trusted he existed. He did. She liked the security of the cat. Who would argue with her when she had a gigantic cat beside her? No one.

She closed her eyes again. As she drifted off, she began to dream. A dream of Aslan? She swirled in the darkness, looking for him. He was beside her in bed but could come to her in her dreams as well. *"Aslan?"* Now that she knew his name and that he wasn't a mystery, she'd relish every second with him this way.

"Not Aslan, sweet girl." Her father stepped out of the darkness. *"But I sent him to look for you. I see he found you."*

She stared at her father. She hadn't seen him since the funeral after his death. He didn't have the gray hairs or lines at the corners of his eyes. He looked like the day he'd married her mother. *"Dad?"*

"You used to call me Thomas."

She had when he'd irritated her. The tips of her ears burned. She'd been a brat. *"I shouldn't have done that."*

"*You were always a rebellious child. If you'd have been any other way, I'd have been shocked.*"

Still, she shouldn't have been so rude. "*I'm sorry.*"

"*No need to apologize.*"

She supposed not. "*You're here. You haven't visited me ever.*"

"*It wasn't time until now,*" Thomas said. "*We should've, but your mother isn't ready to come across the threshold.*"

There was so much she didn't know.

"*You want to question me. We loved that about you.*"

She stared at him again. "*Tiernan's dead.*"

"*About time. But he's why I'm here.*"

"*He is? You delivered me to him.*" Or vice versa. Either way, she'd been miserable. "*He tried to kill me.*"

"*And now you also know why he didn't succeed.*" Thomas sat on a bench and patted the seat beside her. "*Rest a minute.*"

She joined him on the planks. "*I don't understand.*" So much of it was a jumble.

"*We didn't know what your ability would be when you were born. You were the child of a clairvoyant and conjurer. You could've been anything. We didn't want to direct you, so we waited to see what would develop. When your mark appeared, we knew, but we weren't allowed to help you. That's the magic. It wants us to help but won't tell us how or give us permission.*"

"*You're my parents. You're supposed to.*"

"*I agree, but phoenixes are also tricky creatures. You need hardship to grow.*"

"*So you let everyone treat me like an outcast?*"

"*No. That can be chalked up to children being bullies and parents not wanting to correct them. We tried to get that stopped many times and ran into walls instead.*" He shook his head. "*The teachers ignored us.*"

That figured. She'd been told she cried wolf too many times.

"*But that treatment made you stronger. Made you more empathetic. You were quirky and an individual, which made you the best version of you.*"

He sounded like a motivational poster. She'd shied away from her uniqueness.

"*But he changed you.*"

"*Aslan?*"

"*He did, as well, but for the better. He brought out what you've been trying to hide,*" Thomas said. "*No, I meant Tiernan.*"

"*He did.*" She winced. "*He was awful.*"

"*Agreed.*"

"*Why did you let him get close to me?*" She would've been just fine without the abuse. "*He treated me like dirt.*"

"*I know, and I regret it.*"

At least he did. "*You told him we had money, which is why he was so destructive.*"

"*I never said money. He saw the perceived wealth we had and thought that was his ticket. He never directly asked me for money or if it existed. He assumed,*" Thomas said. "*If he'd have asked, I would've told him the money wasn't as good as we projected.*"

She shook her head in disbelief, but also frustration. "*So he lied -- again.*" Just like a troll.

"*He fabricated to get what he wanted.*"

"*Me? What a catch.*" She held up her hand. "*More specifically, he wanted my blood.*"

"*In a word, yes.*"

Her stomach roiled. "*I should've guessed,*" she said. "*You and Mom never told me about my immortality.*"

"*We couldn't.*"

"*Why not?*"

"The same reason we couldn't tell him what it truly meant," Thomas said. "You had to earn the mark."

"What?"

"When you fully stood up to him, you felt power. You changed, yes? That was your phoenix rising. You embraced your true self. We expected nothing less, though we had no idea when the change would happen. Hard to explain what you can't depend on happening."

"But…" She wanted to be irked, but he had a point.

"Let me finish," he said and held up his hand. "You had to change. Until that moment, if he'd killed you for your blood, it wouldn't have given him what he wanted. You weren't immortal yet."

"I wasn't?"

"You never felt you had magic, and that's why. You hadn't come into it yet."

"Oh." Well… when he put it like that…

"He felt the change was coming, but couldn't pinpoint when it'd come, so he married you to ensure he'd be there when it did."

"You could've stopped him."

"What if I had? You were in love with the idea of love. Would you have listened to me?"

"No."

"Correct. I saw no point in wasting words."

She nodded. "I hate when you're right."

"I didn't want to be. I wanted him to truly love you."

"He didn't."

"No." Thomas hugged her. "But you survived. You found a way to get out and be you. That's the most we could ask for. We saw the change coming, but not when."

"And then it did."

"Aslan, the Princess, and fate all helped."

"They did, and I'm glad." Her voice cracked. "I wish you could've been there to meet Aslan. He's what we *thought Tiernan could be."*

"I know. He will be a staunch partner and protector to you and give you what you need. He's your mate."

She considered his words. Aslan was indeed her mate. *"You do know we met because I thought he was a cat. When Tiernan attacked us, Aslan abducted me."*

"He secreted you off to safety, carried you to his home. Not quite the same thing."

"No." She laughed and the sound released some of the tension. *"Where is Mom?"*

"She can't cross the threshold."

"Why not?" What threshold?

"When I step into the spirit realm -- the dream space -- it silences my mind. I can think clearly because there isn't the onslaught of human noise. For her, it's the opposite. She's overwhelmed with the various types of magic. It's chaotic. Too busy for her."

"Like being in the middle of a crowd with the noise and action, but you can't be heard and can't focus?"

"Exactly. For me, it's the other way. It's finally quiet," he said. *"She wishes she could be here with us. She misses you."*

"I miss her."

"You blame her."

"A little." She hated to admit it.

"For not standing up to me?"

"Yes." Shame washed over her.

"You know it had to be this way?"

"I do." She didn't like it, but she understood.

"We never wanted you to be hurt. If I could've stopped him before he abused you, I would've. No one has the right to treat my daughter that way."

She appreciated hearing that. *"Aslan won't."*

"I know. I trust him. I never trusted Tiernan."

She felt the same. *"Why was he able to visit me in my dreams? Cat magic?"*

"*Tiernan? He terrorized you there, too?*"

"*No.*" Thank God. She never would've survived. "*Aslan. Does he have cat magic?*" she asked, repeating herself.

"*He has the magic of his mate. That's what Tiernan wanted. You and Aslan have a bond and had it before even knowing each other. Now you share some abilities -- not to shift, but to communicate. To put it bluntly, you're both immortal now.*"

Holy shit. "*No way. Does he know?*"

"*Not yet. I suspect the Princess will tell him. If he knew too soon, then it might have swayed his heart.*"

She supposed her father could be right, but she doubted it. Aslan had risked a lot for her. He had a kind soul and big heart.

"*My girl, I must leave you. Your mother misses me, and I need to care for her.*"

"*Is she still sick?*" She had been before she'd died. "*The cancer?*"

"*No. I spoil her.*" He flashed a wicked smile. "*When you love someone, you do your best to care for them all the way. She needs support right now because it's killing her not to see you. I'll do whatever she wants to help ease her pain.*"

"*She's okay, just sad?*" she asked, still concerned.

"*She's sad she's not here, and misses me like I miss her. We're a strangely matched pair.*" He left the bench and stood. "*We watch you. We've tried to protect you and send people into your life to help. We never forgot.*"

"*I know.*" She remained on the bench as her father walked away. "*Dad?*" She had one more thing to say.

"*Yeah?*" He turned to look at her but had started to fade.

"*I love you.*" She hadn't said it much when her

parents were still alive.

"We both love you, too." He smiled, then turned and walked away as he disappeared.

Chapter Twelve

Her heart ached. She'd learned so much and was grateful for the information. Too bad it'd come so late.

"Meela?"

She glanced about, looking for Aslan. *"Where are you?"*

"Meela, wake up."

She opened her eyes, surfacing from the dream. Aslan was no longer a cat but remained beside her. Muscled, tousled and handsome in his human form. He was a beautiful sight. "Hi. Sorry."

"Why are you sorry?" He stretched back out beside her. "You were talking in your sleep."

"I was?" She heated all over with embarrassment. "Sorry."

"Again, not needed." He draped his arm across her belly. "Are you okay?"

"I am. What was I talking about?"

"I couldn't understand most of it. To be honest, I thought it might be a spell and I worried that you were entranced," he said. "You're okay, which is what matters."

"Yeah." She rolled onto her side. "It was the strangest thing. I dreamed I saw my father."

"I'm sure you did." He half-smiled. "I bet it was nice."

"Yes and no. I got some closure with them, which helped because they died before we ever got a chance to talk."

"So that's good."

"But I also found out why they didn't protect me from him." She refused to say his name. "To make me stronger."

"An odd way to accomplish it."

"They knew he'd treat me badly, but that I'd be able to handle it. So screwed up."

"A little." Aslan nodded once. "Did he mention the changes?"

"What changes?

He chuckled. "Your hair is flame red."

She'd rather liked her blonde hair. "Is it awful?" Would she have to fix it?

"No, it's beautiful and looks natural, if you can believe me."

"I don't."

"It's powerful, too."

She'd thought about herself that way, but not out loud. "Is that it? I'm simply a ginger?"

"You're paler, but it's pretty."

She glanced at her hands. Sure enough, the tan she'd worked hard to achieve was gone. "I guess it's the new me?"

"I like it."

"You do?" She needed to hear him say it again.

"Uh-huh. I loved the way you were before and the way you've become. You've grown into yourself. That's sexy and powerful. You're more controlled and mature but still have a wild side. It all turns me on, and I'm honored to be at your side."

She laughed. She loved everything he'd said. "Then I guess you've got me." She sobered. "My dad told me I'd always had this power, but I had to grow into it. Had to go through hell to be stronger. I guess he was right."

"He was and you have." Aslan winked. "Are you happy?"

"I am, but I'm also relaxed. I can think, breathe, and exist, which is nice." She stretched out on the bed, luxuriating in the sheets. "I'm home."

"And you said I'd kidnapped you."

"I was wrong." She threw herself into his arms. "I'm glad you cared that much to risk yourself and help me."

"Always for my mate."

She leaned back enough to stare at him. "You're really sure?"

"I am." He grinned. "My cat figured it out first, but we're in agreement. Don't even need the Princess to bless us. When you know, you know."

She couldn't argue. She twined her legs with his and rubbed on him. "We need to see the Princess, don't we?"

"We do." He brushed his nose along hers. "Why? What are you thinking?"

"I'd like to seal this mating and start the process of falling more in love with each other." She kissed him. "Enjoy each other?"

"And see where this road takes us? Until I don't have any more days?" He nodded. "I can't imagine being anywhere else. You're where I want to be."

"Even if you don't die?" She sucked in a ragged breath, wondering what he'd say, now that he'd been let in on the truth.

"Honey, I might have nine lives in theory, but I've surely used a few. Besides, I've got a shelf-life. Everyone does -- except for you." His smile didn't change. In fact, it seemed more genuine. "I can live with knowing I've only got so much time with you. Means I have to make the best of it, and I love that kind of challenge."

He didn't know... Her hands trembled. She had to be blunter, but she appreciated his honesty. "What if when we make love and seal the mating, you gain immortality, too? Would that change your mind?"

"Don't think it works that way, sweetheart." He chuckled. "And no, it doesn't."

"You don't think there's a transference?" she asked. "Aslan, how do you know us talking in our dreams wasn't part of it?"

He frowned, crinkling his brow before shaking his head. "It was magic, sure, but we didn't know we were mates. Did we?"

"Did you know? In your gut?" She stared at him, memorizing his features and falling more for him. "That magic knew something."

"I'm sure it did. I don't understand the magic or even claim to know what it might do. I simply followed where it sent me." He paused and caressed her hip. "Do you believe it intended for us to find each other and to do what we did? Like some higher power watching us? I don't think I wanted anyone to be watching us. That's creepy."

A little. She hesitated a moment. "I realize this is a strange moment to mention this, but when I visited my father in my dream, he said he sent us to find each other. He knew you'd be the protector I needed and expected us to merge. Not sex but come together. I don't understand the magic, mostly because I still don't understand what he can do, but I don't think it was him, per se. The magic knew and he helped direct it. We had no choice but to comply."

Aslan didn't say anything right away. Instead, he continued to caress her bare skin. His gaze flicked away, then returned to hers. "The more I consider it, the more I'm not sure I understand, but what I do know is that I don't care. My heart was drawn to yours and it found you. That's what matters."

"Matters to me, too." She splayed her hand on his chest. "If your cat wants me, if you're both drawn to me in the same way I am to you, then we're expected to be together. We are mates."

"Then we are." His smile returned. "Nothing's going to change that for me."

"Dad told me one more thing."

"You had quite the conversation." He tugged her closer. "Anything good?"

"Very." She toyed with his nipple, teasing him with her fingernail. "Coming together in our dreams and mating means you've gained immortality with me. This doesn't have to end."

Once again, she'd rendered him silent. He frowned, then tipped his head. His cock twitched between his legs and bumped her sensitive pussy lips. "You're serious?"

"I am." She resumed flicking his nipple. "I can't imagine sharing it with anyone else."

"But..." He shook his head. "That's what... and he didn't get it."

"He wasn't going to because he wasn't my mate. He could've torn me in two, draining me, but he wouldn't have gained what he wanted because it wasn't time. There were so many things that had to happen -- I had to find you, had to find my power and had to realize he wasn't a good man or troll. Once I figured that out and you showed me your true heart, then it was all ready. That's when the magic happened. I gained my immortality the moment I stood up to him, and you must've gained it when you prayed. Is there a God? I have no idea, but someone was listening. You proved yourself worthy."

"I'll never be worthy of you. I'm a shifter and lived on the prowl for a long time."

She stared at him, considering his words. "You're not going to prowl any longer, are you?"

"Not when I've got the love of a good woman beside me." He kissed her. "Don't need to."

"Then we're set." When they made love, she had no idea what the magic would do, but they'd be sealed, mated and have forever together. Not too bad for a girl who believed she didn't possess any magic. Hadn't felt like she even belonged in Eerie. Now she had a home, her magic, and the love of a wonderful shifter.

"What are you thinking?" he asked. He tugged her to his chest and rolled onto his back so she straddled him. "Can't be how much you're dying to ride me."

She laughed and shoved the blanket out of the way. "You'd be wrong." She reached between her legs and stroked his cock until she lined him up with her pussy. A moan escaped her lips as she slid down onto his shaft.

For the first time since she could remember, she didn't need to hide. She slid her hands over her breasts and tweaked her nipples. "Yes, baby." He splayed his hands on her ribs, holding onto her as she rode the length of his cock.

Each time she settled fully on him, more coils around her heart snapped. She let go of the shackles in her mind. The past didn't matter. She had freedom and it felt good. Better than good. Hell, she trembled with excitement and desire. She couldn't think straight.

The orgasm started in her brain this time. She embraced the love coming from Aslan. She finally loved herself. She saw herself as the woman she'd always wanted to be, the woman she had the right to become. She cried out, "Fuck."

"Yeah?" He held onto her waist, bouncing her harder. His cock throbbed. "I'm close."

So was she. She groaned and her body went

limp. Magic settled around them. Like a fog, but fluffier. Pink, blue, green... like they were in a soft cocoon. Nothing else existed but the two of them. She locked gazes with him. As she did, she tipped over the edge. The climax shot from her brain to her core, then to her limbs before settling in her pussy.

She knew in her heart where she belonged. The cat, the human, the connection... it was all real. "I love you, Aslan."

"I love you, Meela."

She came harder and he cried out with her. The final coil snapped. Everything within her released as she swayed, then collapsed on his chest. The fog lifted and it felt like an explosion.

She panted on his chest and her heart hammered. "Holy fuck."

"Ditto." He shuddered. "I think we've been sealed. We're sealed."

"How do you know?" She liked it, if it was true.

"That fog wouldn't have come if we weren't. We're official. We're sealed."

"You've said that." She rested her head on his shoulder. "It still feels like we're strangers -- a little." She couldn't deny the truth. They'd only been together for a few days. They had so much to learn about each other. But she wanted to learn it all.

"We are in many ways. You don't know what my favorite color is, what bands I like, if I sleep late, leave clothes on the floor, how I made my money..."

"You're right. I don't." He wasn't wrong. "You don't know much about me, either. How do we know this will last?" She'd asked a silly question that wasn't entirely funny. She still had fears.

"Nothing is certain, except magic. I don't understand how mating works or how sealing is decided, but I know when it happens, it's real. We have a long time to discover the little things about each other. It's okay."

"You make it sound so simple." She lived in Eerie. Things there were easier and complicated at the same time. Magic happened in this town. They were safe here and did have time to sort things out.

"You're scared -- I get it. I do. I never thought my dream woman, the one I got to know in my sleep, was real. Then I saw you and knew you were. When we talked, things clicked," he said. "I felt like me again."

"I feel the same way," she admitted. "But you're right. I'm scared."

"Why? Let me in. I'm here and I'm not running." He held her. "Please?"

She had to be honest. Had to do this. She'd made love to him and her heart was in his hands. Now he needed to know her feelings. "After him, I swore I wouldn't let anyone in. Then I met you and it happened fast. Everything's been so quick. I'm scared you'll end up being like him. That I'll get hurt again. What if my judgment is wrong? What if the magic is wrong?" She was reaching, but it didn't matter.

Aslan held her. Not super tight and he didn't argue. He didn't convince her she was overthinking this. He let her voice her fears. His patience amazed her. His strength was more than she could handle. Maybe her fears were wrong. Maybe not. But he gave her a chance to have a voice.

"Aslan." She balled her hand on his chest. "Why are you being so kind to me? Why aren't you yelling or getting angry? Why?" She lost her control. Her fears ran rampant. Time to regain herself before she did damage that couldn't be fixed.

"Meela." Aslan brushed her hair from her face.

"I'm here. I'm not going anywhere."

"Why?" she whispered. "Why?"

"When you care about someone, and you know you belong there when they hold your heart -- No matter how long it takes to earn your trust, I'm here. I don't give up on people and won't give up on you. Yes, we just found each other. Yes, it's fast. Yes, there are trust issues between us, but I'm not him. I'm strong enough to be right here beside you. I don't quit on those I love. Those who are my friends and you mean a lot to me."

She closed her eyes and sobbed. She'd needed to hear those words for so long. Needed to be cleansed. This was her fresh start. Her chance to have the life she deserved.

She had time.

She cried on Aslan, allowing him to hold her as she dealt with her issues. It'd be a while before she'd be fully okay, but that wasn't a turn-off.

When she opened her eyes, a bubble floated into the room. She noticed the sparkling, iridescent object and froze. "Who or what is that?"

Aslan tensed. "That is a summons from the Princess."

"In a bubble?" That didn't seem possible or make much sense.

"It's her way of letting us know she wants our attention without having to come here herself. *And* her way of saying we're expected to comply," he said. "She's trying to be courteous."

"Oh." It was time to embrace her new life -- the one she'd had before it'd been ripped from her. She'd have to do a lot of letting go. Her previous life, the one with *him*, didn't matter any longer. She could embrace this one and be where she was welcomed. Be where she was loved.

"You okay?" Aslan asked. "The Princess has sent a message to us, but we don't have to respond right now."

She stared at the bubble. He was right -- they could ignore the summons, but why? She'd lived with her past and in fear of it. Now, this bubble, the mating, the change in her life was the push to move forward. "No, let's respond."

Chapter Thirteen

"If you want to respond right now, then pull the blanket up or better yet, how about we get dressed?" Aslan covered them with the bedding. "I'm not wild about being caught in the buff." Good God. He'd nearly been caught a few times after shifting and wasn't in the mood to show the royal court his junk.

There was so much work to be done with Meela. She'd been hurt and abused. He had to gain her trust and help knock off the layers around her heart. He wasn't afraid of the scars or crust. Never had been. He refused to give up on her. She'd become his friend first, his protector, then the one who owned his heart. He couldn't give up -- not on her and not ever.

She tugged the blanket to her chin. "I suppose you're right. She doesn't need to see what we did, but the moment she sees us, she'll know. Is there a filter we can use? A spell or something?"

"I don't know one, but I have a T-shirt you can borrow and a pair of my sleep shorts." He left the bed long enough to get the clothing. "Here."

"Thanks." She hurried into the garments. "How do we get the message?"

"Pop the bubble after I get dressed. You can have the honor." He yanked on a shirt and pair of sleep pants, then gestured to her. "Go ahead."

"Does it hurt?"

"No." He sat up a bit, adjusting the pillow behind his head. "The one other time I've had one of these summonses, it was from the Princess and arrived just after she assumed the role of Princess. She wanted to meet all of her people and I'd been one of the elusive ones, as she put it." Back then, he'd been in the midst of a shift and hadn't been wearing anything. He hurried to shift before he answered and met her for the first time while he wore his pajamas. Not cool.

"So you touched the bubble?"

"I did." Why did that sound sort of odd and gross? "You get to do it this time."

"Will it explode?" She reached out, then stopped.

"No, so touch it." Her hesitation amused him, but so did the light in her eyes. She might be scared of this, but she wanted to give this moment a try.

"Think we're in trouble?" she asked. She pulled her hand back. "We could be at the precipice of being arrested."

"For what?"

"Killing him? Violence in the court? I don't know," she said. "We did something terrible."

"She knows what happened because she was in on helping you. Remember? She said she had eyes everywhere," he reminded her.

"Even now?"

"Stop." He held her free hand. "You're stalling out of fear. It's going to be okay. Take care of the bubble and answer. I'm right here beside you."

"Okay." Defeat clouded her voice, but humor filled her eyes. She popped the bubble and yanked her hand back. Sparkles flew through the air. A scroll unfurled with a thick ribbon and wax at the bottom. "Wow."

The whole thing was pretty dramatic, he had to admit. He waited for her to read the paper.

Meela grasped the scroll, stretching it out. "Meela Durning and Aslan Maine, you are hereby summoned to the castle tonight at seven. Everything you will require for this official visit will be provided. Simply tug the ribbon on this scroll. Your presence is expected, and you should be prompt. All questions will be answered upon your arrival." She shifted her gaze to Aslan. "Pretty fancy stuff."

"It is." He snorted. Everything would be explained tonight. Fine. He didn't need much explanation. He'd found Meela, they were together, they were sealed and mated. Now they had a future to fall deeper in love.

"So… we pull the ribbon and we get… what?" She crooked her brow. "Our wildest desires?"

"We're going to be outfitted for a visit to the royal court. Probably designations to get us to the main throne room and maybe some answers. You have questions and want answers. You have since I met you."

She blushed. "You're starting to know me too well."

"Just observant." He sighed and nodded to the scroll. "So do we do this?"

"It appears to be an all-expenses paid trip to the royal court. How do we not?" She grasped one of the ribbons. "You take the other and we pull together."

"Deal." He pinched the second strand. As if on cue, they tugged the ribbons. The room filled with smoke and glitter. He wished he'd have reached for her before they did this. Then he could be holding onto her. Was she scared? Did she need him? Fuck. He'd messed up.

"Aslan?"

He froze. He wasn't even sure where he was. "Meela?" His heart thundered in his chest. "Where are you?"

"Turn around." She laughed. "Aslan, it's beautiful."

He didn't realize he was standing. He turned and caught sight of her. Meela stood before him, swathed in a form-fitting crimson sheath dress. The garment accentuated her curves and the deep red of her hair. Her eyes sparkled.

She smoothed her hands down her hips. "What do you think?"

"I don't know what to say." She'd stolen his breath. He wobbled and reached out to her. "I'm… Wow."

"You're pretty 'wow' too, you know." She crossed the short expanse to him. "Nice suit. Fits you like a second skin."

He hadn't noticed. All he saw was her. He reached for her.

She nodded toward the clock. "Don't we have a deadline?"

He glanced over his shoulder. Well, shit. "The summons said to be at the castle tonight at seven. We should go." He'd have to delight in the vision of her while riding to the castle.

"I've never been this pretty in my life." She laced her fingers with his and walked with him through the house. "I didn't even dress up for my wedding."

"Why not?"

"It was too quick. Tiernan just wanted the piece of paper and for everything to be legal. Pretty had nothing to do with it."

"The fool." He opened the door to the garage. "After you."

"Thank you." She stepped onto the concrete and made her way past his car. "There's a limo out there."

"Not shocked." He should've guessed when the Princess said everything would be taken care of, it would be. He followed her to the driveway, then closed the garage door. "Shall we?" He opened the limo door for her.

"Thank you." She slid onto the back seat.

He joined her and closed the door. There wasn't a driver. Instead, magic swirled around them. In seconds, they were in front of the castle.

"We're already here?" She leaned forward. "I didn't even get the chance to be naughty in the car."

"We're probably being watched." He couldn't be sure, but didn't want to run afoul of the Princess. Instead of opening the door himself, he waited for an attendant. Aslan stepped onto the red-brick-paver drive. He held his hand out to Meela. "My love."

"I love when you say that." She grasped his hand and fell in step with him as he walked into the castle.

Would there be trumpets? Some official welcome? The last, and only, time he'd been to the castle, the feeling was much more informal. Another attendant met them at a pair of wooden doors.

The attendant opened the doors without saying a word. Should he give the man a tip? Meela nudged Aslan forward.

He fought off a wave of nerves and wished his cat could be in charge. The cat would go forth boldly, without a care in the world. He, on the other hand, had lots of cares. He worried he'd trip.

The lush dark wood created a sense of warmth, despite the room being cavernous. The carpet muffled their footsteps. Like walking on plush clouds. Soft music filled the air. When he spotted the instruments, he noted they were playing themselves. Had to be an enchantment, but he didn't care. The tune filled his head. He'd never forget a second of this night. He had a beautiful woman beside him, love in his heart… things were as they should be.

There weren't horns, but a few other people, dressed in lush gowns or suits milled around the throne room. He didn't know most of the others in attendance, except Diesel.

The cyclops wore his standard sunglasses and cowboy hat but paired them with a crisp black suit. The Princess wore a gown similar to Meela's, but with a little more flair in the skirt and a champagne color. She grinned when she spotted Meela and Aslan.

Another couple joined them. "Hi," the woman said. "I'm Belle and this is Azel. We're so glad you're here at court. I'd like to introduce you to Michael and Lia. She's a siren."

Aslan hadn't known their names, but he'd seen the cast of characters around. "I've fished near Michael's cabin."

"Oh, yeah. The cat. We thought you were a cougar," Michael said. "Feel free to catch whatever you need."

"Thanks." He probably should've asked before he'd trod on the property, but he'd been in his cat form and thought he'd been invisible. So much for that.

"We live in the spire of the castle hotel," Belle said. "Azel watches you."

"Oh." His stomach lurched. He'd forgotten about the gargoyle. "I've tried to stay on my best behavior."

"You're fine," Azel said. He stood behind Belle, barely moving.

"I didn't know any of you, but now I do and I'm thrilled. Until I picked Aslan up, I didn't believe I belonged here. Now it feels like I've got family." Meela blushed from her hairline to her chest. "I figured you'd all think of me and my past with... *him*... and not want me around."

Aslan caressed her shoulder, trying to give her strength.

"The troll?" Lia snorted. "No one's judging you.

We're glad you're here and have found each other."

"Thanks," Meela murmured. She leaned into Aslan. "Thank you."

"May I have a turn?" Piper joined the group. "I still don't know how to plan these events. Diesel tells me to let someone else plan them, but when they're this small, it feels wrong to pass it off."

He didn't understand what was happening. Aslan remained next to Meela. "Well, thank you for the invitation."

"You're welcome," Piper replied. "So, did you figure things out? You conquered your fears, didn't you?"

"I did," Meela said. "It's a good feeling. A release."

Piper nodded. "And?"

"We realized we were mates," Aslan said. "Might have done something to cement it." He didn't want to tell the Princess they'd had sex. Christ.

"I knew you did. The magic around you has changed." Piper clasped her hands together. "Did you realize the other stuff?"

"What other stuff?" Meela asked.

"Yeah?" He felt so clueless.

"I see you don't know." Piper stepped back. "First, you're both immortal. I suspect you knew that but weren't ready to accept it."

Aslan tamped down his continued shock, but she was right.

"I told him," Meela whispered.

"It's okay. It takes some getting used to," Piper said. "Second, you are indeed mates and it's a wonderful thing that you've cemented it. You should've by now. You've got a long time to fall in love and discover so much about each other. Discover everything, really."

Good. She'd reiterated what he already believed.

"Third, you don't have to worry about the monies the troll owed you. They've been deposited into your account and your balance with Norm Slone has been settled. He's taking the win and has decided to work with the public to advance the rights of paranormals."

"It's over?" Meela asked. "All over."

Relief washed over him. Thank God. She'd never have that dark cloud over her head ever again. About damn time. "Thank you."

"You're both welcome." Piper held up her hand. "There's one more thing. I want to welcome you both to join the royal court. Meela, we need you as we don't have a phoenix or anyone so adept at handling trolls -- although Lia's a pretty good second. Aslan, we don't have any shifters and you've got a keen sense of what's going on in the shadows. Will you accept this invitation to the court?"

"Yes," he blurted. He hadn't believed he would be worthy of the court. "Thank you."

Meela opened her mouth, but no sound came out. Her eyes widened and cheeks flamed red.

He caressed her back. "I won't speak for her, but I'd say she's agreeing."

Meela's eyes widened a bit more, then her lip trembled. "I'm sorry. Yes. Thank you. I... wow."

"It's a lot to think about." Piper applauded. "Wonderful. I knew this would be the best day. Shall we dance? I've got the band queued up and there's plenty of wine. After all we've been through, it's time we enjoy ourselves." She grasped Diesel's hand and tugged him away from the small group.

Lia beamed. "It's fantastic to have you on the

team. You won't regret it." She allowed Michael to whisk her toward the middle of the room.

"That's how they roll." Belle shrugged. "I mean, when you've got someone special, you might as well enjoy them. I'm glad we all met and are now friends." With Azel beside her, she stepped away and began to dance.

"I guess we should join in." Meela clasped Aslan's hands. "You don't have any doubts?"

"Nope. Not a one." He kissed her temple. "I found my heart when I found you."

"You found me." She allowed him to whisk her into his arms. "I've been taken by the Maine Coon and I love it. My mate."

"My mate." He swept her up in the swell of the dance. Finally, he had a place, a purpose and a love to last a lifetime. He had taken her, but she'd saved him right back.

Taken by the Huldra (Taken 10)
Paranormal Women's Fiction
Megan Slayer

A Huldra and a human collide in the forest...

Hunter came to Eerie to give up on his life. Nothing's gone right and he's ready to quit. Then he sees the most beautiful woman in the world, but she wants him dead. Talk about bad luck. Until he meets Annika, a Huldra -- a Norse protector -- and the woman he can't seem to forget.

Unlike her twin sister Runa, who wants only to destroy, Annika is a nurturing spirit. The moment she sees Hunter she has to save him from her homicidal sister. He's too pretty to kill, but he's got a secret. He's not solely human, although he doesn't know what paranormal blood runs through his veins.

If he can survive Runa's wrath, the scars of his past, and allow himself to have a future with Annika, he might find the best things in life aren't exactly what they seem -- they're better.

Chapter One

"I've had enough." Hunter Hallahan drove past the line separating the town boundary of Eerie from the rest of the world. To anyone who didn't have a drop of paranormal blood, the road went through untouched woodlands. Unlike most beings, he had the very cells permitting him to be there -- paranormal blood. More specifically, shifter blood. By the time he'd cropped up on the family tree, the strain of paranormal magic coming down to him had been diluted enough he wasn't able to shift.

Didn't matter to him.

He had the keen senses of the wolf -- sharp hearing, keen eyesight, a sixth sense to detect danger, and lightning-fast reflexes. His abilities to read other beings had served him well. They had in the past.

Not now.

He'd read Sally so wrong. He'd thought she loved him. Thought she wanted to be together forever. All she'd wanted was a boyfriend for now. He flexed his hands on the steering wheel and drove straight to the woods. His eyes burned from shedding too many tears over her. Her words burned into his brain.

"Oh, honey. You're good for now, but you're not marriage material. You're a mongrel."

How could someone say those things?

No, he knew how they could. She'd wanted to get back at her now-fiancé. Making him jealous got her a bigger diamond. Got her attention. Got her the house in the suburbs with the large yard and the chance at having kids.

He'd never be able to give her children.

He turned onto the gravel road leading deeper into the woods.

When he'd set out for Eerie, he hadn't planned on going to the forest, but the second he crossed the city limits, he'd been drawn here. He couldn't even explain it. Like the car was being driven by itself.

Impossible.

Yes, he had magic, and Eerie was full of spells, magic and everything else paranormal, but the car wasn't driving itself. He wasn't rich enough to have one of those vehicles. This was something different.

Something stronger.

He continued farther into the woods, shocked by the darkness. This wasn't his first time venturing into the forests of Eerie. The area that hid the town appeared to be only a few hundred acres on a map. But that was the magic of Eerie. It might not appear big, but once one started exploring, the place was huge.

As he drove, he noticed a woman walking among the trees. Seeing someone in the woods wasn't strange. The fact the woman wore a filmy dress and had flowing blonde hair was the eye-catching part. He slowed his pace and cast a longer glance at her. Her pale skin practically seemed transparent. Gods, if a stiff breeze blew through, she'd fall over. She had no meat on her bones.

Some might find her gorgeous. She had that stick-thin look going for her, with more bones than curves. She cut a striking figure among the trees.

He liked women with a little more curve.

The woman rushed up to him. "Come to me."

Part of him wanted to. Just stop the vehicle, leave, and follow her. The rational part of his brain refused to comply. This had to be a spell. Had to be something to bring him to his doom.

Except he'd initially set out for Eerie with the plan to end his life. He'd thought that was what he wanted, but he'd never followed through with his spur-of-the-moment intentions. Gods, he'd loved Sally, but she wasn't worth him doing something so drastic. Never had been.

The woman stopped in front of his car and pointed to him, then crooked her finger. "Come with me."

He flicked the button to lock the car. Why in Hades had he done that? If this was magic, she could come into his vehicle despite the damn locks.

"Come with me," she repeated. Then the woman winked.

As she did, he collided with something hard. Not just hard, but immediate. He rocked forward, smacking his face into the airbag. The wind rushed from his lungs, and he groaned. His limbs ached. What in Hades had just happened?

He blinked to clear his vision. Smoke wafted through the air and the bag deflated.

"Odin's sake." The door opened and a person reached into the car.

When he looked at the speaker, his blood chilled. "You're determined to get me to come with you." The woman who'd pointed to him was yanking him from the vehicle. "I'm not going with you."

"If you know what's good for you, you will." The woman, almost too thin to be manhandling him, tugged him free of the seat belt. "You're dying, you fool."

"Dying?" He'd come to the woods to do himself in but hadn't wanted to -- not for real. "How?"

"You hit the fucking tree." She hauled him against her body. "Come on. Use your legs -- or are they broken?"

"I don't know." His brain swam. "I've got to be

concussed."

"Probably." She grunted, then tossed him against the side of the car. She waved her hand across his forehead and spoke words he couldn't understand. Her brow crinkled and her green eyes flashed. Her mouth twisted into a frown. "Can you walk now?"

He hadn't bothered to try. He stared at her. She looked a lot like the woman who'd called to him, yet nothing like her. After a moment, his brain cooperated, and he forced his legs to move. "Yes," he managed. He allowed her to slide her arm around him. "What happened?"

"I'll explain in a moment." She fumbled across the underbrush to a large tree. When she knocked on the tree, a hunk of the bark opened like a door. "In here." She didn't give him a chance to argue. Instead, she shoved him into the tree before closing the door behind her.

"What's going on?" He leaned against the wall. "I'm so confused. I've got to be concussed."

"You probably are." She raked her hair back from her face. "You'd better thank your lucky stars I got there in time."

"Why?" He understood so little.

"That woman who called to you? That's my twin sister," she said. "That's some bad magic you don't want to mix yourself up in."

"Jealous?" He'd tried for a bad joke, but it hadn't worked. "I'm sorry. I don't get it."

She flipped a switch, sending light across the space. "Here." She helped him to a chair, knelt in front of him, then stared at him before tipping her head. "I get it."

"I'm glad you do, because I don't." He didn't like riddles or misdirects. "What's going on?"

"You crashed your car into a tree."

"I did? I didn't see anything in front of me." He'd destroyed his car? Fuck.

"That was the point."

"What?"

She sighed and folded her arms before sitting back on her heels. "What brought you to Eerie? You're here, so you must have magic. Why are you here?"

"I..." He didn't know this woman from anyone else, but something within him wanted to tell her everything. "I've been having a bad day, and it got worse, so I came home to Eerie to regroup." It wasn't entirely a lie.

"I see." She scratched her forehead, smoothing out the lines between her brows. "You intended to be here, but did you intend to visit the woods?"

"Yes." The tips of his ears burned. "I've been low."

"Ah, wanted the woodlands to recharge you? That makes sense," she said and nodded. "Except, there's something darker in you. Depression. Sadness. Foolishness."

"No." She'd read him way too well. "Some of that's wrong."

"Uh-huh. Runa doesn't care that you're down, but she'll exploit it." She rocked forward on her knees, then stood. Her dress, more opaque than the one on the woman in the forest, still clung to her body. The garment hugged her faint curves and accentuated her bosom.

He longed to touch her. To feel her again and be sure she was real. "You've saved me from Runa?" Whoever that was.

"Yeah, I did." She rested her hands on her hips. "You're paranormal, but I can't detect what yet. I will.

I'm guessing Runa did, too, but she didn't strike. Just made you run into a tree."

"A tree?" Hades, he hadn't seen it. "Will you be plain with me? What's going on?"

"Fine," she said. "My name is Annika and my twin sister, Runa, lured you here. We are Huldra. Some of us are guardian spirits and others are a bit more... nefarious. She detected your pain and wanted to use it for her own ends. She feeds off your sadness and anger. She felt you arrive in town and brought you to her. You weren't even on the path when you collided with the tree. Probably thought you were driving along on the road and doing just fine."

"I might have." He massaged his temple. "No wonder my head aches like a son of a bitch."

"You hit that tree at fifty miles an hour. I'm sure everything hurts." Annika sighed. "I cast a spell on you to help you heal a bit faster, but things will ache."

"Thanks," he mumbled. "You said your sister wanted to take me. To feed off me?"

"Take your soul." She shrugged. "Huldra can be terrible beings. I mean, she did allow you to crash hard into the tree."

"And you brought me into a tree." He couldn't wrap his mind around the situation. "Why, if she wanted to steal my soul, did you save me? Or are you going to steal my soul instead?"

"I don't do that." She frowned. "You're bleeding. I hoped I'd gotten to you before you drilled your head through that window. Wrong. You probably have glass in it."

"Sure." His vision blurred. "I don't feel well."

"I know." She scratched her forehead again. "I didn't want to bring you here, but you can't stay where you are. Let me..." She flicked her fingers.

He wasn't sure what was going on, but before he could gather his bearings, he was stretched out on a bed. "What the Hades?" he murmured. "How?"

"I have a bit of magic and can move you easier than I wanted my sister to believe." Annika stood beside the bed. "You need to rest. I'm surprised you haven't slipped right into shock yet. I'm here and I'll take care of you. I don't want you to sleep, but you'll need to. May I invade your mind to communicate with you until you fully heal?"

"You can do that?"

"I can." The corner of her mouth curled in a slight smile. "When I saw you in the woods, driving so oddly through the trees and underbrush, I knew my sister was involved. She probably wanted you to collide with other trees and you simply didn't cooperate. It's a good thing you didn't. But she would've won. Now, you're safe in my tree house where she can't get you. You can sleep, heal, and figure this all out."

"You're being too nice to me."

"I feel protective of you. I can't not help you." Annika rubbed his forehead, caressing his skin with the pad of her thumb. "It'll be okay."

"I shouldn't trust you. Shouldn't trust anyone here." Eerie wasn't a bad place, but there were plenty of individuals here that wanted nothing more than to take advantage. Going to the wrong areas of town and coming back unscathed wouldn't be possible.

"I want to talk you out of distrusting me, but you have to decide in your own time. Until then, sleep." She continued to caress his forehead. The smile on her lips softened along with the ice in her stare. "You've been through a lot and need to rest. I don't know your story, but I see a man in pain -- not just physical, but emotional. You're in a safe place. I've got you and no one will hurt you here. Promise."

He allowed the darkness of sleep to envelop him. He shouldn't trust her, but he did. Anyone else might have left him there to die, left him to the wild animals or even to her sister. Annika was a mystery to him, yet she made so much sense.

As he swam through this dream-like state, wandering through the darkness, pieces of his life floated in his subconscious. Meeting Sally, seeing her face for the first time, the moment he realized she'd break his heart. His stomach churned and he groaned. How could he have been so foolish? He should've seen the signs. Should've trusted his gut.

Where had that gotten him?

A thought occurred to him. If he hadn't been through the rough time with Sally, he wouldn't have come to Eerie. Might not have met Annika.

Was this truly a turning point in his life? Could be. Could be another dead end or a huge detour before sorting things out.

Hades, this is too confusing.

His body ached. He still wasn't sure how he'd been enchanted enough to hit the tree. He should've seen it. His head hurt. If he wasn't concussed, then it was pretty close. He could've died out there. No one would've found him. But he'd been saved.

His mind turned to Annika. She'd not only located him but given him aid. She helped him to a place where he could rest, heal. No doubt she didn't know she'd helped not only his body, but his soul, too. He'd needed that rest. He'd been through the wringer, though no one understood the extent. He'd turned his life upside down by coming back to Eerie.

His heart ached from the breakup with Sally, but

also the accident. A sense of calm settled in his brain. Because of Annika? She'd said she was his guardian spirit. Or was this connection more than that? It was too soon to tell.

But he could finally rest. Could sort this out eventually.

For once, he just might be okay.

Chapter Two

Annika sat with Hunter and watched the rise and fall of his chest. The bruises on the visible areas grew darker. He was lucky to be alive. Lucky he didn't have broken bones.

He could lock her sister up for her behavior. There was no need to grab another being. Runa could've killed him. Probably wanted to. She lived for destruction. If she couldn't cause trouble, she wasn't happy. Then again, she never had been.

Annika stared at Hunter. He was a pretty man. Not just handsome, but pretty with his long lashes, dusting of freckles on his cheeks, dark blond hair, and all that muscle. She wanted to stretch out on him and snuggle against his chest. He was the kind of man she'd longed to meet. To find someone who understood her. Someone who wasn't afraid of her. Her tail slipped free from her dress, becoming visible. She'd almost forgotten about the blasted thing. Would he be disgusted when he saw her tail? Her strength hadn't bothered him, but the abnormality might.

She hated complications, and her tail was a big one. She hated the way Hunter twitched as he slept, too. So unsettled. Like he had too much on his mind. Probably did. She'd never met anyone who was completely carefree. If they acted like they were, they were damn good at masking their problems. Good at hiding, too.

Runa couldn't hide a thing if she tried. She wore her disgust on her sleeve. Her sister believed herself to be the better actress, though. Huldra were expected to play the part of the vixen. To lure men to their doom. Annika had never been good at the act. Runa loved it.

Killing never had pleased Annika. She'd rather

help people. She sat beside Hunter and watched him sleep, despite it being an odd feeling to keep vigil this way. She should be helping him. Healing him. But what should she do? Call a medicine man or witch? Someone with spells? There had to be someone.

"So you saved him?" Runa stood at the window, on the outside. "You took mercy on him."

"I did." She left his side to speak to her sister through the glass. "You have none."

"Don't need any," Runa replied. "You and I aren't so different, you know."

"We aren't?" They were complete opposites.

"Nope. We're carbon copies. You look like me." Runa's eyes twinkled. "One push and you'll come to the dark side."

"I doubt it." It wasn't in her nature to be cruel.

"We could have so much fun. Prank the unsuspecting, have all the sex we want without any guilt. You know humans will give it up that easily. They see beauty and think they should have us, then allow us to do whatever we want."

"That's the life," Annika said dryly.

"You get it."

"I really don't. I don't get it at all." She stared at her twin. They did look exactly alike with the same figure, hair, eyes, face... but Runa always looked angry. There wasn't any tenderness in her eyes. When she got irritated with someone, her true form showed. Annika wondered if she had the same gruesome face and soul within herself. She hoped not.

"You're deep in thought." Runa narrowed her eyes. "Why?"

"No reason." She hated discussing her feelings with her sister. The past didn't matter. Besides, the conversations always turned to arguments, which turned to mentions of Erik -- the one person she never wanted to mention again.

"You lie."

Maybe she did.

"You hate me."

"I'm not doing this." Annika hated this argument, too. "Stop."

"You're trying to get rid of me."

"You're being paranoid." For being twins, they sure didn't share the same thought wavelength. Not even close. "I'm thinking about him."

"My prey?"

"The man." He wasn't prey. "You said humans are easy, but he's not human."

"I know that," Runa snapped, and crooked her brow.

"Then what is he?" If her sister was so smart, she'd know. If her pride got in the way, she'd admit what she knew.

"Old magic."

"I guessed that. What kind?" She wanted to hear Runa say it. He was of older magic than even they were.

"No."

"No?"

"You know," Runa said with a growl.

"I'm asking you." She had an idea. His magic was indeed old, but so far along that it'd been diluted. Traces were still there, which permitted him entry to Eerie, but not enough to be blatant. "So?"

"You don't need me to say."

"Runa. You thought he was human. How could he be and exist in Eerie? No truly full human can."

Runa rolled her eyes. "I was testing you."

"Liar." Not a good one, either. "Is he dead?"

Nice subject change. "He sleeps."

"Vampire?"

"No." Then her sister didn't know, either? Interesting. Annika had an inkling but wondered about his origins. "Animal."

"Fuck. I never toy with *those* kinds. Too chewy." Runa tossed her hair over her shoulder. "You can't deny we're alike. We're twins. What you like, I do. What you are, I am. We're intertwined." She splayed her hands on the glass. "You need to accept it."

"Runa." Acceptance wasn't that easy.

"If you want him, then I do, too. I won't rest until he's mine." Her eyes flashed. "Oh, the things I could do with him."

"What if he's not interested?" She didn't like talking about Hunter like he wasn't there. He'd hear and be upset. Who wouldn't be? Any reasonable being would. "He might not want to be with me." Thinking he might was an overreach.

"He could want me," Runa said. "He's got good taste."

"You just said he was too chewy."

"Meh." Runa shrugged.

"What about Aleksandr? Erik? What about them?" she asked, knowing she'd opened the door to trouble.

"Spit those names out. You never speak their names in front of me ever again. Vile men. They wanted to break me. Wanted to use me, then lied to you. No man breaks me or uses my family." Runa curled her lip in a sneer. "They thought they were smart. Fools."

"So you want to break Hunter? In return?"

"You know his name?" Runa's eyes widened and her sneer softened. "Have you formed a bond?"

"I saved him from you after you ran him into a tree at full speed. So, no, there hasn't been time." Her annoyance flared. "He should be dead."

"He should be. I wanted to eat his soul. Feed from his energy."

Oh, they were back to that… "Drink the blood of innocents and bathe in it, too? I don't care to do those things."

"You're jealous," Runa said. "No matter. He will wake and have to choose, like Erik and Aleksandr. He will perish like them, too. He's too bold, like Erik, and too foolish, like Aleksandr. I must go. I'll return when the time is right." Without another word, Runa vanished.

Annika hoped that never happened. She sighed. She shouldn't have left Hunter alone, but she wanted to help. Now his bruises were too dark and deep. He probably had internal bleeding. The animal within him had the ability to heal him, but nothing could work this fast. She had to focus. If anyone could help, the Princess could. She'd know what to do.

Annika snapped her fingers. She needed a bubble. She hadn't made one in years. She flicked her fingers, creating sparks. After three tries, the bubble formed. Relief swept over her. She hadn't forgotten. Good.

The image in the bubble grew clearer. The Princess stood at a table with her arms full of blankets. She'd picked the worst time to interrupt the royal court.

"Annika?" Piper dropped the pile. "I'm glad you contacted me."

"I'm bothering you, aren't I? I'm sorry." She apologized too much for her own good.

"No. Well, you are, but I'm thrilled to be

interrupted. Stacking blankets isn't fun. Besides, I never get to talk to the Huldra. How are you?" Piper asked.

Annika would never tire of the Princess's positive attitude and nature. The woman was so upbeat, she brought everyone up with her. She was the best change of pace from Runa. "If you're not upset with me interrupting, then I'm glad I contacted you. I'm well. You?"

"Other than this job, I'm good." Piper grinned. She had a thousand-watt grin that could light up a room. "Let me go into the other room. I love a good chitchat, but this feels bigger than small talk." She moved out of the larger room to another one.

The castle was so spacious, the Princess could be anywhere -- not that Annika had much knowledge of the building. Annika waited as Piper settled in a chair. "Okay," Piper said. "Better. Been on my feet all day. So, what's up? You look stressed."

"I am." She wasn't sure how to ask for this kind of help. "Runa tried to capture a being in the woods."

"As many Huldra would do."

"Except me." She prided herself on not luring anyone.

"I know," Piper said. "You're a good soul. You stepped in?"

"I did." She explained how Hunter had ended up being in her tree house. "The thing is, he's hurt and I can't fix him. He's got broken bones, and I'd be shocked if he didn't have internal bleeding. I don't have the magic to heal him."

"I do."

"I know." Yet she didn't have the words to ask Piper to help her.

"You want my assistance?"

Her throat ran dry and her heart hammered. "Yes, please?"

"All you have to do is ask." Piper sat up taller and wriggled her fingers.

Annika wobbled. Defeat ran through her veins. "I feel helpless. I know what to do -- to ask -- but I keep fumbling. He needs help, I'm trying to get him help, yet I can't seem to find the words or the courage."

Piper tipped her head. "You're interested in him."

"No. Maybe? He's so beat up."

"I'd imagine he would be. He crashed into a tree."

"I can't fix him," she repeated. "I want to because it's not right that he was hurt. He was there for a reason, but I don't know what it is and even if I did, it's not enough to destroy him. He deserves the chance to keep going." She wasn't sure why she was so upset.

"I get it."

"Then explain it to me." She balled her hands in frustration. "I'm sorry. I hate seeing anyone hurt for any reason, especially malicious ones." Whereas Runa simply wanted to hurt anyone to keep from getting hurt first.

"I've sent a potion that should help heal him. He'll sleep for at least twenty-four hours as it works. Anything instantaneous will not help. It might even kill him or cause more trouble."

"Okay." She wasn't in any position to argue. "Thank you." She shouldn't be so bold, speaking for him, but she assumed he'd appreciate that someone cared enough to aid him. She hoped he would do the same for her if the roles were reversed.

"It's on the way. Give it, and him, the time needed to do what should be done and keep an eye on him. You're interested, which is good. He'll have excellent care. Just keep in mind that your heart is involved already. You could get hurt."

She could, but she'd risk it. It wasn't like she'd never had her heart broken before. Erik and Aleksandr came to mind again. "I'll be okay." The potion appeared in front of her, and she slowly dripped it between Hunter's lips.

"I hope you will."

Piper's words sounded so ominous. They could be a foretelling of a bad ending -- which she didn't want. "I'm sorry."

"Why?"

"I don't want to hurt him. Maybe I screwed with fate. I should've left him there." That didn't feel right, though. "I don't know. I'm afraid I made the wrong decision."

"Who says you did?"

"Who says I didn't?" She glanced back at Hunter's sleeping form. "It's all so messed up."

"Maybe it is, but you were drawn to him. You did what you did for a reason. Don't question that," Piper said. "He's out cold, isn't he?"

"He is." She checked again. Still breathing, but out to the world. "Very much."

"Then the potion is working. Good." Piper sighed. "You're embarking on a very important, but scary, journey."

"I am?"

"You've found your mate, so yes, you are."

"No." She hadn't *found* him. She'd rescued a person in distress.

"You have. You found that one person who will make you tick, twitch, sigh, and feel gooey inside. He'll do all that while driving you nuts. You'll be glad you found him, and you're destined for each other, but right now it'll be tense because only one of you knows, and you're unsure."

"Yeah, I am." Realization swept over her. This was all a disaster. He had no idea what was going on. He might not even like her. "Do I tell him? What do I do when he freaks out? He could dislike me!"

"You can't wake him right now."

Not when he was asleep. "I mean, should I say something when he comes around?" What was she supposed to do? Dance naked for him? Show up in a flimsy nightie? Couldn't wake him with a kiss. That seemed too forcible and not romantic. Still, she wasn't sure what to do. Erik had said she was too cold toward him. Aleksandr didn't like that she had a twin. Hunter could be the same way. "He might not like me. I don't want to push it. I should tell him and let him choose right then."

"Nope."

"No? What do you mean? He deserves to know. Then he can be rational about what he wants. He could have a woman at home. Could be engaged. Married." She hadn't seen a wedding ring, despite looking, and he hadn't mentioned anyone. But there hadn't been time. "If I can't tell him, then it's sure to be a fuckup." Why make this ten times harder?

"He has to figure it out on his own," Piper said. "If you tell him, that's guaranteed to make him run."

"I can sway him?" Entice him? Show him what he might have if he was with her? "Be the best version of me I can?" And let fate handle the situation?

"I'd hope so. Use those feminine wiles, girl. You're adorable and sweet. If he's not suffering from permanent paralysis of the heart, then he'll see that. Something drew him to you. Drew him here. Use it."

Her brain hurt. "I suppose."

"Runa will strike again. She's got him in her sights because it's in her nature, no? You've got other reasons. You know what to do to get him to see who you are inside. It's up to him to choose, but the magic will work if you trust it."

"What if I don't trust it?" she murmured. "What if I'm still afraid?"

"Would you believe the magic is smart enough to know what to do? Go along for the ride," Piper said. "Yes?"

"Okay." She could do this. Had no choice.

"That said, don't be surprised by his initial freak-out. He's in over his head and will be afraid, too. Be strong for him and for you." Piper hopped up. "Shit. I hear Diesel. I need to get more supplies. Apparently, we need to prep for an invasion."

"What?" Her blood chilled. "I didn't know we were under siege. Is there a war happening?" What did she have to do to protect herself?

"Children." Piper shrugged and grinned. "The home for orphaned children was flooded this morning, so the kids are coming to the castle for the weekend to rest while the building dries out. It won't be too bad. See you." She disappeared, leaving Annika in shock… and a bit of relief, as well.

At least the invasion was something simple. But how had the home been flooded? It was on a hill. She shook her head. The more pressing issue was that she and Hunter were destined. Use her feminine charms and win him over. Easy. She massaged her temples. It wasn't easy. But if she'd learned anything in her life years, it was tenacity. If she wanted something or someone, she had to take them. She had charm, grace and could be sweet. She might have lost out on

Aleksandr and Erik, but they weren't her mates. If Hunter was, then this would work. She'd make it work.

She had little choice. His life depended on it.

Chapter Three

Hunter groaned. In his sleep? In a dream? Or was this all real? He had no idea. All he did know was that everything hurt. He'd never ached this much in his life. Was he even still alive?

Oh, Hades. He could be dead.

No, if he could think then he must be alive. Or a spirit…

Nothing much made sense.

Except Annika.

She'd saved his butt. It could've been a way to screw with him, but he doubted it. He tended to be able to read people well.

That is, until he'd gone to the forest. Then everything seemed wonky. Not her, though. The one who looked like Annika. That was the one who'd messed with him. He'd felt the darkness in her presence. The bloodthirsty quality within her. She'd destroy him and smile while doing it. He wasn't in the mood to be destroyed.

He wanted to talk to Annika. Get to know her. Get to know Eerie again. Like he'd never left, but also like he'd never been there before.

First, he needed to wake up. His brain was foggy. His limbs felt heavy. Like he couldn't move. Had she enchanted him?

"Hey."

He recognized that voice. Annika. She jostled him.

"Hunter?" She nudged him again. "Honey, wake up."

Her voice reassured him. "Yeah?" he managed. He opened his eyes a bit and blinked in the dimly lit room. The lethargy was still there but not as bad. He turned to the sound of her voice. "Hi."

Annika smiled. Her blonde hair flowed freely, and a pink stain infused her cheeks. Her smile warmed his heart. She still wore a white dress, but the fabric accentuated her breasts and her nipples. He shouldn't be looking, but she was too beautiful to ignore. Too enticing.

He had to be losing it. He'd just met her and had to be rescued while in her presence, yet he was lusting after her. He should be sorting out his life.

"You're staring at me," Annika said. "Am I hideous?"

"No." He fumbled for words. "Not at all."

"The dress is too much, isn't it?" She averted her gaze. "I wanted to look sexy, but it's too much."

"No." He placed his hand on hers. "It's fine. You're fine."

"Good." She sat a little closer to him. Her dress strained against her breasts, giving him quite the show -- not that he minded. He liked what he saw.

Blood rushed to his cock. He adjusted the blankets to hide his growing erection. She'd think him a perv. But she was on display and something about her drove him crazy. "So..."

"So." She rested her free arm across her lap. "You've been out for a while."

"I bet." There was something rational he could talk about. "I'm guessing a few hours?" He still ached, but it wasn't the bone-deep hurt as before. She must have a spectacular ability to heal, even if it was only in his mind.

"Try three days."

"You're joking." Three days? That had to be wrong. He would have sworn he'd laid down to take a nap. Had to be more like three hours. "Are you sure?"

"Positive." She shoved him his phone. "I charged this because I happened to have the same cord. Your phone appears to chirp when the battery is low. It chirped, I wanted you to be able to rest and not have the annoying sound, so I charged it. I hope you don't mind."

"I don't." He'd forgotten about it chirping. But he prided himself on keeping it charged. He understood what she'd done, though and appreciated her thoughtfulness. He looked at the screen. She was right -- three days had passed. "Well, shit. I don't know how this happened."

"I do." She tipped her head and braced her hand on the bed. "You hit a tree tree."

He vaguely remembered that.

"You crashed right into a tree and collided with the steering wheel. It's a miracle that your face isn't broken. The airbag worked, but you hit pretty hard," Annika said. "My sister caused the accident."

"She did?"

"She did. She determined you were prime for her enticing and lured you to the forest," Annika said.

"No." He shook his head. "I'd planned on going there."

"Why?"

Why, indeed. He snorted. He wasn't ready to sit up, but he liked watching her. Liked listening to her talk. "I was upset."

"Why?" She blushed. "I'm sorry. You don't have to tell me."

"I don't mind telling you. I thought my former girlfriend -- who hasn't been my girlfriend in over a year -- wanted to get back together. Turned out she wanted to fuck with me. Made my heart ache." He met her gaze. "I was foolish enough to think she might want me back and when she didn't and laughed in my face, I wanted to hide. I thought for a few minutes about doing something terrible to myself when I arrived at the forest. If I wanted to follow through with my ideas, then the forest was the best place to hide. No one would find my body until it was dust."

"That's terrible." She squeezed his fingers. "You have more to live for than someone who was rough with your heart."

"Yeah?" Would she be willing to help him heal his soul, too?

"Yes. I know how it feels to have someone tear your heart in two. My former lover shredded my heart because he didn't want me. He wanted my sister. The other one never wanted either of us, and knew it, but toyed with us both."

"Men," he said, despite being a man himself. "We can be cruel."

"You can."

He watched her, marveling at her beauty. She wasn't pretty only on the outside. She seemed to glow from within. Like she had a light in her. Had fight in her, too. She struck him as the type who'd love hard and fight even harder for the one she loved. He wanted her in his corner.

In his bed.

Dear Zeus, he had to stop thinking this way. She wasn't an object. She was a warm, sensitive, sexy woman.

So why did he want so much to kiss her?

She snickered. "You're staring again. Brain damage?"

"Might be." But he doubted it. There was something between them. A draw he'd never felt before. When he looked into Annika's eyes, he forgot all about Sally. Forgot about the women in his past. They didn't matter and held no importance now.

"You collided pretty hard."

"I did." He reached for her. "You saved my butt."

"And the rest of you."

She had a point. "Why?" he asked. She didn't have to step in. She could've left him there. She certainly didn't owe him anything.

"My sister, Runa, would have killed you if I hadn't intervened. I didn't want you to die. No doubt she'd have destroyed you," she said. "She loves destruction."

"Some do." He'd bet her sister was related, even if only in spirit, to Sally. "Has she always been that driven?"

"Ever since I've known her." Annika chuckled and shook her head. "She wants you."

"She's interested in me?" He had no interest in Runa. "To do what? Go apple picking? I'm beat up, but not ignorant."

"No, you're not. She also doesn't want to do nice things with you. She wants you dead and to have your energy," Annika said. "We're Huldra. We're Norse beings who can either save or destroy. Those who want to are protectors. Those who wish destruction will do so at any cost."

He hadn't known it, but that made sense. "You're strong like Valkyries."

"But we don't take you from the battle."

"Right. Runa *is* the battle."

She nodded. "She is."

"What about you? Are you a battle, too? Are you going to nurse me back to health only to kill me?"

"No."

He liked hearing that. "Will I make a full recovery, doctor?"

"You will. I got help from the Princess to bring you around. I'm glad because I enjoy talking to you."

"We could do more than talk." He wasn't sure why he'd said that. It was too suggestive, even if it was true.

"Aren't you the smooth talker?" She blushed. "Is it bad that I don't mind?"

"No." He liked hearing that. It gave him hope he might be able to entice her into giving him a chance. "Will I get back to myself soon?"

"What do you mean?"

"Will I be able to move around soon?" he asked. He struggled to sit up. "I feel like I'm made of lead, but I'd also like to properly thank my rescuer."

"Me?" She helped him into an upright position. "I'm not sure how long it'll be until you're at full power."

He'd struck a tree. No one bounced back from that in a few days. Still, he liked having her close. He liked a lot of things about her. "I can't explain why, but I want you to lean closer."

"Like this?" She rested her forehead on his. "Close enough?"

"No." He curled his fingers under her chin, touching her. Her soft skin, the tenderness in her eyes made his spirits soar when he looked at her. "I want to kiss you."

"Me?"

She asked that a lot. "Yes, you." He feathered his mouth over hers. The second he did, something within him both righted and felt off-kilter at the same time. He bumped noses with her. She smelled so good. He reached out to her, cupping her jaw. Holding her felt so right. Destined.

That had to be wrong. No one was destined. They were bodies coming together. Souls crossing paths.

If anyone was truly destined, then it was a big secret.

He kissed her, tasting her and memorizing this moment. He'd never felt this way before.

She broke the connection first but remained close. "Whoa."

"Yeah? Felt the stars explode and your belly churn?"

"I did."

He slipped his hand down her shoulder. "I want to touch you."

"You may," she whispered. "I hope you do."

He shouldn't be wanting to undress her this way. Shouldn't be so desirous for her. Not so fast. He couldn't help himself. He smoothed his palm over her breast. The heat of her body relaxed him. He cupped her breast, loving the way her nipple beaded under his touch.

A groan rumbled in her throat. She arched into him. She placed her hand on his. "Oh, gods."

He liked this, too. He brushed his mouth across her jaw. The longer he spent in her presence, the more he wanted to stay here.

She woke something in him that had been long dormant -- his heart.

He brushed his thumb across her nipple. "You confuse me."

"How?" She balled her hand on his chest. "Because I want to crawl into your lap already?"

"That's not it, but I'd like it if you did." His body might be broken, but his dick still worked. His sex drive was quite intact. "Come here." He wasn't wearing anything and was not ashamed to show himself off, not when he craved her this much.

"I can't."

"Why?" He saw no reason why not.

"You're hurt. I shouldn't push you." She smoothed her hands over his chest. His nipples reacted as hers had. He needed her. Like now.

He reached for her, nudging her toward his lap. "Come here and go for a ride." It'd help them both.

"I'm not that kind of girl." Her dress parted high on her thigh, revealing a lot of leg.

He'd never seen such pale skin. She was almost translucent. "You don't see the sun?"

"No. The canopy is too thick." She hesitated. "When you're better, we can explore this. First, you've got to heal."

"You'll leave me hanging?" He hated being tossed aside, but he understood exactly why she'd done it. He did need to repair himself. "You drive a hard bargain."

"I do." She sat beside him but rested one hand off to the side so she faced him. "My sister will attack you. She will push you if you give her a chance."

"I need strength, then, to fight back." Maybe he needed another reason to fight back as well. Annika was a good reason. He'd keep going forward if he could have a few more minutes with her.

"You do. She's wiry and dangerous," Annika said. "I can't defeat her alone."

"Then you don't have to." She'd made his mind up for him. "I'm ready."

"To do what?" Her eyes glittered. "You can't get out of bed yet."

"Maybe not, but I'm planning on staying here --

unless you want to join me."

"You're going to die trying to get me into bed with you."

"Will it work? Will I die a happy man?" He caressed her bare arm. "I'm captivated by you."

"Why?"

"You're strong. You stood up to a bully for me and did what was right." He smoothed his hand over hers. "I've never had someone do that for me."

"You've been around the wrong people."

"I have." Now he'd found one of the right ones. "Will you at least recline with me?"

She smiled. "I thought maybe we'd test your strength and feed you."

"We?"

"You and me."

He liked that. The more time he spent with her, the more he fell for her. It had to be lust, but he didn't care. He loved hard, fell even harder, and threw himself one thousand percent into whatever he did.

"Besides, I want to get to know you." She left the bed. "What do you like to eat?"

What a loaded question. He wanted to sink between her thighs and delight in her. It wasn't the time yet, though. Soon. "Is it day or night?"

"It's two in the afternoon." She folded her arms, bunching her breasts. "Too late for breakfast, but nearly right between lunch and dinner."

He nodded. He wasn't much of a breakfast person.

"I suppose you want to know what I have?" she asked. "Or what I can scrounge up?"

"No." He sank back onto the bed. "I was thinking I'm not all that hungry. Tired, though."

"I'd imagine you are." She remained next to him.

"Well?"

"I don't want a woman who works for me. I'm not incapable. I'm simply temporarily broken. You don't have to take care of me. I'd rather you be my equal."

She stared at him but said nothing. She parted her lips, like she wanted to say something, but didn't.

"You expected me to be more of a chauvinist?" He sighed, his body heavy. "I want to disrobe you and taste every inch of you. Want to kiss you. Make you moan. See you blush and feel you bounce on my lap. Want to sink so deep into you that I forget where I left off and you began." He'd never been good at romance. Never seemed to know what to say. Right now, he led with his heart and trusted he sounded somewhat intelligent. "I'm not like everyone else."

"No, you're not." She left the doorway and disappeared.

Had he been too bold? Had he said too much? He wasn't great at holding back. He scrubbed both hands over his face. The scrapes and bruises on his arms and hands burned. His wrists hurt, except when he touched her. He could keep doing that -- touching her. She was like a drug. A balm to his soul. He needed more of her tender care.

Annika reappeared, this time her eyes wide. "Oh, man."

"Man?" he asked. "Who are you talking to?"

"Sorry." She closed the drapes, darkening the room. "It's bright out there and the house is visible, and I don't want anyone to find us."

"Why?"

"I don't want to be interrupted," she said.

He could appreciate her bluntness, but worried about her meaning. She had the power to help him or kill him. If she took after her sister, he was in big trouble. Huldra were tenacious and dangerous. Vicious.

He had to believe she was different. His heart already did -- now he needed his mind to be in agreement. Easier said than done.

Chapter Four

Annika closed the last of the curtains. To anyone passing by the tree, they wouldn't see the house among the leaves. It appeared to be just any old tree, which is how she wanted it. No one to bother her.

Until he'd come along, she hadn't wanted anyone to be with her. He changed everything.

"Are we going to do something fun?" Hunter asked.

"We may." She debated what to do. They couldn't have sex. Good Gods, if they did, he'd get hurt and he needed to heal. That didn't mean she couldn't entice him and give him pleasure. She switched off the lights, save for one small lamp.

"What are you doing?" He scooted back down on the bed. A tent formed in the sheets.

Her enticing had the right effect. So far, so good. She danced for him, moving her hips to make her skirt swish. The soft fabric rubbed her tender nipples. Electricity ran through her veins. She slid her hands over her chest, then down to her hips.

"Yes," he said, his voice thick. "Come here."

"Not yet." She danced more, then turned her back on him. When she did, she allowed the straps of her dress to ease down her shoulders. The bodice loosened and revealed most of her back.

"My Gods, yes," Hunter said.

She glanced over her shoulder, before allowing the dress to tumble to the floor. She sucked in a ragged breath. Being this vulnerable made her happy. It was freedom.

But he could reject her when he noticed her tail. The fur receded when she undressed, but it was still a jarring sight.

"I need you," Hunter said. "You tease me too much."

She did. She glanced back at him again. Raw hunger shimmered in his eyes. He reached for her. She kept her back to him for another moment, hoping he'd see the remains of her small tail, almost completely receded by now. If he was going to turn her down because of her unique attribute, then she wanted it to happen now rather than after her heart was fully involved.

"I see you." He offered a lazy grin. "You're incredible. All of you."

"All of me?" She embraced her boldness and turned to face him. Her breasts jiggled. She licked her lips as the chilly air in the tree house swirled around her.

"You're dynamite." He kept reaching for her. "Please? Put a damaged man out of his misery."

The neediness in his voice spurred her on. She inched up to him, taking her time. The closer she got to him, the more powerful she felt. Not dominance, but a belief in herself that she could be bold. Could have what she wanted. Like she'd come into her own. She crawled onto the bed. Her hair slid over her shoulder and her breasts swayed. Heat enveloped her.

"Yes, baby." Hunter curled his fingers under her chin again. "You're a vision."

"You're not too bad yourself." She kissed him. The taste of him pleased her. When he cupped her breast in his free hand, she arched into him. It'd been so long since she'd been touched this way. Since she'd been needed. Desired. She'd almost forgotten how it felt.

"Ride me," he whispered. "Get yourself off on my cock."

"Not yet." She kissed her way down his body, feathering her mouth on his chest, up to his nipples, careful not to press too hard on his bruises.

When he groaned, she moved lower. The closer she got to his dick, the more anticipation ramped up within her. His moans and the way he thrust his fingers into her hair excited her. He touched her with reverence and tenderness. He held her like she mattered.

She yearned to please him. She kissed down to his navel. He wasn't as hairy as she'd expected from a shifter descendant -- or he shaved. She splayed her hand over his abs. The taut muscle flexed under her fingertips, like she touched silken steel.

A moan vibrated within him. "Sweetheart, you know how to drive a man crazy." He nudged her head. "Put me out of my misery."

"Going to come just from me touching you?" She'd give him relief eventually. She nuzzled along his inner thigh and breathed him in. The spicy aroma of him -- animalistic and sexy -- increased her need. Her hair slipped over her shoulder and her breasts skimmed his thigh.

"I'm fucking close." He tugged on her hair. "Please?"

Precum shimmered on the tip of his erection. She took a moment to drink in the details of him. Was it wrong to lust after the chance to ride his thick shaft? No. Terrible to want to feel him ripple within her? Not at all.

Her pussy creamed and anticipation filled her brain. She wrapped her fingers around his girth before stroking him.

He pulled on her hair. "Yes, baby. More."

She couldn't deny him. Not when they were both

this vulnerable. She brushed her lips over his blunt head, then took him in her mouth. The taste of him exploded on her tongue. The spice and salt of him added to the moment.

"Take me in," he murmured. "Make me come apart, Annika."

She'd never had her name used during sex. Hearing him call her by her name both excited and comforted her like she mattered. This wasn't just an act, but a union.

She shouldn't be thinking in such deep terms already. Pleasure should be enough, but she'd always wanted someone who got her on a molecular level, someone who appreciated her. Could he be the one? She'd never know until she crossed the line and took this next step.

Did she want another man? No. He was plenty exciting. Besides, there was more to explore with him. This was just the beginning.

She increased her speed, bobbing faster.

He seemed to meet her thrust for thrust. "Babe." He growled. "I need to come."

Then he should. She moved even quicker, pushing him closer to coming apart. As he shivered, she teased him more.

"I can't." He shuddered, then trembled. He rammed his cock deep into her mouth. He whimpered as his dick throbbed.

She swallowed him to the root, not wanting to miss a drop. The musky taste overloaded her senses. She swore she heard a wolf howl.

He loosened his grasp on her head and let go of her hair. "Jesus H. Christ in a bucket."

She let go of his erection with a pop. "I guess you liked it."

"Liked? I loved it. If that's your version of nursing, then I'm all for it."

She bit back a laugh. Trust him to liken a blow job to nursing. He would, though. She wiped her mouth with the back of her hand. "You're awfully coherent for a guy who just came." She didn't hear the wolf any longer and must've heard one passing by the house. "You need to rest."

"Is the house locked up tight?" he asked. "Enough your sister isn't going to infiltrate while we're asleep?"

"We?" A bit pushy, wasn't he? "Why do you think *we* will be sleeping?"

"Because I'll heal a lot better and faster when I have you here beside me. You're a good influence."

"How?" She snapped her fingers, locking the tree house up with the power of a spell. "We're good -- if I decide to sleep with you."

"Please?"

"You're begging."

"I *do* need to rest." He batted his eyelashes. "Besides, we need to strategize."

"On what attack?"

"The one your sister is planning."

"I'm not killing her." She wasn't sure she could. "And I can't convince her to change her mind."

"No one says you should," he replied. "But I need to know what I have to do to stay here, get more chances with you, and prevent her from killing me." He reached for her.

She shouldn't succumb to him. She'd been a fool for other handsome men and paid dearly, but Hunter felt different. More like a real man where the others were clichés. Still, she'd been burned.

"You're worried, yes? I would be, too," he said.

"This guy does a crazy thing in front of you and you have to save his ass. When you do, he acts all dippy for you -- all while your sister, the homicidal nut, wants me dead. It's a lot to take in."

"That's an understatement." But succinct.

"I'm not the type of guy to make rash decisions and run off to the woods."

"Yet that's what you did -- unless you're saying my sister pushed you."

"Even if she did, I was there for a reason and I think I know that reason."

"You do?"

"And if I follow my heart, I'll find my path. I know why I should be in Eerie."

"Because of me?" She didn't believe him.

"Maybe." He shrugged. "For now, let's rest and sort it out when we've had a night to recharge."

"Says the man who slept for the last three days."

"Don't give such a good blow job."

Flatterer, but she liked him and his words.

"Will you stay with me?"

She should toy with him a little longer. It was in her nature to do that, but she couldn't let him suffer. "I'll stay." It might be the craziest thing she'd ever done -- being this vulnerable -- or it could be the best.

* * *

Hunter needed the rest. He refused to tell her just how bruised and battered he was -- and not just on the outside. He'd been through so much in his years. He settled into relaxation, but his mind didn't. The more he tried to calm his thoughts, the more they churned up. Was this some of the magic of the Huldra? A way that Runa might get into his brain? It didn't seem possible -- yet was completely plausible. The magic of Eerie was crazy. It could do things no mere mortal could do because it was magic. Plus, the Huldra were old magic. Ancient magic.

Did Annika have anything to do with it? She might, but he doubted it. But if she did, then staying put would enable Runa to find them. Or she was protecting him from danger.

His head ached. He'd thought too hard about this already. But this was his problem. He overthought things -- too much. He let his mind run wild because he wasn't sure of so many things.

Sally had called it his indecisiveness. She'd hated when he second-guessed himself. According to her, the one time he made a choice and stuck to it, she'd die.

He'd bet she wasn't dead. Not even close. But she had a point -- he sucked at making decisions.

He'd never told anyone else why he'd been so bad at choosing. She wouldn't have understood anyway. Sally could only think about herself. She had no decency when it came to others and being kind. Sally wanted anything and everything she could get for herself without putting in any work on her part. She'd do whatever it took to benefit herself. How could what someone else did benefit her?

He shuddered. He'd put up with a lot of shit from Sally and the rest of the world. The kids at school taunted him for being different. He heard things no one else did, detected scents others couldn't smell. He'd been quick in gym class -- he loved running in short bursts. He'd been good at sprinting and track events but was never the star of the team. He hadn't been wanted that way. Why would the rest of the team want to shine a light on the orphan kid? Because his adoptive family wasn't a wealthy one.

He did what he did best. He operated at his best levels but flew below the radar. No attention meant no teasing.

Hades, he was so screwed up. He should've used his abilities and been the man he'd been destined to be -- not the second-guesser. But he had no information on his past. No idea who he belonged to, other than he could come and go in Eerie. He felt like he belonged in the paranormal town.

The realization struck him. He knew damn well why he'd felt so much indecision. Never knowing his past made him question everything.

Would knowing the truth help him heal? Yes. Help him make better decisions? Not necessarily, but it might give him insight. It could help him trust people despite his tendency not to.

He needed to talk to Annika. She might be willing to help him figure out his past or could send him in the right direction. She might not know where to send him. Maybe she couldn't leave the woods. Hades, he didn't know enough about Huldra.

Did anyone, except the Huldra? There had to be someone. But who could help him?

He paused. What if all this second-guessing was because of Runa trying to get into his mind? About her trying to turn him against Annika and everything he knew? Was she making him question what he did know?

There was too much to think about, and he should be sleeping. He had so much recharging to do.

He shook his head. When he awoke, he'd speak to Annika to figure out what he should do to get answers. He needed to get to the bottom of his past so he could move forward.

Hopefully, Annika would come with him. He'd grown too fond of her. He liked having her in his orbit because she captivated him. He wanted to know if the captivation would last beyond the honeymoon phase. If it did, then he wanted to keep exploring it.

"Go to sleep," Annika said. "I've never had to work this hard to keep someone in bed."

Chapter Five

He froze. She wasn't supposed to know he couldn't relax. He was supposed to be putting up a good front. His senses were supposed to be honed to keep him vigilant. So much for that. He'd done a piss-poor job of hiding his frustration.

"What's wrong? I'm really doubting my ability to make you happy," she said. "When you're not thrashing, you're talking in your sleep."

Oh, good gravy. He sighed. "I can't get comfortable."

"Why?"

"Can't shut my brain down." He shook his head and opened his eyes. "Can you leave the forest?"

"What?" She faced him. Pink infused her cheeks and sleep filled her eyes. "What are you talking about?"

"Can you leave the forest or are you bound here?" he asked. "I want to ask you to come with me on a date." It was a crazy idea and could implode, but he had to ask. He needed a better ending this time around. Why not have wonderful memories with a sweet woman to blot out the crap ones from his past?

"I can leave. I'm not bound here."

"Would you like to go with me on a date?" He smoothed his hand down her shoulder to her arm. "At least give me a chance?"

"You act like I'll tell you no." She smiled. "I'm not so sure it's safe to be out."

"I'm sure it's not." For all he knew, Runa was waiting right outside the door. "Can we get out without your sister knowing? We can't hide from life because we're scared."

"She's always lurking, but I suppose you're right.

We can't stay cooped up forever. We'll get bored and you might miss your old life. Probably already do."

"No, not at all." He hadn't thought about that life.

"Anyone missing you?" she asked. "Guess I should've asked that before we got naked." She blushed and averted her gaze.

Her instant show of embarrassment amused him but also broke his heart. She didn't deserve to be hurt. "No one." Not that he had anyone waiting for him -- he hadn't lied.

"You're sure? You're not fibbing to me because I gave it up?" She covered her face with her hand. "I should've thought of that before now. I get so caught up in helping that I don't think."

He held lightly to her wrist. "You're a caring being and have a tender heart. If you weren't upset right now, I'd be shocked. I like that you care."

"Okay." She sighed. "No one is waiting on you? Looking for you?"

"If she is, then it's too late," he replied. "Sally only loved herself. I was the unfortunate guy who couldn't see she was using me. I was a wallet. Sad, huh?"

"Some people don't know what they've got until it's gone." She smiled again and the sadness tinged her eyes.

"You're right. Some will never figure it out." He kissed the back of her hand. "And others simply don't care."

"True."

"The woman in my past didn't love me in the way I did her. If she misses me, it's only because she's in financial straits and wants money, not love." He hated to admit this out loud.

"You were running from her?"

"Running away from bad memories." He propped himself on his elbow. "I thought I'd found the one, but she thought I was one of the many. It sucked because she never returned my love."

"She was a fool."

"Could be. Could also be full of herself." He didn't like thinking about Sally, but also wanted to let go of the past. "I met Sally at a club. I was there with friends because they felt I needed to get out."

"So you did?"

"I did." He chuckled and basked in her sweet smile. She gave him courage. "We went out and had a good time. When I bought a round of drinks, she decided I had lots of cash, which I don't."

"Doesn't matter to me."

"Good to know," he replied. "I'll make you feel like the luckiest girl in the world if you'll allow me to."

"Yeah?" She grinned. "How about you treat me with respect?"

"Done." He respected her for who she was and what she'd survived.

"You're too kind to me."

"Anyone who cares about another person should be kind. It shouldn't be a question, either. If you and I are together, then we're kind to each other. We might not agree on everything all the time, but we'll talk and be understanding while we sort it out." He expected no less.

"You're right. She didn't respect you? That's terrible."

"It is," he said. "I knew she'd never be good to me, but I thought it could work."

She nodded. "I get that. I had a thing for a man named Erik, who never loved me. I hoped I could sway him, but no."

"His loss." Good thing the guy hadn't been what and who she wanted. No, it wasn't good because he didn't want her to be hurt, but good for him because he got the chance to show her what proper treatment entailed.

"I will never understand what makes someone treat another person so terribly," she said. "He had a thing for Runa."

"I'm sure that went well."

"Oh, yeah -- he's dead."

"She killed him?" Hades, Runa didn't seem to have any qualms about destruction.

"What do you think?"

Such an odd conversation to be having while in bed, but oh well. He appreciated her honesty. "She wants to destroy stuff. Was it bad?"

"She eviscerated him."

He bit back a groan. He wanted to leave the house to explore, but was now having second thoughts. He wasn't exactly a fan of evisceration. "Why'd she do it? To be tough?"

"I'll never understand her, but I don't get destroying someone." She shrugged. "She does it to toy with them, then thrives on killing. I protect, but she loves the screams, the fear, and the panic."

"You've done a great job. I'm still alive." And damn grateful. She'd saved his butt and given him a new lease on life. "You did a great job."

She blushed. "I did what was needed."

He stared at her. She captivated him, and he wanted these moments to last. Was he falling for her? Sure felt like it. A little quick, but he wasn't ready to tell her that. "Do you like me?" he blurted. Embarrassment hit him like a truck. He should've kept his mouth shut. Why would she open herself up to him this way or give him head if she didn't like him a little bit?

"Yes, I do." She brushed her fingers over his cheek. "You need to work on your confidence."

"What? Me? I've got lots of confidence."

"Uh-huh. Want to try for the truth?" She laughed and the sound brightened his mood.

"If we're going to risk our lives with your sister loose, then we should have the time of our lives, you know?"

"Are you feeling up to it? You've been so unsettled."

"I have." She had a point. "But I'm healing. Look." He held up his hand. The bruises were indeed faded, and not from the simple passage of time.

"May I ask a question?" Annika settled beside him. "Do you know your magic?"

"What I am?"

"Yes."

"Not entirely." She might want him to rest his body, but these conversations worked out his mind and he appreciated it. He hadn't been challenged in a good way in so long.

"What do you know?"

"My mother was from here, but she was an enigma to me. I never knew anything else about my folks. I was told once I was stardust, but I never really knew what that meant. I've never even seen a photo of her. All I've got are some secondhand stories."

She crinkled her nose. "Aren't you intrigued by where you're from?"

"It's a constant wonder."

"I should ask more, but you don't know, so there's no point. I don't know your magic either, but I can tell somewhere in there is shifter."

"Wolf."

"I thought you didn't know."

"I only know there's wolf in there somewhere. I was told I had the sign of the wolf, so I'd be protected, but where the stardust comes in... I have no idea. I guess it's where I got my heightened senses, which seem dull right now, but I don't shift and never could."

"Shifting isn't all it's cracked up to be."

"And you know?" He laughed. "I bet you do."

"Not much, but I've had shifter friends. Some consider it a pain."

"It's a pain *not* being able to shift. Made me feel odd all these years."

"Why?"

"People who can shift ask why I can't. Other kids gave me a hard time about it, and my not having any idea who my parents are."

She rolled her eyes. "Kids are terrible."

"They can be." He wanted to hide away. He hadn't ever talked to Sally about his past -- not that she'd have listened. But with Annika, talking was easy.

"I know why," she said, pulling him away from his thoughts.

"Oh?" He'd like to hear the reason. He'd never been able to figure it out.

"Kids pick on anyone who is different, and in a town full of people who are different, the one who is the most normal-ish is the oddball. You were odd and they chose to be mean. They didn't understand so they were cruel."

"And the bit about my not knowing my parents?" He couldn't deny she was right. He'd been teased for being what was otherwise considered average. "Is that why you live here?" Didn't she feel included? He might not be right, but it had to be asked. "Because of Runa?"

"I don't want to talk about it." She left the bed. "You need rest, so rest."

"Whoa." He sat up. The strength which had been sapped from him returned. He felt renewed. He wasn't sure he wanted to run a marathon, but he certainly felt better. "I talked. You can open up."

"I did." She dressed in another of her shimmery dresses. "And I'm done."

"You infuriate me." Yet he wanted to hold her. He wanted to help her heal. "Why are you afraid?"

"What am I afraid of?" She twisted her hair back and secured it with a clip. "I'm immortal. I don't fear anyone."

"Stop." He left the bed and strode naked to her without a care that anyone could see his ass. For the first time in a long while, he felt free. "You're scared."

"And infuriating. So what?" She turned her back on him. "You didn't quit."

"Why should I? You won't tell me something I have the right to know. Why are you afraid of Runa, besides the obvious?" He folded his arms. "I won't let up until you tell me."

"You need to stop."

He stepped into her path. If he had nothing else, he had tenacity. "Why?"

"I don't want to talk about it."

"My ass is on the line here. If you don't want to leave because your sister is a homicidal maniac, then fine. I do want out."

"I knew you would. The door's over there."

He stared at her, gobsmacked. "You'd let me go? Like that?"

"I have no right to keep you."

Hades and Zeus be damned. "What are you not telling me?" His blood pressure spiked along with his fury. "I won't be a prisoner here." As soon as the words left his mouth, he regretted them. He also instantly understood. "She's got you trapped here."

"No," Annika managed, weakly.

"She knows you're tender and sweet -- all the things she's not, and she's trapped you here. You're her toy, Annika."

"We have an understanding."

"What? If you're not under her foot or visible, she won't kill you? That's not an understanding. That's punishment." He turned her around and forced her to look at him. "Anyone who loves you will not force you to do something like that. I shouldn't have forced you to explain. I was wrong and I'm sorry."

"Don't say you love me. You can't."

"I don't know if it's love or lust, but what I do know is that I want to protect you. I need to. I need to be sure you can have a life and be happy -- even if it's not with me." But he sure hoped it could be with him.

"You're acting foolish."

"So?"

"It'll get you killed."

"I beg to differ." He needed some time and space outside of the tree house to show her. He also needed the threat of her sister to go away. There was a strong, graceful, sweet woman beneath the fear. She came out every so often and he longed to see her again. He craved her kiss but also wanted to see her blossom. If she could be free, she'd be dynamite.

"Hunter."

He enfolded her in his embrace. "I don't have conversations or arguments in the nude. It's not my style, but I'm doing a lot of things out of my usual because of you and I like it. Let me show you what it's like to live with a little less fear."

She eyed him but said nothing.

"How about if we go down, we go down together? We'll crash in flames, but we'll have a great time in the process." He grinned. "Sounds like fun to me."

Finally, she cracked a smile. Small, but it was there.

"What do you say?" he asked. "Will you give me a chance?"

"Okay."

"Okay?"

She nodded. "Okay. Flames it is."

It wasn't the most romantic way to get out, but there was a possibility they'd be okay and he intended to take it. He'd show her a fantastic time or die trying. There was the chance he'd die, too, but he'd take the gamble.

Chapter Six

Annika shivered. She'd made some quick decisions in her life, but this one could be deadly. It also could be a lot of fun. Her sister didn't own her. Annika had allowed herself to be a prisoner in the forest for too long, and it was time to get out. Time to start reclaiming her life.

But what about his? She didn't want to risk another being because of her sister's wrath. Runa had killed many times before and never seemed to regret it. Annika regretted allowing the men to be lured to their death.

"I need to get dressed." Hunter let go of her. "I didn't bring clothes."

"I can help you." She strode to the closet. "We'll get you something better while we're out, but you can use this for now." She pulled a pair of jeans and a T-shirt from the drawer.

"Your dad's?" He accepted the garments. "Or is it best I don't know?"

"Suffice it to say they haven't been used in a long time and won't be missed." She balled her hands. The owner would never be coming back. "And my father wore robes. He was a Viking King."

"Whoa." He nodded. "So you're a princess, too?" He shrugged into the shirt. "They fit."

"Good." It was odd to give him a dead man's clothing, but whatever. She'd prefer not to think about the past -- not when she could let it go.

"You know, it doesn't bother me where these came from. We need to shed certain parts of ourselves, our pasts. That's okay. There are parts of me and my past I'd like to get rid of, so I can't pass judgment. I won't." He held out his hand. "But shoes would be good since mine were beat up in the fray. I'll manage."

"I can't help you with shoes. I don't have any." Her embarrassment ebbed a bit, but she wasn't much of a protector this way.

"Don't sweat it." He grinned. "I grew up on a farm and spent a lot of time barefoot."

"Not in these woods. It's dangerous." She squeezed his fingers. "But I can help you. You'll have to hold on pretty tight."

"Why?"

She shrugged. "I'm kind of a cheetah. I've got speed in bursts, but I can't go for a long time." She wrapped her arms around him.

All she had to do was run. Her magic would secure the tree house behind them as she left. She summoned her energy and courage. One foot in front of the other and her sister couldn't hurt her. She burst out of the tree house and focused on moving forward. Just get out of the woods.

She lived too deep in the thick trees. She kept her ears open in case she crossed paths with her sister. If at all possible, she wanted to go undetected. The second Runa knew she'd broken free, her sister's fury would overflow.

If Hunter spoke while she ran, she couldn't hear him. That or she'd tuned him out. She kept going forward, doing her best to dodge the trees in her path.

"*You dare defy me.*"

She couldn't see Runa, but she felt her. For goodness' sake. Her sister didn't own her. She needed to have her own life. Living in the tree house and woods without escape was too stifling.

She ignored Runa and moved as quickly as she could. When she reached the edge of the woods, she forced herself to keep going. Runa wouldn't leave the woods.

Not yet.

Her energy waned as she rushed to the center of Eerie. Gods. She let go of Hunter and dropped to her knees. "I shouldn't have done that." She'd worn herself out and she had no idea how she'd recharge.

"Are you okay?" Hunter scooped her into his arms. "I pushed you too hard. Someone help me!"

"Don't shout like that." She tried to fight him. "You'll draw attention."

"Of course, I will." He carried her to the hotel. "I need help."

A red-haired faerie rounded the desk. "Oh my. What's wrong?"

"She's overexerted herself." He carried Annika to a sofa. "She got us out of the woods, but it took a lot out of her. She's Huldra."

The faerie grabbed a blanket. "I've contacted the Princess."

Gods. They were talking about her as if she wasn't even there. "I'm fine."

"You are not." Hunter paled. "I never should've asked you to get out of the woods. We didn't need to leave. We should've stayed there for a date."

"Stop." She placed her hand on his. "I'll be okay." She tried to get up but couldn't manage it. Because of her sister?

A blinding light filled the air. "Excuse me."

The voice didn't sound like Runa, but it was still commanding. Annika struggled to turn enough to look at the speaker. She should've known -- the Princess.

"I've been called and need to offer assistance." Piper wiped her hands on her trousers. "I haven't been able to use that spell in a long time. I kind of like it! Lots of razzle-dazzle. Now, Miss Annika, what'd you do?"

She groaned. "I got cut."

"I see that. Was it worth it?" Piper asked. She might be a Princess, but she was still blunt.

"What do you mean?" Hunter asked. "'Was it worth it'? Who are you?"

"You should bend the knee, young man," the faerie said. "She's our Princess."

"So?" He grasped the back of the sofa. "I bow to no one."

Piper's brows rose, but she said nothing.

"Hunter." Annika grasped his fingers as she sat up. "You should be kind. She's trying to help." The word *help* kept coming up so much. It almost seemed silly.

"Then do something," Hunter said. "I don't get it."

"Few do." Piper snorted. "Look, I know she's not supposed to leave the woods."

"No, I'm not, but I had to." Annika shook her head. "I couldn't be a prisoner there any longer."

"Who says you should?" Piper knelt next to her. "You've been there a long time."

"I don't understand," Hunter interjected.

Piper snapped her fingers. Everyone around her except Annika froze. Piper sighed and wiped her hands on her jeans again. "So much noise."

"He means well," Annika replied. "And he's scared."

"I know he does, but he's annoying me. He won't let me talk," Piper said. "Now, about you."

"Is he okay?"

"He's fine. He can hear us but can't interrupt. Sometimes it's better to listen. I'm hoping he takes note." Piper folded her hands. "Now back to you."

"What about me? I should've stayed back in the woods. Runa will find out where I am and kill him." Her worry got the better of her. "I kept telling myself it'd be fine, it'd be an adventure, but it's not. He's scared and so am I."

"Runa won't harm you."

"She'll steal him." Yes, she trusted he could be her mate, but she didn't trust her sister. "She's done it before."

"She has, which is shitty. You didn't deserve what she did, but she doesn't care. Never has."

"No, she hasn't." She stared at Piper. "How are you so cavalier? You seem like no one bothers you. And... don't you have to deal with kids?" There was so much Annika didn't understand.

"The kids are handled. It was a short visit and they're fine. As for my attitude, I got tired of being scared. What's the point?"

"I guess you're right." Being scared was getting old. "But here's the thing. I'm tired of losing people. I thought I loved one of them and I thought I could be happy with the other, but it was a disaster."

"It's hard to have love when Runa gets involved."

"Yes." She liked Hunter too much to risk him. "My sister still wants him so she can destroy him. I won't stand for it."

"You shouldn't," Piper said. "But you also shouldn't be a prisoner."

She shrugged. "I did go too hard when I got out of there. But I wanted to have the chance to woo him."

"You did, and now you're resting." Piper tipped her head. "I can help you have some time." She paused. "Did you say woo?"

"Yes." She liked the term. "So?"

"Nothing. I just haven't heard that word used in a long time." Piper drummed her fingers on her arm. "I can give you a few hours without obstruction."

"What?" It wasn't possible.

"I can help you. I've got a cloaking spell that will mask your identity, allowing you and Hunter to go for a ride, spy on your sister, create a battle plan... or whatever you want. It's up to you."

Most of the ideas sounded good -- except the spying and battle plans, but now that she'd been given the idea, she liked it. "We could be out without a care?"

"For about six hours, yes. I can't make it last any longer. If I do, there's a window of time that your sister could find you early."

"Don't want that." There were so many ideas of what she and Hunter could do. They'd have fun.

"You two enjoy yourselves and woo. If you do other things or come up with other plans, then even better." Piper stood. "Once I enact the spell. It'll seem to everyone except me and a few others that you and Hunter are just another couple at the hotel."

"Will we know each other?" It wasn't any good if they didn't.

"You will." Piper straightened her clothes. "I need to get back to the castle. Diesel hates it when I leave for too long without him. He's afraid I'll get into trouble."

"You could." She supposed if anyone had the potential to get into trouble, it'd be Piper. "If he can't help you, or swap in, he's not happy."

"He's my big, scruffy protector." Piper grinned. "I'm a sucker for him."

"You can be." She wanted a love that deep and lasting. "I'd like to be one for Hunter."

"You do? You're sure?"

"Of course, I'm sure." She just wasn't sure how to make that love work. "You said he's…"

"I did." Piper glanced about. "Give me a moment."

She could do that. If nothing else, she could handle the request.

"Okay. When I snap my fingers, you and Hunter will be able to move about without being detected. You've got about six hours, so make the best of them. If anyone can see you, it's because there's a debt owed to you, and I don't mean money. Doesn't mean Runa will see you. She shouldn't. Are you ready?" Piper snapped her fingers, and the room hummed to life.

Annika gasped as she realized what was happening -- and not the world going back into motion. She'd admitted she wanted Hunter and he could hear her. She'd all but told Piper, and him by extension, that she loved him. She hadn't thought she was ready to say such things, but given the chance, she'd revealed her heart. Now she could have what she wanted with Hunter, if only for a few hours. At least the opportunity to try to have something was in her hands.

Hunter wobbled. "I'm free? Where is everyone? It's like we don't exist."

"You are free, and so am I. The people around us are busy. We're sort of cloaked, but they're busy with their own lives." She left the couch and stood. "Still want to go out?"

He stared at her a moment, like he had to think this through. After a couple seconds, he grinned. "You bet your shapely ass I do. I refuse to pass up the chance to go about town for some wooing." He winked and offered his arm. "Shall we?"

She wished he'd forgotten he'd heard her say that word. She wished she'd never said it. "Hunter, you're not shocked we have the time to do this?"

"All I know is that you and I have a few hours to be alone without the threat of your sister, so I'm taking it. I've never felt this way with anyone else, and I don't want to lose it. Not sure if I can."

She hesitated, then linked her arm with his. She had nothing to lose and the assistance of the Princess. She might as well take advantage of what she'd been given. "We shall."

"Good." He strode with her to the doorway. "Wait. How did you manage this? It's like no one knows us."

"They sort of don't." She lowered her voice. "We've got a spell on us that masks us from everyone except the Princess."

"I remember because there's a restriction."

"Right. We only get six hours." She didn't budge. "Did you change your mind?"

"Hades, no." He kissed the top of her hand. "I'm with you. That's all I need for as long as we've got."

"You're... I don't know what you are." But he made her skin tingle, her heart race and the future seem possible.

"Yours."

She wanted that to be the truth. "We might not last."

"We might." He curled his fingers under her chin, forcing her to look at him. "You keep trying to remind me of finite things. Doesn't mean we are."

"No." But she wanted him to be sure he wanted to do this. "You might change your mind."

"I might," he replied. "I learned a long time ago that you don't always get a second chance at love.

Some don't get a first chance. So when someone comes along to knock you off your feet, you don't think twice. You leap and enjoy the ride."

"I'm a ride?" She was reaching. The more he spoke, the more she believed him, despite her protests.

"No, but this adventure is." He pulled her in close. "You're trying too hard to push me away. I don't give up that easily."

"You did with Sally." She shouldn't be so mean.

"Keep pushing," he replied. "Sally never deserved my attention. I gave so much more than I should've and held on longer than anyone else would've. It was silly."

"You loved her." She really needed to stop reaching. It wasn't a good look for her.

"I loved the idea of her. I'd fallen for the notion that someone would love me -- and before you ask me if I doubt how I feel about you, my heart may be faulty at times, but not now."

She had no more arguments. Nothing else seemed possible to change his mind. Secretly, she loved and appreciated his determination to convince her he liked her. Now she had to figure out how to tell him she knew they'd be together. He might not be thrilled that she hadn't said anything yet.

"Are you convinced yet?" he asked.

"Yes." Very much so.

"Good. I've got a full set of clothes now, shoes, and the most beautiful woman beside me. We've got plenty of time to head out and I'm famished. Are you?"

"I could eat something." He had a sense of adventure she couldn't deny. The longer she held onto him, the more she looked forward to the next few hours. They could have so much fun.

Chapter Seven

She walked along the sidewalk with him and basked in the sun on her face. She'd forgotten how warm it could be without the canopy of the trees to hide in. Her cheeks burned. If she wasn't careful she'd be red all over, but the pain would be worth it.

"Question," Hunter said, jarring her from her thoughts. "Are we invisible?"

"Not exactly." She nudged him forward. "We appear to everyone else like we're someone else, but not ourselves."

"So we see us as us, but each person around us sees someone else?"

"They see whomever they want." She shrugged. "It's camouflage so Runa can't see us."

"I'm in." He walked with her to the front of the castle. "Do we have to return here when the time is up?"

"I'm not sure." She should've asked more questions. She'd been so excited about having time that she hadn't thought about the end. "Sorry."

"We'll figure it out as we go along. Where shall we go, my beauty?"

His question amused her. "Your beauty?"

"Yes." He laughed. "For the first time since I met Sally, I can laugh and relax. It feels good to let go."

"Wonderful." She leaned into him as they walked. "I like you relaxed."

"How do you feel?"

She hadn't expected the question. How *did* she feel? "Part of me is on edge because I'm sure my sister will find us."

"She always did before?"

"Yes." She tensed. "I'm waiting for her to figure

out the ruse. She's very smart and she's my twin, so I can't run too far away from her."

"She'll find you." He sighed. "I've never had a twin."

"It's not all that exciting. I'm convinced she feels more from me than I do from her. Maybe I block her out more." She wasn't sure.

"Or you just aren't interested?"

"It's possible." She hadn't thought about it much. "I'm convinced she simply wants to track me because it's easier to chase me and whoever I'm with, rather than hunting for someone on her own."

"If someone wanders into the woods, she'll jump at the chance."

"Yes." Without question. "She's not above an easy catch." She kept going forward. Birds chirped, a harpy flew overhead, and a car horn honked. She barely heard the roar of the car engines as the vehicles raced by.

"What does she do with the men she catches?" he asked.

She walked with him to the first shop. "We can go in here. They've got delicious stew."

"That sounds yummy." He opened the door for her. "Wait. How do we pay for it? And you owe me an answer to my first question."

She paused. "To be honest, I'm not sure how we'll pay, but I'll tell you the other when we get a table."

"Deal." He patted his pants. "I'm guessing the Princess thought of everything. I've got cash in my pocket."

"Well, then." She appreciated the consideration. She'd have to thank Piper later. "How about some stew?"

"I'd love it." He followed her into the shop.

The scent of the stew, roasting potatoes, onions, and spices filtered through the air. Her mouth watered and her stomach growled. "I didn't realize I was this hungry until now."

"I get it." He nodded to one of the free tables. "We seat ourselves?"

"Yes." She joined him in the small booth. The table was quaint and quiet, despite the conversation around them. "I haven't been here in so long."

"When was the last time you left?"

She folded her hands. "I'm ashamed to say." He'd never believe her.

"Tell me. I won't laugh. It's been what... five years?"

"More like fifty. I screw up my courage about every fifty years or so and break loose."

He stared at her, then nodded. "I forget you're immortal."

She shrugged again. "I came to Eerie to escape my sister and she followed me. She won't leave me alone."

"The twin thing?"

"Yes." She smiled. The more she tried to forget her sister, the more she had to worry about her. "She's ever-present."

"Not right now." He held her hand. "She's not important."

She laughed out loud. "If she heard that, she'd be red with fury."

"Let her." He flagged down a server. "We'd like to order."

"Yes." The elf grinned and pulled out her order pad from her pocket. "What'll you have?"

He nodded to Annika. "Sweetheart?"

"Stew, monster beer, and a slice of cotton candy pie," she said and laced her fingers together. "Thank you."

"I'll have the same," Hunter said. "Thank you." He turned his attention to Annika. He smiled and held his hands out to her.

"Got it," the elf replied. "Be right back. We haven't had cotton candy pie in fifty years. Cook will love making it. He's a sucker for cotton candy pie."

She paused. Cook loved making it -- fifty years ago? Couldn't be.

"So, what does your sister do to them? I didn't forget that I asked," Hunter said.

She'd tried to forget it. "She rips them limb from limb after kissing them until they're breathless. She tells them they're wonderful and holds them, then digs her claws into them. They think she's the most beautiful woman ever, until she shows her true form and they see the monster within." She tensed and a shiver ran the length of her spine. "Are you sure you want to see that?"

"No. Never." He held onto her hands. "I'm glad I met you. You've restored my faith in person-kind."

"Thank you." She fought her better judgment and glanced over her shoulder at the person in the kitchen. She knew only a few people who liked cotton candy pie, and even fewer who knew how to make it. The person at the grill kept their back to her. When he turned, she gasped. She knew that face.

Aleksandr fiddled with the spatula. His hair was white and his frame thinner than she remembered. When he turned, he stared right at her. Did he remember her? She couldn't tell.

She'd once thought she'd loved him. Thought he'd loved her sister. She'd believed him to be dead, too. How was this possible? How could he be standing there? Her thoughts raced back to the time she'd spent with him. When he'd held her, it was nothing like the tingle she felt with Hunter. She hadn't noticed the sparkle in his eye, either. She'd forced the romance with him. She wanted to make something out of nothing, so she'd have anything to hold onto.

"What's wrong?" Hunter asked. "You're a million miles away."

"I am." She hated wasting so much time on the past. "I know the cook."

"You do?" Hunter's eyes widened. "Someone important to you?"

"Sort of." She returned her gaze to Hunter's and studied him. He was handsome and rugged, but hard to forget. He was nothing like Aleksandr. "He was trouble for me and a thorn in Runa's side."

"Trouble?

"Remember Aleksandr?"

He shook his head. "You never mentioned him."

She wasn't sure if she'd said his name or not. Didn't really matter. "I thought I loved him, but he loved Runa, who tried to destroy him. I thought Runa succeeded, but if he's here, then she was thwarted. I didn't even know he could be here. He wasn't part of Eerie last I knew. Neither was Viv. This is the first I've seen them in a long, long time."

"Thwarted?" Hunter tipped his head. "If he won, then it's possible we could, too."

She hadn't thought of that, but he had a good point. Sort of genius, really. "I doubt he'd talk to me. It's been so long, and I didn't help him."

"Could you have, if you'd have wanted to?" He stared at her. "Let's be honest. If Runa wanted to get in your way, she'd do it."

"True." Runa had thwarted every other attempt she'd made to stop her.

"But maybe we can talk to him and sort out how he managed to get here," Hunter said. "Can't hurt to try, right?"

"No, it can't." She liked how he thought, even if she wasn't convinced Aleksandr would speak to her. He might talk to Hunter, though. At least to warn him.

The elf returned with two brew mugs. "Here are your beers, and I'll be right back with your stew. Cook asked me who ordered the pie. May I tell him?"

"Yes, please," Hunter said. "Thanks."

"I'm so happy you came in," the elf said. "We've had so many grumps today. It's nice to have a pair of diners who are kind." She shook her head and walked away.

"Wonder if Runa's anger is spreading?" Hunter asked. "Can she do that?"

"I'm not sure," Annika replied. She picked up her glass and sipped the bitter brew. "I haven't had this in forever."

"Fifty years?" a voice asked.

She looked up to see Aleksandr standing next to the table. Her breath lodged in her throat. "Oh!"

Hunter nudged his drink aside. "Hi. Are you the chef?"

"Chef?" Aleksandr snorted. He dragged a chair over to the end of the table. "I'm no chef. I sling food. What I'd like to ask you is, how'd you do it? You're out."

"You're not supposed to be able to see me," Annika said, opting not to deny the truth. "How?"

"Guess we're all full of questions," Hunter said.

"I'd say I asked first, but it doesn't matter." Aleksandr straddled the chair and sat facing them, resting his arms on the back. "So you're the new victim?"

Hunter frowned. "Victim. It sounds so terrible. How about I'm the one trying to get away from her?"

"Good luck," Aleksandr replied. "She'll stop at nothing to kill you."

"We know." Annika picked at her napkin. "You're here, so you didn't die."

"No thanks to you," Aleksandr snapped. "You never tried to assist me."

"I did try!" He'd never believe her. "The more I tried, the more she intervened."

He sighed and shook his head. "I know."

"Then why are you angry with me?" she asked. "Doesn't matter. How'd you get loose? Why aren't you fighting or in some battle? You were a warrior."

"I remember." Aleksandr bowed his head. "I hoped you weren't her. I hoped I'd get to see you again, but that you weren't here to drag me back."

"Why would I do that?" He'd shocked her. "That's not how I felt."

"She used to love you," Hunter said. "If she truly cared, then killing you would've been ridiculous."

"He's right," Annika murmured. Her head hurt from thinking about the situation. "You still haven't told me why you can see me."

"He might be right," Aleksandr said. "Or you wanted me for yourself and if you couldn't have me, you wanted me dead."

"That's honestly ridiculous. I thought you loved her." Annika's belly churned. "Nothing makes sense." She rubbed her forehead. She hated complications, and this was one gigantic complication.

"I'd like some answers," Hunter said. "How about it?"

Aleksandr shifted his gaze between her and Hunter. "I'll tell you, but you have to promise me something."

"What?" Hunter asked, not skipping a beat.

Annika knew she should argue, but nothing seemed fitting. "What promise do you need?" Was her voice clouded with that much disgust or heavy memories?

"Promise me you'll make it out together. Be good to each other and never let go. That's my mistake. I let go. I knew I shouldn't have, but I lost my faith," Aleksandr said.

"Then how are you here?" Hunter asked.

"I lost my faith in Runa, too."

She practically smacked herself in the head. That was it -- losing faith in Runa. The love had died and faith evaporated, so her power over him died. But if Hunter didn't believe in Runa, he might not believe in her, either. His heart wouldn't survive the hurt. Not again.

Annika watched him, and something Piper had said came to mind. She'd be seen by someone who owed her a debt. When she'd first spotted Aleksandr, she wouldn't have thought he owed her anything. Now she understood. He needed to redeem himself. By giving her the key to possibly defeating Runa, he had.

She hoped he'd be able to move on soon. The diner wasn't terrible, but it was no place for a warrior. Hunter might not be a fighter like Aleksandr, but he could be her champion and she welcomed his assistance.

She had to believe he wouldn't hurt her. She had no choice.

* * *

Hunter stared at Aleksandr. He didn't see what

Annika had seen in the man. Aleksandr reminded Hunter of an eternal playboy. He might have been a warrior -- and thanks for his service -- but that didn't make him any better or greater than anyone else.

Still, Hunter wouldn't let Aleksandr down. He refused to let go of Annika. She made him happy. More than that, he hated to see a bully win, and Runa was a bully. If it took holding on tightly, he'd do as Aleksandr asked and keep Annika close.

"So what did you do?" Hunter asked. "You lost your faith?"

"I did," Aleksandr said. "Anni, I'm sorry. I'm sure I see you now because I don't believe in the love we might have shared. I never should have, but I thought I knew better and was smarter than everyone else."

"It happens," Annika said. "It's fine."

No, it wasn't. Hunter reached across the table to her, but she didn't take his hand.

"No, it's unforgivable." Aleksandr shook his head again. "I was so angry with Runa. I felt cheated because she lied to me."

Hunter studied Aleksandr, sizing up the man. For a fighter, a warrior, he seemed brittle, and he acted like he had no stamina. "So you took it out on Annika?"

"Yeah." Aleksandr narrowed his eyes. "I used her to keep Runa at bay. It was a dick move, and I knew it. Knew it then and now. That's why instead of going to Valhalla or anywhere else, I'm sentenced to a sort of purgatory here at the damn diner. I don't want to be here, but I am."

Good. The jerk deserved to pay for his stupidity.

"You might have told me," Annika said. "I wouldn't have gotten my hopes up again."

"I have to live with that mistake." Aleksandr sighed. "Just... don't believe in her. Don't give her power. Each day she feels she's got control over you and everyone else, then it's another bit of power she gains."

Hunter nodded. That explanation made so much more sense. Runa needed to be believed to have energy. Men wandering into the woods believed in her because they were drawn to, then feared her. They noticed her beauty and bought into the allure. Her sister had given into the fear by way of retribution. All that belief in her powered Runa.

Time to end her reign of terror.

"Are you ever getting out?" Annika asked. "Or are you trapped here for the duration?"

"Unless something's changed, the duration," Aleksandr said. "I didn't know what I had until it was gone, and had no clue how good it was."

"Now you do," Hunter said. "Are you remorseful or repentant?"

"If I had it to do all over again, I'd probably follow the script, but with more kindness and honesty." Aleksandr stood and put the chair back. "You both wanted stew. Viv's got it about ready. Be good to each other."

Hunter stood. "You, too. Thanks for the help."

"However much it was." Aleksandr disappeared into the kitchen.

"What?" Annika asked. "You're thinking."

"I am." He sank back onto his chair. "I had a thought or two."

"You have?" She leaned into him. "About?"

"Us, them, him, the situation..."

"Oh?"

"I think I'd like to get you alone, so I can show

you how much I believe in you." He bobbed his eyebrows. "Then we make up a plan."

"Okay."

She didn't sound convinced, so he'd convince her. "Aleksandr said the way he defeated your sister was to stop believing in her and to not let her have power. Well, I don't believe in her and she can't hurt me. It's way too simple and easy, and for all I know it may not work, but I'm willing to try. She wants me to fear her. No. Wants me to run. Forget it. She wants me to give myself to her while she takes my essence or whatever, and while she hurts you. Fuck no. I don't play those kinds of games."

"No?"

"Nope, and you shouldn't either. She might be your sister and might have power over someone else, but not me and not you."

She didn't speak right away. "You make it seem so simple."

"Maybe it is. Maybe that's what she's banking on -- that we won't see the simplicity of ignoring her."

"It is kind of genius." She grinned as Viv brought the stew. "And dinner is here. Time to feast?"

"I'd rather feast on you."

"If your plan works, then we'll have plenty of time later." Annika nodded to the food. "Eat. We'll need our strength."

"We will."

Chapter Eight

Hunter finished his stew. Belly full, spirit renewed, he swore he could take on the world. Viv brought over two plates. Whipped cream, piled high on the plates, obscured the delicacy underneath. He smoothed his napkin on his lap. He'd never seen cotton candy pie before.

"What's it taste like?" he asked. "Sorry. First timer."

"Sweet, light, and fluffy, when not covered under this much whipped cream." Annika grinned and picked up her fork. "I highly recommend it."

"Then how could I resist?" The pie didn't smell like cotton candy, though he wasn't entirely sure what cotton candy should smell like. He sliced his fork into the concoction and the pie cut easily.

Annika took a bite first. She groaned. "It's still like a slice of heavenly perfection. Not something to eat every day, but a definite treat."

He dug into the pie and enjoyed the first bite, but the sweetness reminded him of something else -- of her. A surprise, a brilliant twist, and unforgettable.

She finished her slice before him and pushed the plate away. "I haven't eaten like this in so long."

"Yeah?" He finished his piece, then wiped his mouth. "Glad you did?"

"Absolutely." She piled the dinnerware at the end of the table in a tidy stack. "You said you have cash?"

"I do -- if she brings the bill." He'd gladly pay.

"You leave some money on the table," she said.

"They don't lose money that way?" he asked. "They're not cheated or anything? Seems sketchy."

"Anywhere else, yes, but here there's a spell or

something that ensures you pay the right amount and don't dash. Trust me, even if I don't understand it."

"I do." He left a few bills on the table. He'd only been back to Eerie a handful of times, but the currency seemed odd. "Is this new?"

"Updated. New royalty, so we have new currency. It needed to be upgraded. It'd been fifty years since we got better cash. Most of the other stuff was clunky coins."

Now he remembered. He left the table and offered his arm. "I haven't been able to go on a stroll with a beautiful woman in forever. I said we should go fuck, but let's take it slower with a walk and enjoy ourselves."

"Yeah?" She threaded her arm around his. "Where do you want to go?"

"Up and down the main street." He had no particular destination in mind. He simply wanted to be with her.

"I'd love it." She left the restaurant with him and stepped onto the sidewalk. "It's a beautiful day."

"It is." He started north through the main square. "Question."

"Yes?" She leaned into him. "What do you want to know?"

"How old are you? I'm thirty-five. I don't know what it translates into in magic years," he said. "I guess I should find out."

"The Hall of Records would know," she replied. "They know the story of everyone in Eerie."

Good. He had a starting point, finally. "Thanks. We should go there sometime."

"It's open today."

He wasn't sure he wanted to waste precious time in a foolhardy search. "Maybe later."

"Suit yourself," she said. "I'm five hundred years old."

He stopped in his tracks. "Really?"

"Yes. Does that upset you?"

"No." He liked older women. "It's intriguing."

"Well, it's the truth."

"Then how old is Aleksandr?"

"I'm five hundred and seventy-three years old and he's a little over four hundred years old. I like to round my age down because it sounds better."

"Either way you go is good for me." Anything with her was good. "What about your favorite meal?"

"Wow. That's tough. I used to love anything seafood because it reminded me of home, but I've developed a love of noodles. Pretty much anything with noodles," she said. "You?"

"Tacos. I'm a sucker for tacos." He held her close. "Do you miss home?" He thought he did, but the more time he spent with her in Eerie, the more he didn't miss his old life. He'd found a place to belong.

"I used to," she said and rested her head against his shoulder. "But not now."

"Things have changed?"

"In the last hundred years or so they did." She shrugged. "The more I left that home behind and in the past, the more I don't want to go back. Being there reminded me of my sister, the endless battles between us, and my not feeling like I was part of the family. That's probably sad, but it's true."

"It's not sad at all. It's life. You think you've found this absolutely fantastic thing or place. Then life steps in and you realize what you thought you wanted and deserved isn't what it could be."

She stopped and stared at him. "Yeah."

"What?" The look in her eyes fascinated him. He

wasn't quite at the point of reading her mind. He shouldn't -- it'd only been three days, give or take a few hours. They needed a lifetime to get used to each other. Some people never did. He wanted to know her inside out.

"You understand. You seem to get me in ways that others haven't. Like you've walked a bit in my shoes." She grinned. "Part of me wishes you'd have come into my life earlier, but I'm glad you showed up when you did."

"I'm glad I did, too." He'd always believed things happened for a reason. He'd come to Eerie again for more than just to be lured by Runa. "Come here."

He tugged her into his arms and kissed her. He'd tasted her a few times, and needed more.

She draped her arms around his neck. She opened to him and whimpered as he sucked on her tongue. He splayed his hands on her lower back. The more he touched her, the more he needed to hold onto her even tighter and never let go.

She ground against him, brushing her torso over his. The move sent tingles through his body. His cock throbbed and pushed against his zipper. Hades, he needed to get her alone. Somewhere he could delight in her.

She slid her hands down his chest and brushed his nipples as she grasped the front of his shirt in both hands. She broke the kiss. "Hunter."

"Hush." He didn't want to use their names and raise suspicions. If word got out they were around, then Runa would find them. He didn't trust anyone not to tell her where they were. For all he knew, Aleksandr already had. "Don't need to blow our cover."

"I forgot." She blushed. "Got caught up."

"So did I." He guided her around the corner to the closest building. They could hide in the Hall of Records. It wasn't a great place to have carnal knowledge of each other, but it'd be quiet and private. Maybe they could steal a few moments together among the stacks of scrolls.

"We're going to get busted." She laughed softly. "I don't mind. I'll take that kind of trouble."

He pushed the huge metal doors open. When he stepped into the building, he listened for anyone inside.

"Are we alone?" she whispered. "I know people work here. Or at least they used to."

"Maybe they're on a break?" He ensured the door closed and tugged her through the Hall to one of the darker corners.

"Wait." She kept going deeper into the building. "I know where we can be alone but also see if anyone's coming."

"I'm hoping you're coming soon," he murmured. He captured her in his arms and pinned her to the wall. "I can't wait."

She laughed and kissed him. The frantic pace thrilled him. She clawed at his shirt before moving to his jeans. She opened the zipper, parting the denim.

He shivered. He glanced around to ensure there was no one close. He popped the button on her jeans and unzipped her pants before pushing the garments down her legs. She helped him, then leaned into the kiss.

"Gods," she whispered. "You know how to get what you want."

"I do." Mostly. He worked the pants down her legs until she kicked her shoes off. She stepped out of the leg of her jeans.

He patted her hip, finding the side seam of her panties. He tugged, trying to tear the lingerie from her body. As he tugged, the flimsy fabric gave way.

Another gasp ripped from her throat.

"Yes." He eased his hand between her legs. Her liquid heat pleased him. He liked having her on the edge.

She shivered. "For a guy who was pretty beat up only a few hours ago, you're kind of dangerous."

"Yeah?" He stroked himself, smearing her cream on his dick. Holy shit. He'd never last. Not like this. He needed to be inside her.

"Please?" The desire and pleading in her eyes spoke to his soul. She panted. "Need you."

"Got me." He pinned her between his body and the wall. As she held onto his shoulders, he hoisted her up enough to fill her in one thrust.

This wasn't the way he'd imagined making love to her the first time, but to be honest, he hadn't been sure he'd get the chance to sleep with her.

Now that he had her in his arms, he couldn't believe he had her. He sank deeper into her. The tight heat blew his mind. She held him within her body like he was made for her. Maybe she was made for him, too. He'd like to think so.

"Yes," she murmured. "Feels good."

"Yes, you do." He wanted to lose himself in her. Being one with her on this deep a level made his heart beat faster.

She rocked against him, creating a perfect rhythm. The blue of her eyes deepened. Her cheeks reddened and she parted her lips. Her hair slipped free from the clip and gave her a mussed look. She reminded him of a goddess or a warrior. Didn't matter. She made him happy.

He tried to listen for anyone coming near, but she required all his attention. The scent of her cologne wrapped around him. He loved the feel of her in his arms.

She tipped her head back. She dug her nails into his shoulders and cried out. "Can't hold back." She tensed. "Please?"

"Yes." It wasn't a question. He needed to come, too. His thrusts turned frantic. He tried to remember and memorize every detail of this moment. If he never had another chance to be with her, then this was enough. She buoyed him.

She made him better.

He pistoned into her. "Mine." As he pushed deep into her, he swore he heard footsteps. It wasn't like he could stop. He was too far gone at this point to do much more than finish.

Whoever walked up to them could just wait.

He buried his face against her neck to cover the cry as he came. He rammed his dick into her, filling her with his seed. She required every bit of his energy and focus.

"I --" She pressed her lips together and gritted her teeth. The moan vibrated in her chest. She tightened her grasp, then relaxed. She sagged against him. "Wow."

Yeah, he had to agree. She was pretty wow, too. He held her, allowing his senses to settle and his breathing to return to normal. Damn.

"Excuse me."

He knew he'd heard someone. He didn't bother to look up. "Yes?"

"This isn't the sort of place for that kind of behavior," the female voice said. "Will you please use some decorum?"

"Yes," Annika replied. She patted Hunter's shoulder.

He didn't need words to know what to do. He pulled out and placed her on her feet. "Sorry." Not really.

"It's fine," the woman said. "You're not the first couple to decide it's sexy to... do things here."

He helped Annika right her shirt and find her shoe, then glanced over his shoulder as he tugged his pants back up. "Sorry." He didn't know the woman. She appeared to be a faerie with bright red hair. "We didn't mean any harm."

"No one ever does." She smiled. "I'll give you a moment. I get the feeling you need to speak to someone." She walked away, leaving them in silence.

He stared at the space where the faerie had stood. "That was odd."

"Yeah." Annika pulled up her jeans. "Wonder how long she stood there and watched."

"Hopefully not long." His irritation with himself grew. His senses were supposed to be sharp, but he hadn't really noticed her nearing. What if she'd been Runa? He'd have been fucked. "We're sorry," he called.

The faerie returned and crooked her brow. She folded her arms. "Oh, please. Do you think you're the first to do that here?" she asked. "You're not. Not even the first ones this week."

He stared at her. "Now, I'm even more sorry. Hades, I had no idea."

"You saw a big old building that seemed unoccupied and available?"

"Sort of," Annika said. "The last time I was here, only the Historian was here."

"Yeah, he's not the only one now." The faerie

sighed. "So what's your deal? You've got a fetish for risqué sex?"

"No," he said. "We were trying to get some privacy."

"For sex?"

"No," Annika said. "I'm being chased and we wanted a respite. The other sort of happened and wasn't entirely planned."

"It was in mind, but we did need a place to breathe for a second." It was the half-truth, but whatever. "Since we're here, I've got a question." It could blow their cover, but the chance was right before him.

"Oh? Where else to have sex?" the faerie asked.

Annika groaned. "We got the hint. We won't do that here again, so you can stop the browbeating."

"Good." The faerie nodded. "As long as you know."

"Tasia, stop. You don't have room to talk," a man said as he rounded the corner. "You're riding their asses, but we were the other couple to have sex here this week. Hi, I'm Thaddeus and this is my wife, Tasia. How can we help you?"

He hadn't expected the man to be kind. It could be a ruse, but he had a sixth sense about Thaddeus. "We're here to find out who I am."

"You don't know?" Tasia asked. "You seem like the kind of guy who has a firm grasp on reality.

What an odd thing to say, but whatever. "I do, but it's not all that crystal clear."

"And we're in a bit of a time crunch," Annika said. "We can't explain much, either."

"Nope." Tasia held up her hands. "I won't do it. Unless I get names and a purpose, I won't help you. I don't like liars or cheats."

"You used to be one," Thaddeus said. He turned his attention to Hunter. "But she's right. We can't help unless you give us your name."

"How about this?" Annika asked. "We'll tell you what we want to know -- sort of -- and if we survive the mission we're on, then we'll come back and tell you everything."

"That makes no sense," Tasia replied. "What's the mission? You're not law enforcement or soldiers."

"No." Hunter groaned. They should tell them, but it could bring Runa in and the last thing he wanted to do was wreck the Hall.

"Wait." Thaddeus frowned. "You look familiar."

"Nope. Not us." It was probably time for them to leave. "We're late and we've only got six hours."

"Not even," Annika said.

"Six hours to what?" Tasia narrowed her eyes. "You can't rob us. Nothing in here is valuable."

"Who said anything about robbing?" Hunter asked. "I'm just trying to figure out who I am because I don't know. I was adopted and my biological mother was adopted, so I know nothing about my past. I can't tell you who I am or who she is because we've got a homicidal immortal on our tail. Now, do you see why I can't give you any details?" He'd given away too much as it was.

Tasia nodded. "I shouldn't, but I follow you."

"Me, too," Thaddeus said. "I don't know who it is you're running from, but you're safe here. How long are you hiding?"

"We have less than six hours to shore up our defenses before we're seen," Annika said. She adjusted her shirt. "I'm sorry we're wasting your time."

"Not at all." Thaddeus rubbed his chin. "Can we help? A bully is a bully, no matter how you slice it."

"Cute," Hunter muttered. He liked the turn of phrase, even if it was a little close to the mark.

"How do you know they're not the ones who should be chased?" Tasia asked. "I mean, they might not be innocent."

"No," Thaddeus said. "But I trust them. I've met enough lowlifes in my time that I can pick them out. I've run with too many, too. They're not that kind. How can we help you?"

Annika nudged Hunter. "If we know what or who you are, then we can help you use your particular skills to prevent our demise."

He debated what she'd said. The knowledge would assist them, but it risked their exposure, too. "We know how to defeat her."

"Her? Who her?" Tasia asked. "Which her?"

"Runa," Hunter replied, not realizing he'd answered until after he'd spoken. His heart lodged in his throat. He'd said her name. That could be enough to summon her. "Forget I said that."

"The hell I won't," Tasia said. "Runa? As in the woman who terrorizes the woods?"

"As in the one who abducts and kills men for sport?" Thaddeus asked. "Or pleasure?"

"She's got a twin," Tasia said. "I heard the twin is three times as dangerous, which is why she hasn't been spotted in years. I heard she lives off the blood of the men she's killed and bathes in it."

Annika gagged. "I do not."

Thaddeus's eyes widened. "You, what?"

Annika straightened her shoulders. "If you're going to spread a rumor about me, then get your facts straight."

Tasia jumped in front of Thaddeus. "He's mine."

Hunter rolled his eyes. "Hades, you're paranoid.

No one wants him dead."

"I don't want his essence, his blood, or his bones," Annika said. "I don't chase or kill, either. I help the victims of my sister to get out before they do die. I've been shunned and gaslit into thinking I had to hide from and bow to her. I don't. No one else is going to die because my twin is out for blood and vengeance... or whatever reason is given."

He stared at Annika a moment. What she'd said took guts and determination. It also outed her. But she seemed to stand taller, like the weight of the situation was off her shoulders.

"You're Annika?" Thaddeus asked. "*The* Annika?"

"What do you mean *the*?" Hunter asked. "Is she legendary? To me, she is, but what's the deal?"

"Runa's been charging through town, swearing on all that's livin' that she will find Annika, will destroy her, and will fillet Hunter," Thaddeus said. "Which must make you Hunter."

Tasia snorted. "Either you're both brave or foolish."

Hunter sighed. Runa now knew where they were and was pissed. Lovely. Fucking lovely. "Maybe I'm a bit of both."

Chapter Nine

Annika shook her head. This ridiculousness had to end. "Running through town? Like a spoiled child? Unreal."

"A bit, yeah," Thaddeus said. "It's nice to meet you, though."

"Sure." She held up her hand. She had to think. "First, I'm sorry we were dodgy with you. It's a bit of a habit for survival."

"I know," Tasia said. "It's okay."

"Really?" She stared at Tasia. "A moment ago, I was the devil."

Tasia squirmed a little. "I may have been in similar shoes to your sister -- with less killing -- and I understand your need to make up for it."

"I see." She turned her attention to Thaddeus. "It's nice to meet you, too -- both of you -- but I wish it were under better circumstances."

"Agreed," Hunter added. "It's not our idea of fun to be hiding out here from her."

Annika nodded and made up her mind. She and Hunter had experienced sex, enjoyed each other's company, and were in the Hall. Time to be honest. "I hope we figure out who you are, Hunter. But I need to tell you something."

"Will it kill me?" he asked.

"Let's give them a moment." Thaddeus nudged Tasia away.

She waited for them to leave before speaking. "Hunter, when you were out cold and healing, I summoned the Princess."

"Oh? Okay." He leaned on the wall and crossed his ankles. "So she met me while I was comatose?"

"Sort of." She wasn't sure how to say this. "She

told me something I should've told you right away."

"And that is? What about me?" He tipped his head. "What, if you know whatever it was, didn't you tell me before now?"

"I couldn't."

"Because of magic?"

"Fear."

"Of me?"

"Yes." Her stomach clenched. Why was this so hard? Because she could be rejected.

"What? Why?" He shook his head. "I don't understand."

"I'm your mate," she blurted. Oh Gods, she'd said it with no chance of taking it back or erasing it. The question was, how would he take it?

Hunter's eyes widened. He opened his mouth, but no sound came out. He paled as he backed away from her.

She leaned on the wall for stability. Her knees buckled and her skin itched. She wanted to run away. Just hide and never be seen again. The longer he remained quiet, the more her heart sank. She'd made a huge mistake in holding back as long as she had.

She wanted to say something, but what was there to say? She sank to the floor. "I'm sorry."

He scrubbed both hands over his face. He still didn't speak. Instead, he dropped to his knees beside her. He stared at her.

Her nerves got the better of her. "I'm sorry. I should've told you when I found out, but I didn't. Piper told me to let you decide if you liked me, too, before I told you. She told me to when I hadn't even asked. I didn't push, but she told me and I told her I'd fallen for you, but you weren't awake, and I really should've been honest, but I didn't know how to tell you…" She was rambling.

"Stop." Hunter sighed. "Just stop."

"Yes, sir." She bowed her head. She tended to over-explain and rationalize when under stress.

"Slow down and explain what happened. Breathe. I'm listening. I'm shocked and confused, but I'm listening," he said.

She gulped in a deep breath to center herself, but it did little to work. Her heart hammered and she bowed her head again. She balled her hands. "When you were out cold, I needed to heal you. Piper could do that because she has all the magic in the world. She knows how to use that magic, so I asked her to help me."

"Breathe," he said again. "Look at me."

She forced her gaze to his. She needed so much more confidence than she had now. "I was fascinated by you and asked Piper to heal you."

"Why?"

"So I could talk to you and get to know this man who'd wandered into my woods. This man who hadn't shied away from me. You didn't seem to be afraid of me."

He nodded. "You helped me."

"I did."

"It's in your nature to help, so I appreciate it. But what did she say?" he asked.

Her hands shook. "She told me you were my mate."

"So you lied to me?"

"No." She forced herself to stay calm. "I never lied to you."

"You withheld."

"Yes." She struggled to keep her poise. "You don't understand."

"Then enlighten me." He folded his arms. "I don't know who I am, or what I am. Don't know what I'm doing here, but you knew something and didn't tell me. That pisses me off."

"I know."

"So you admit that you didn't tell me the truth?"

"I never lied to you about that. I said I didn't tell you because I wasn't permitted to."

"What?" Fury shimmered in his eyes.

"You're angry, and I understand why, but will you please listen to me?" She needed to make him understand. "I can explain."

"Sure." He stood. "I'm all ears."

She sucked in a ragged breath to steady herself. Something had to work. She needed to speak without a wobble, but also from her heart. "I didn't tell you about you and I being mates because I couldn't." She held up her hand. "Piper told me to let you come to the conclusion on your own. If I'd told you too early, then you might not return my affections, and I couldn't sway you."

"Why?"

"You have to decide on your own. While we are meant to be mates, you're the wild card. You can decide you don't want us to be together, and could walk."

"What?" He frowned. "That makes no sense."

"How does it not?" she asked. "You can say you're not interested. You could reject me."

"Why? Mates don't reject each other." He asked so many questions.

She gritted her teeth. "You're part human."

His eyes widened again and his lips parted a second time, and again, no sound came out.

"Yeah, I wasn't sure, but it dawned on me just

now. Part of you is human and part is shifter. The human side of you will fall in love, but it's left to chance. The shifter side knows it's a mating thing."

His gaze narrowed. "And you saw it?"

"I didn't say anything about that because I'm not permitted to tell you. I know others who've dealt with it, though."

"But have you been through it?"

What an irritating man! "I have not. I've been misled before, but not on this."

"And Aleksandr?"

"Wasn't true. Remember, Aleksandr even said that." Why was he being so dense? Was he scared? Could be.

"You're sure?"

She growled. "Goodness' sakes, yes. I know my heart and I'm not unsure this time. I know we had the chance to go the distance, but you have to fall for me. If you don't, then I'm still beholden to you, but you owe me nothing. You could walk, but I'll watch and protect you forever." Something within her snapped. Tears sprang from her eyes, and she shivered. She wasn't much for offering her heart. She preferred to keep herself protected. Not with him, though. He made her want to open herself up to him.

He didn't speak right away. "I don't know what to say."

"You don't have to say anything." There wasn't much to say. Mostly, he needed to understand and digest.

He sagged against the wall. "I didn't know the truth, but it explains so much now."

"Yeah?" She turned her back on him. "Then digest it."

"I am."

She stood, then wandered away from him toward the Scrolls. He needed space to think. She made her way past Tasia.

"Are you okay?" Tasia asked as she caught up to her. "Hey. Wait up."

She didn't want to. The numbness overwhelmed her. She'd opened herself up and told him everything, but now she could lose it all. Everything she hoped to have and had earned was slipping through her fingers.

Life could be so cruel.

And she wasn't even worried about Runa any longer.

"You'll be okay." Tasia stopped her. "He's stunned, but it's not the end of the world. I promise."

"Yeah." Somewhere in her brain, that made sense, but she needed some time. "I created a mess."

"You did not." Tasia stood in her way. "I couldn't help but hear you -- you were both kind of loud and this place has great acoustics. Everyone hears everything. That said, I heard the argument. You did what was asked and what was needed which was best for the situation. It wasn't for you, but good for both of you and that's a big thing. Many people would've given up or given in a lot faster than you did."

"He hates me." He had to, now.

"Who said?" Tasia shook her head. "I watched him with you. For a guy who is mixed up, he does care about you. He's just all sorts of confused, so give him a minute."

"I am."

"Give yourself a minute, too. You're jumping right to the conclusion he dislikes you and you can't prove it. You're guessing and flailing. Stop doing that because he looks at you with love and adoration. He's irked at the moment, but it's not hate. He's scared. You just laid a pretty big info drop on him. He's stunned."

"I know." She sighed. Everything made sense, but it was hard to make it plain in her mind. "I just screwed up his entire world and should've told him the truth from the beginning."

"And what would that have done? Rushed the process, sure, but would that have worked? What if he hadn't fallen for you? What if the news freaked him out? What if he ran away?"

"I don't know." She pondered all of it and had no idea.

"You do, too."

"Do I?"

"Yeah, you do. You know he's nuts for you, and you're nutty for him. Have some faith in him, but yourself as well." Tasia met her gaze. "Please. I know you don't believe me right now, but try."

"I do." The odds were against them, but she had no other choice. "Do you know who or what he is? Where he comes from?"

"I do, but he has to ask me. I can't tell you," Tasia said. "I wish I could."

"I figured as much." So much for trying.

"Oh, fuck!" Thaddeus sprinted into the hallway. "We have to stop her."

"Who?" Tasia asked. "I can lock this joint down."

"Not here." He pointed to Annika. "You have to stop Runa. She's got Hunter."

Her blood chilled and vengeance surged through her veins. She'd lost too much to her sister, and this was far beyond what Runa deserved. Runa couldn't have Hunter, too -- not that Runa couldn't give this her best shot. And lose.

Annika made up her mind. There was no greater spirit than that of a woman on a mission. Hunter was her mission.

* * *

Hunter stormed through the Hall. The various scrolls and books of information annoyed him, but he wasn't even sure why. The books hadn't hurt him, and the scrolls hadn't lied.

Neither had Annika. Not really.

The rational part of his brain understood. She'd done what she needed to for his sake. She'd been good to him and let him decide for himself how he felt about her. He should be grateful.

But her not telling him annoyed him because it reminded him of the way Sally had been. Except Sally was cruel. Annika hadn't tried to be that way.

"Come out here. We'll talk."

"Annika? He twirled around to look for her but stood at the entrance to the Hall. He wasn't even sure how he'd gotten there. Had she followed him? He'd been walking without looking where he was going. "Anni?"

"Come here."

That sounded like her, but not exactly. "Anni?" He left the Hall and stepped into the sunshine. "Where are you?" She surely hadn't followed him outside. He'd have heard her footsteps.

"Annika?" When he turned, he practically collided with Runa. Fuck.

"Nope. Not your precious Anni." Runa grasped his shoulders. "You thought you could get away from me? Thought you could hide? Ridiculous."

"I don't believe in you." He tried to sound as forceful as he believed. He didn't have feelings for her either way, not any longer.

"Yet, I smell fear on you." She crinkled her nose. "I do, and I detect uncertainty. Not so sure about my sister, eh? I wouldn't be. She's useless."

"No." He struggled in her grasp. "You underestimate her."

"Do I, though?" Runa dug her fingers in deeper. "You see a beautiful woman, but have you ever seen her true self?"

"Yes."

"Oh? It didn't stop you cold?" Her eyes blazed. "Didn't make you want to scream?"

"She's unique, and I like that."

"Unique?" she spat. "I'm her twin. She's a copy of me."

"Not hardly." He refused to back down. "She's got ten times the heart you have -- if you even have one."

"I don't."

"Didn't think so."

She scratched her nails into his skin, tearing his shirt. "And that woman you think is so beautiful isn't even coming out to help you. You thought you had friends. Nah. You only have me."

"I'd rather have Annika or no one."

"You're making me sick." Runa yanked him to her chest. "Want to see what I can do?"

"Nope. You can't do shit."

She snarled at him. "Watch me." She cackled. Before he could think, she surged into the woods, leaving Eerie proper behind them. The trees blurred around him and the speed at which she moved made his stomach roil.

He had to fight back. He hadn't come this far just to be beaten by a paranormal being bent on death. He'd been at the precipice of finding out who he was, and it had been taken from him.

He might have even found his mate. Yet, she'd

tried to take that from him, too. Unreal.

He debated wriggling from her grasp, but she was too strong. Besides, she might drop him. At this rate, his own speed wasn't enough to counteract her. A thought occurred to him. She shouldn't have been able to see him -- yet she'd found him.

So much for the spell.

Did he believe in Runa? No. He refused to believe in a bloodthirsty monster.

But he wondered how she'd found them. As he considered the situation, her grasp on him slipped. Odd, really. She should've had stronger magic than that of a Princess. Unless this was about a debt.

He tumbled out of her grasp and onto the forest floor. The wind rushed out of him as he landed with a *thud*. Runa zoomed away, either not realizing he'd fallen or using this as a way to mess with him.

He didn't care. Either way, he was free.

"How?" Runa thundered. She landed just in front of him and her hair whipped around her face. Her eyes blazed again. "You can't run from me."

She was right. He couldn't -- and that was the key. He stood tall and stared at her. "I'm not."

Chapter Ten

He refused to back down from Runa. He'd come too far to let anyone best him. Besides, he needed to get back to Annika and make amends.

"You're right, you're not running from me." Runa stared at him and curled her lip in a sneer. "And you won't survive the hour."

"No?" He'd bet he would.

"You dare challenge me?" she growled.

"Yep." The longer he kept her talking and distracted, the more time he bought for Annika to find him. He refused to force Annika to save him. He'd save himself, but he'd love her backup help.

"You're a fool. You think people care, and they don't." She lunged at him, colliding with him and drawing a deep groan from him as she slammed him into a tree.

He whimpered. He'd feel the impact later. Right now, he couldn't succumb. "You don't scare me."

"You lie." She dragged him through the underbrush, scraping him against the bark of fallen trees and the pricks of the thorny bushes and slapping him with the saplings.

"Get angry with me all you want." His left eye was swelled shut, and he was pretty certain she'd broken his arm. "But I don't believe in you. You're nothing to me."

She screamed and the sound split the air. The trees quaked. Birds flew off and animals in the general area ran away. "The last man who claimed I had no power is dead." She picked him up by his ankles and slammed him into a tree.

He groaned. He still didn't believe in her, but some force had shattered his right shin bone. A shudder of pain ripped through him, but he refused to give up. "You have no power."

"You lie."

"And I'll die?" He snorted, trying to hide his agony. Too much more of this and he'd have bigger issues. The mortal side of him could win out and he just might die. "Like Aleks?" It was a foolish challenge, but he had to try.

Her eyes burned red, and she snarled. "Never mention that name to me."

"Why? Because he didn't believe?"

"No."

"Or because you used him to find your sister?" He staggered, then dropped to his knees. "You enchanted him? Raised him from the dead to draw out Annika? Come on. What a wonderful party trick you can do."

"Shut up." She blasted him with a shaft of light, pitching him backward.

He swore he passed out for a moment. When he came around, Runa straddled him. Instead of the flaxen-haired beauty, her true form came out. Her hair turned black and her skin ashen, almost green. Her eyes blazed red, ringed with black. Her teeth and nails blackened and her tail, now a thick oxtail, swished. The veins in her temple bulged. As she breathed, spittle rained down on him.

"Gonna kill me now?" he asked, taunting her.

She held a gigantic broken tree branch almost as thick as his arm, sharp at one end from being torn from a tree. "I like to play with my kills a bit before I finish them off. You will beg for death, and it won't come soon enough."

"Suit yourself. I can wait." He shrugged as best he could.

Out of the corner of his non-swollen eye, he spotted Annika, Piper, and what appeared to be a herd of elves marching through the trees.

Elves? What'd they have to do with this? How'd Runa manage to piss them off, too?

He had no idea, but welcomed the help if they could give him an assist.

Annika thrust out her arms. "You want me to be afraid? Want to hurt me? Come and get me."

Runa jerked her head up and snarled. "Must we do this again? You know I always win."

"Not this time." Annika surged toward Runa, knocking her off Hunter.

"Come with us," Viv said. She and half a dozen elves carried him away from the fight. "You'll never last here."

He couldn't believe Viv had come to him. Had she appeared from the diner? Or was she a figment of his imagination? "I can't leave her." He refused. "Stop."

"We won't. You'll be torn limb from limb." Viv shook her head. "I'm tired of seeing this damage. We can't go into the woods, and Anni deserves to be happy. You being alive will help with that."

"She'll be killed," he whimpered, pain flooding his body. "Please."

"She can handle herself. Besides, she's got the Princess to help her now." Viv nodded. "Runa fucked her last meal. Just you watch. She's in deep shit."

"I'd rather be helping Anni."

"You are, by staying alive and out of sight. Runa forgot you existed the second Annika showed up. The battle is now between them," Viv said. "But you gave Annika something to fight for. Just watch."

He wasn't sure he could, even with a swollen

eye. He wasn't sure he could stomach it. "I can't leave her."

"You can and are. You've got no choice." Viv gestured to the other elves. "Get him out of sight. Anni needs to focus."

He wanted to argue and fight more, but the ability left him. "Is Runa killing me?"

"No, but you've lost a lot of blood and it'll be a tough job for Piper to get you fixed. Sleep. You don't have much choice, so stay still. All will be well."

He opened his mouth, but no sound came out. He closed his good eye and swore a weight settled on his chest. He had to trust that Annika had this fight in hand. If he could give her his heart, love, and soul to help her fight, then he would. He'd been a fool to walk away from her.

"Now you're starting to believe," Runa said. "I feel the power coming back. Yes, yes."

He didn't believe in her, but he did in Annika. If anyone could save him, it was her.

He bowed his head; sadness filled him. He'd let Annika down as the fight left him. He slumped to the ground.

Help me, Annika. I love you.

* * *

Annika gestured to Piper. She refused to take her attention from Runa, but she also had to get Piper's attention. She didn't believe in her sister, but seeing Hunter so abused annoyed her. How could Runa be so destructive?

Eventually, Piper would confront Runa, too. "I don't like how this is unfolding, but I also don't care. She's not playing fair." Being a bully and devious being, Runa could do as she pleased.

She'd talked to Piper about what to do, but that

didn't make this any easier. She didn't want to kill her sister, but it'd be nice to have her locked up a while. To have her somewhere she couldn't hurt anyone. She'd asked Piper to make her sleep, like a hibernation. It was better than an outright killing.

She'd wasted enough time and had to help Hunter. At this rate, he was dying. She stood tall in the woods, facing her sister. She summoned her courage. She'd stood up to plenty of bullies, but Runa would be tougher. She opened her arms and magic crackled on her fingers. "Runa."

"I wondered when you'd finally wake up." Runa shook out her hair. "You never did have the toughness I do."

"No, I don't." She wiggled her fingers. "But I don't want to be like you."

"Because you love this fool? Where did he go?" She glared at Annika. "Had your minions take him? He's almost dead anyway, so stop wasting your time."

"I won't waste anything because he's fine. He sleeps." She shook her head. "But you want him dead because he's my mate and we found each other."

"Aleks?"

"No." Not a chance.

"Aleksandr has been long dead," Runa replied. "Bet you didn't know that." She brandished a dagger.

"I don't care." But that made sense. He must've been brought back from the dead to make them believe he was alive.

"I raised him to get you to come out and it worked. The fucking elf and that bastard Aleksandr are figments of my imagination. They did their job, though. Viv always was his shadow. But she and Aleks got you to come out and told me right where you were."

That made so much more sense and explained why she'd seen Viv. She'd been trying to save Hunter, too. She might have been a figment, but that spirit wasn't entirely gone. A bit of her goodness had shined through. "Aleks was a lie. Figures."

"Yes." Runa grinned. "And you fell for it."

"I did, but he gave me strength, so I guess it didn't help you much. He let me move on." She nodded to Piper. Whenever she was ready, she could strike. "He showed me I could move on with my life and embrace what I have now. Didn't expect that, did you?"

"Lies. I gave him life, but he has no heart. None."

"I know he has no heart," Annika said. "You didn't have to tell me. You may have destroyed his body, but you can't destroy his spirit. That's what saved me."

"You're making me sick," Runa said. "He's dead, and so is Hunter. I've absorbed his spirit."

"Fine." She knew better. "I'm tired of the lies. You punish because you're upset. Don't take it out on me." She remembered the man who'd pissed Runa off and the reason he'd done it.

Runa glared at her. "You know nothing."

"Don't I? You want everyone to love you and when they don't, you kill them. It's shitty because not every man will love you. It's normal." She knew that quite well. If her sister simply faced her past, she'd be fine or at least on the road to healing.

"He loves your tail?"

"He does." No question.

"Your true form?"

"Yes." She knew for certain.

"Even the darkness?"

"I don't have the same darkness you do. I'm your

opposite. I don't have hate and vengeance in me. You thrive on those." She held her head high. "What are you going to do? Huh? Thrive on the anger? Let it drive you? One day it will destroy you and that's silly."

"No," Runa growled. "You lie."

Piper appeared. She opened her hands and shot sparks from her fingers. "You have two choices, Runa. I can destroy you myself right now, or you can sleep and think about your past."

"Fuck you," Runa spat. "Never."

She knew her sister would say that. "You have a chance to fix things with Baldur. What would you say to him if you could see him again?"

"To fuck off," Runa snarled at Annika. "He turned me away because I wasn't right."

Annika remembered quite well. Every other man who'd ventured across Runa's path were pale comparisons to Baldur. No one had had the same impact. Baldur offered Runa love and marriage until he saw her dark, vengeful form. He hadn't been able to stomach seeing the monster. Annika swore there was more to the story than Runa claimed, but she'd never been able to talk to Baldur to find out.

"Ah. That hit the mark. She misses him," Piper said. "Then that's it. You and Baldur get to be together for eternity. Got any last words before you're sent away?"

"You go to hell," Runa thundered. "I refuse."

"You've terrorized this town for too long and have half of my people in fear. But that doesn't mean you have power. The ones you believe to control the most don't believe in you."

"Prove it," Runa challenged. "My sister fears me. Hunter is dead and I win."

"I'm not scared," Annika said. "I haven't been scared of you for quite a while. I'm not living in fear or as a prisoner in my home because I'm worried you'll kill me. You won't -- because if you do, a piece of you will die."

"You'll let me die?" Runa screamed. "You can't kill your twin."

"Who says you're dying?" Piper asked. "I'm not killing you. I don't kill."

"Then I refuse. I'm not letting you destroy me. You can kill me before I give in to you." Runa whipped her arms out. "I summon the power of the underworld and all that is evil to destroy these fools who dare to argue with me. Death to the fools."

"Please." Piper snapped her fingers. In an instant, Runa dropped to the forest floor. She crumpled in a heap, unmoving.

"Gods," Annika murmured. "Whoa."

Piper flicked her fingers. A box appeared in her hand, and she opened the lid. "This is where she will exist. She isn't dead and won't die, but will be suspended in a limbo of sorts where she has to think about her past. Baldur is joining her." With that, Piper snapped the lid shut on Runa's box and affixed the clasp with a golden lock.

Annika collapsed. "I can't fathom this. It's really over?"

"It is." Piper offered her the box. "This is yours to keep. She's your twin. If I kept her at the castle or somewhere else, you'll feel incomplete."

"Because she's my twin." Annika sighed. "I never wanted to have custody of her."

"It happens." Piper plunked the box in Annika's lap. "It won't open unless you break the lock. It's not easy to break, either. You have to truly want it broken, so it won't open by accident."

"No tripping and it's on the floor, then it's open?"

"Nope. It's not that easy."

She stared at the box. A million thoughts ran through her mind. "Will Hunter make it?"

"Yes. Viv's spirit guided him away from the fight. He's at the tree house, where he is healing. It'll take a few days this time. Maybe even a week. She really tore him up."

"I saw."

Piper stared at her. "You have more questions. Ask."

She might as well. "Why did you help me save him? Why are you being kind to me?"

"You could've done things the way she did." Piper nodded to the box in Annika's hands. "You do have a kind heart, and you care about Hunter. You deserve the chance to be with him, so you should be. I've helped you because I see your courage. I need people and beings like you in my court. I need you to protect these woods."

She didn't know what to think. "Thank you. I'm honored and don't feel worthy."

"It happens." Piper grinned. "You're a great addition to the court, and so is Hunter."

"He's not sure who he is."

"He'll figure it out -- after he heals."

Annika tapped her thumbs on the box. "How were you able to defeat Runa so easily? She's been terrible for so long. I get that you're the Princess and are all-powerful, but she's the one I thought couldn't be felled."

"Not me. *You* did it."

"I did?" She didn't understand. She shook her

head. "I didn't. I couldn't have."

"You sure could, and did," Piper said. "Annika, you didn't believe in the power of her anger. That's what did it. You quit giving her power through your fear. Once she didn't have that power, she weakened. Hunter stopped believing as well. He took a beating for you and for himself. He stood up to her and grinned. That's real power."

"That had to piss Runa off."

"It did, because she wasn't the one controlling the situation. That's what did her in -- she lost control. That's how I was able to get a foothold, too. I'm powerful, but the way she managed to outdo me was through her anger. I will never have that kind of anger or that anger-driven power. It's not who I am."

"Anger beats joy."

"No, but she stole power from those who were afraid. I don't *want* that kind of power. I'd rather have the spark of joy, laughter, and fun. They are light and exciting. Runa's spirit was heavy and clouded. She didn't win, but hopefully, some cooling off time will help give her clarity."

She shrugged. "I doubt it, but we can hope."

"We can." Piper stood and dusted herself off. "By the way, go back to the Hall. Thad and Tasia will help Hunter. Now that you can be honest, he will get his answers -- once he's healed. Don't rush it."

"I won't." She'd have a devil of a time keeping him in bed if he woke early, but she'd try to follow instructions. She kept hold of the box and stood. "He's in my home?"

"He is." Piper hesitated. "Viv came to him to help him, but she can't see him again."

"And Aleks?" He had to have the same fate.

"That was all Runa. I'm sure she did that to treat

you poorly, but the conversation you had with him was real. His body is gone and his spirit is weak, but he knew to help you. He might not have been pure of heart, but he did try to make amends. Viv was part of her vision, but she did like you and wanted to assist you. I'd like to think her spirit is always with you as a guiding friend."

The notion warmed her heart. The elves were good people. "I'm glad she is. She's a sweet elf."

"She was." Piper brushed her trousers off. "You go home. He's waiting on you, and he'll need care. Do your best."

"Thank you. I will." She debated hugging Piper but kept her arms to herself. The journey wasn't over. She still had to get Hunter back to one piece. Then, she'd have to help him and herself.

She made her way through the woods. She'd see Piper again and could hug her when the dust had completely settled. Gods, she hoped she'd be able to return to her in good spirits. Her heart was involved with Hunter.

Hopefully, he woke up still feeling love for her.

Hopefully.

Chapter Eleven

Annika placed the box in her glass cabinet and closed the door. She'd have custody of her sister while Runa paid her time for her destruction. She'd never expected to have such a heavy burden, but she appreciated Piper's decision to imprison Runa, instead of killing her.

She turned her back on the cabinet and focused on the bedroom. No sound. Was Hunter even there?

She crept across the tree house to her room. She'd spent so much time with him there and would continue to do so. She spotted the bruised form in her bed. Hunter.

She sank onto the mattress and sat beside him. "Hunter."

His face was indeed blackened and his eyes almost swollen shut. He hardly resembled himself. He seemed almost smaller somehow because of his beating. He'd managed to survive a lot. His left leg appeared to be crumpled. He was in one piece, but not by much.

"Oh, Runa," she whispered. "You didn't have to do this to him. You could've left him alone. Could've had the chance to find your own forever if you'd have just given him a try."

It wasn't like her sister was going to answer her or anyone else, not from the box. Just as well. She'd undoubtedly argue.

Annika brushed Hunter's hair off his forehead. "I can't fix you alone. I don't have that kind of magic. What I do have is the power to protect you. I will with everything I am. You're important to me."

She slipped his hand into hers. "You risked so much for me. You really would've died. But you still tried to keep her from hurting others. That's huge."

He wasn't going to reply but speaking to him like this helped. Maybe he could hear her, even if he seemed to be out cold again.

"You keep getting hurt in my woods. It's like you want to get back here. With me? I can hope, but I won't know until you tell me, *if* you do. I do love you, Hunter. I can't imagine my life without you -- even after this short time. You helped me find strength I didn't know I had. Come back to me. Give me another chance to show you how I feel."

She let go of his hand and left him in the bedroom. She made her way through the tree house, ensuring the place was locked up and the lights off. It wasn't late, but she saw no reason to keep everything on. She'd rather focus her energy on him.

She returned to the bedroom and stretched out beside him on the bed. She rested her head on Hunter's shoulder. The silence surrounded her, and she swore her heart thundered. As she listened to the quiet, she noticed his heartbeat. He wasn't entirely dead. Thank the Gods. She could rest knowing he was still alive. He just might make it.

"I'm here," she whispered. "Always protecting you. Always here." She closed her eyes and accepted sleep. She needed the rest. The day had been too much for her. She could've lost the man she loved. Still could. He had to find himself and that could lead him out of Eerie.

Didn't matter. She'd stick with him. She could do nothing less. He owned her heart and was her mate. No question.

* * *

Hunter drifted in and out of sleep. His body ached all over. He couldn't open his eyes. What he could do was discern Annika beside him. She hadn't abandoned him. Not that he'd thought she might.

He believed in love and the power of having a soulmate. He had faith that things would work out, too. First, he had to get out of this green-sludgy-sleepy feeling and explain to Annika that he'd been stunned by her confession because he'd already fallen for her and hadn't expected her to feel the same for him. Shocked that she'd known and kept it to herself. Flummoxed that he'd been lucky enough to find her. Mostly, he was thankful she'd taken a chance on him. Many women would've passed him by.

Hunter knew had to make this right. Annika deserved to be loved and cherished. To be cared for, but also championed and encouraged. He could do those things. He wanted her for as long as he had. First, though, he needed to heal -- again -- and stop getting the shit beat out of him by Runa. He hoped she was finished.

But if Annika was in bed with him, that had to mean Runa wasn't on the loose. Had to. Good. No one else should live in fear.

He shouldn't be worrying about Runa. And he wasn't. Not really. He'd been knocked around pretty hard, yet here he was, back to where this had started -- in Annika's bed. He had to admit that didn't bother him. She made him happy. Besides, if she was here, then Annika must've won out over her sister. He'd known she could do it. She'd needed the right motivation. Hopefully, he'd been able to give her some of that motivation. She'd been through so much.

Hunter's entire being ached. Every time he breathed, something hurt. One day, he'd be healed and not have to worry about being attacked again.

Hunter?

He froze. He hadn't woken up. Could've, though. But he didn't see Annika. *Anni?*

No. Piper stepped out of the shadows. *You know me.*

He did. He must be in the midst of a dream world. Better than being dead. *Princess.* Should he bow? He wasn't convinced as to how to give her the proper respect in this space.

Not going to ask me how you're here? She smiled and laced her fingers together. *No questions at all? Everyone has questions.*

I do. His voice was so weak in his mind. *I was thinking I should bow or something. I don't know what to do.*

She dipped her head once. *I appreciate the honesty. Most people who see me this way have a thousand questions, but questioning what they should do to show deference isn't one of them.*

I have a few others. He couldn't lie. *Should I ask them?*

Why not? Piper laughed. *It's natural.*

I suppose so. He needed to think first. He didn't want to ask the wrong things and waste time.

Well?

Shit. He needed to focus. *How am I here? Am I dying?*

Good questions. At least you led with them, not with something else like how could I not do whatever you think I didn't do, Piper said. *I'm the Princess and damn powerful, but not a miracle worker.*

Nor should you be. He didn't believe so. He snorted. Finally, there was something he believed in besides Annika.

So, the questions. You're here because I need to explain a few things to you. Can't do it when you're out cold and I'm at the castle. Makes it easier to speak to you here.

Understandable. Am I dying?

No.

That relieved him. He had another chance to be with Annika. *Why did I get spared?*

Easy. Your journey isn't done.

That was a little too easy. *What is it?*

I can't tell you what the future holds. Not like that.

He should've guessed. *Will I have one with Annika?*

You should, but it's up to you.

Because I'm partially human?

It's not really that bad, you know. A lot of us are and we're just fine.

He stared at her. He'd need a few minutes to digest this. There were so many characters in town, and he doubted he'd fit in. *I can stay?*

Of course. I've already invited Annika to join my court.

Holy shit. He snapped his mouth shut. He shouldn't curse in front of the Princess, but wow. *I'm honored to know her.*

Why don't you join her on the court? I'd like to invite you as well, Piper said. *We can use you.*

Oh? Why? You know who I am? It'd be nice if she could tell him.

I have an idea, but I can't tell you that. Only the Historian and his people can.

He bit back a growl. Another half-answer. He shook his head. *Okay.*

Piper smiled and crooked her brow. *You haven't asked the biggest question.*

What's that? He already had too much to consider. So much to understand.

How is Annika with you, and did she win? Piper

asked. *You haven't posed those questions.*

I thought of them. He hadn't gotten around to considering them. *Not yet. But yes, how? Did she?*

She did, or she wouldn't be here with you. She got help in saving you. Runa did her best to use every bit of magic to confuse and annoy her. She tried hard, but Annika didn't budge. She wouldn't back down.

Annika's very strong.

She sure is, Piper said. *Runa did quite a bit of damage to you -- as you can feel throughout your body. But it was your lack of faith in her power and Anni's determination that stopped Runa.*

He paused. *Runa's dead?*

She sleeps.

Like me?

No. She's in a prison of her own making. She's locked up with the man who broke her heart. It's torture, yes, but it's a way for her to heal as well. She can't ignore him.

Ouch. But it fit. She needed to learn a lesson.

It's not kind, but it's what needed to be done. That's how Annika's here with you. She stood up to her bully. Piper folded her arms. *As I said, you're here because your journey isn't done. I need you to find out who you are and to join my court. There will be others who will come to Eerie and will need guidance. That's where you come in.*

Will Anni be stuck in the woods, protecting the helpless, hapless men? He didn't want to share her. He craved time alone with her and wanted the next thousand years to learn everything about her.

Why would she? Piper asked. *Runa cannot hurt them.*

There aren't other Huldra out here?

Not yet. Others may join us, but not right now.

Oh. Good to know. *Why didn't she tell me who I am? Why didn't she tell me I'm her mate? It would've saved time.*

What time?

The hours I didn't kncw and could've been using them to romance her instead. I could've delighted in her.

You didn't do that in the meantime?

I did. She's... I can't put it into words how I feel about her.

Then it isn't wasted time.

He groaned, trying to hide his frustration. *It's like you only speak in riddles.*

You're not listening.

Enlighten me.

Her smile faded to annoyance. *You didn't need the connection blatantly told to you. You needed it to be revealed. Needed to come to the conclusion yourself on your own. That's what your heart already knew.*

He pressed his lips together to stay quiet because she was right. The answer had to be revealed like a flower opening, each petal a new piece of information slowly being given the light of day and a way to a delicate inner truth.

Now do you understand? I made her keep quiet because it was the right thing to do. You can still reject her.

I won't.

Not even if another woman catches your fancy and happens across your path, but she doesn't have a tail?

I've seen it and it doesn't change my mind.

Even if she somehow develops a true image that's more like that of her twin?

I won't back down. I've chosen her.

She nodded. *Okay.*

Have you spared me? He wasn't sure where the onslaught of questions had come from, but he wouldn't stop.

Some magic is bigger than mine, yes. I'm currently

using a spell to heal you as quickly as I can, but also as quickly as it's safe to do. You will heal, will have time with Annika, time to find your past. It's here and waiting for you.

Will the journey suck?

More than being assaulted twice in less than a week's time? Piper asked. *My gods.*

I'm scared, he confessed. *What if I find out something that makes me upset or forces me away from Annika?*

Then you have to figure out how to stay with her, if that's what you really want. Piper snapped her fingers. *I won't say this will be easy. You can be a tough customer, but the biggest trial isn't over. Runa wasn't the hard part. Show us all you can handle the difficult parts, and have the future you deserve.*

With Anni? That's what he wanted.

That's up to you. I need to go. I'm being requested at the castle, Piper said. *When you wake, be kind to her and yourself. She's scared, too.*

I will. He watched her vanish into the darkness. The dream enveloped him again.

He didn't have every answer, but he had some and a bit of a map as to where to go next. He could figure this out. Could make sense of it and survive.

If he'd managed to make it through the bout with Runa, he had the strength to face this hurdle, too.

Annika was the ultimate reward and more than he ever deserved. He refused to give up. He'd keep going until he had a chance at a forever with her. She was the one he couldn't live without. Ever.

Chapter Twelve

Annika left the bed long enough to eat. Hunger wasn't on her mind, but sustenance was needed if she wanted to be there when he woke.

She nibbled on two pieces of bread, then drank a glass of water before making her way past the box holding her sister.

"You and I could've been friends. Could've been the best of friends and sharing so much. Maybe one day you'll see me as your sister and not as a problem."

She wasn't sure why she was speaking to her sister. Did Runa hear her? Did she even care?

Probably not, but Annika needed to unburden herself. Someone needed to listen to her. Not believe what she said, critique it or give her advice, but simply listen.

"She never will."

Annika froze. She had to be imagining his voice. Hunter was in bed and on the verge of death. He couldn't be with her right now. This had to be a figment of her imagination. Or one of Runa's machinations. "Don't tease me like this," she murmured. "You can't hurt me with visions, sister. I won't fall for them."

"I know you won't, but I'm real. I'm here," Hunter said. "Look at me."

She couldn't. If she looked at him, she'd have to see the truth that Hunter was a vision. "I won't."

"You will." Hunter stepped into her path and blocked her way. "See me?"

She met his gaze. He sure looked real. Looked as if he wasn't a figment of her imagination, but flesh and blood. She reached for him but recoiled. "Don't toy with me."

"I'm not." He gently encircled her wrist with his fingers and brought her hand to his face. "See? Flesh and bone. Not perfect or even unblemished, but I'm very much here with you, where I want to be. Where I belong."

She caressed his cheek. She hadn't been able to touch Aleksandr, but he'd seemed real. She'd gone through so much since Hunter had joined her universe, but she still couldn't believe he was there.

"Annika." He eased closer to her. "I know you're scared. You want this so much, but you're worried it'll all shatter. It won't, I promise."

Somewhere in her brain, she knew and trusted him. She did feel his warmth, his light and goodness. "Hunter?" she managed. "You're alive?" Seeing him was so much different than seeing Aleksandr. Her heart fluttered and her skin tingled. She longed to throw herself into his arms. It almost felt like she hadn't seen him in years, but he'd returned. She didn't want to let him go.

"I'm alive," he said. "Not going anywhere."

"No?" Tears sprang into her eyes. She swallowed past the lump in her throat. "No?" she repeated, not quite believing.

"No, my love." He enfolded her in his arms. "I'm battered and bruised from the last few days, but only my body. My soul is renewed. My heart beats again. I'm where I belong."

"You are?" she asked, her voice wavering. Her hands trembled. "Hunter."

"You sacrificed so much for me. You fought for me without giving up. No one has ever done that. No one ever saw my worth the way you did. You showed me I'm worthy." He grinned. "That's how I knew what you felt for me was true. We are meant to be together.

We're mates." He curled his fingers under her chin.

She stared at his eyes, memorizing the fall of his lashes, the line of his brow, the crinkles at the corners. These were the details of the man she loved. The man she knew was her mate. He claimed to be her mate, and she knew she was his.

She refused to believe this was a lie. They had a shared truth. "Hunter."

"I know. It's hard to fathom, but I'm here and I'm not going anywhere," Hunter said. "I didn't deserve to need to come back -- well, more like I didn't deserve to die in the first place."

"Yeah." She touched his face, then his hair. He was indeed real. "I knew you weren't truly dead, but I'm not wrapping my head around you being here."

"I understand. I can barely believe it, as well." He cupped her jaw in both hands. "I'm proud of you."

"For what?"

"Containing your sister, finding your strength, and being the best version of you. I knew you could do it. I knew you'd figure it out."

"I gave up trying to hide from my sister." Her hands shook. "I need to sit."

"Sure." He let go and guided her to the bed, where he sat beside her, keeping her close. "Still shocked?"

"Yes." She swore her knees would give out. "It's all too much."

"What is?" He focused on her, like she was the only one in the world, which made her feel special.

"I can't sort out how we're here. We should've been dead by now. We shouldn't have survived my sister."

"You're immortal."

"You're not."

"Not that I know of, but we've got time to find out. That's the best thing. Piper gave me a chance to find myself, and I'm not only taking it, but I'm taking it with you beside me."

Now she understood why her heart still hurt, despite the fact he was there with her. He still could leave her. He hadn't been granted immortality. Right now Hunter believed her to be his, but if he found out he was something special, he'd dump her.

She needed to trust him, despite her better judgment. Why not? He was different.

She'd been hurt before and could be again.

Annika balled her hands. Time to stop being so wishy-washy. If she wanted him, then she had to have some faith. Sure, he could leave her, but at least she'd have wonderful memories of their time together. Besides, why should she immediately jump to the conclusion that he'd go? He might stay.

"Anni?" He tipped her gaze. "I know you're scared and worried. I would be, too, but I'm not leaving. I found a beautiful, sweet, vibrant woman who kicks some serious ass." He smiled.

A twinge of fear remained. She doubted she'd ever truly lose it, but she didn't want to bog herself down with that fear any longer.

"You're still scared?"

"Yes."

"Give me time."

"I will." Without a doubt. "It's the wildcard of you being human that has me bothered."

"Part."

"Part human." She had to concede that.

"We have a job to do."

"Oh?" She had no idea. "What job?"

"We're on the royal court."

"You, too?"

"You missed me saying that, didn't you?"

"I did." She hadn't believed him.

"We are, but more than that, we need to find out who I am. Not just me on this journey. I need you with me. You're the catalyst."

She winced, not wanting to be put on such a pedestal.

"Okay, I wouldn't have gone to the Hall without you. I'd be dead."

"You outwitted my sister."

"Maybe, but I came to Eerie to end my life. At least, I wanted to get lost and never be found." He squeezed her hand. "Then the most beautiful woman in the world with the quirkiest, yet most adorable tail showed up. She captivated me, tearing my attention from the worst day of my life as well as the monster trying to help me end my life. You came to me, saved my ass, and proved there is goodness and beauty in this world. That's why I need you."

"You'd be fine without me."

He nodded. "You're trying to push me away to protect yourself, but you don't need to. I'm one of these peculiar guys because I'm loyal. You'll have to dump me if you want to get rid of me."

She shook her head once and needed a second. "But you left Sally."

"I did."

"You could leave me."

"I could, but I won't. I'll keep showing up, so you'll know how I feel."

"Okay." She should balk again but didn't. "When do you want to find out who you are?"

"How about after I delight in you first?" He kissed her.

As his lips touched hers, a shiver ran the length of her spine. She curled into him. The entire situation was so impossible, but she'd fought him so much and wasted so much time.

No more.

She crawled onto his lap and broke the kiss. "Wait."

"Now what?" His eyes sparkled with mischief, not anger. "What's wrong?"

"How are you able to be this active? You were just beaten all to pieces."

His grin widened. "Piper healed me. I'm good as new."

"You look like you're not well. You're still bruised and there are cuts." She touched what should've been a tender spot on his temple. "This doesn't hurt?"

"It does. Like a dull ache, but I'll live."

"No. I'm not pushing you." She couldn't. "You need to rest and heal on your own some first."

"So you don't subscribe to the theory that sex makes everything better?" He winked.

"No, I don't. You need proper healing time," she said. "But yes, I want to make love to you. I want to do that in a sweet manner, not against a wall in a place where we could get caught."

He tipped his head and nodded. "True." He shrugged. "You've got to admit, it was hot and definitely a story for our legend."

She rolled her eyes, despite loving that he'd called them "our." "You should move around more. How about a walk?"

"I'd love it." He held up one hand. "Oh, and I have a surprise."

"You do?" He was full of them.

"Because we're on the court and my stuff was trashed -- I guess the foragers in the forest got a hold of it."

She nodded. "Scavengers, I guess. If it's left behind, they'll take it."

"They did, so Piper had my stuff replaced. I've got my own clothes, all sent here." He grinned. "And she sent stuff for you."

"Me?" She couldn't remember the last time she'd gone shopping for new clothes. "Even with my tail?"

"Yes. Accounting for your tail." He kissed her again. "Why don't we get dressed, go to the Hall to start my search, then have an actual date? Not in a six-hour rush, but a real date?"

"I'd love it."

"If I show you I'm well enough, can we seal this mating in the proper way?" He patted her ass. "I'm dying to make love to you again."

"The feeling is mutual." She squeezed his shoulders. "Yes, let's try a real date."

"Perfect." He didn't let go.

"What?" She enjoyed being held and didn't mind the peculiar look on his face, even if she couldn't gauge his expression.

"When you squared off against her, I wanted to stay and help you," he said.

"I guessed you did."

"The elves made me leave," he added. "I never got to thank them. Can we visit Viv at the restaurant?"

"I wish we could.'

"Closed today?"

"It was never really open. Everything about that meal was Runa casting a spell. She knew I'd go there and what I liked. She knew who I'd want to see and that I'd want to see it like it used to be the last time I'd been there. She crafted a lie."

He frowned and groaned. "I liked Viv."

"She was a good elf," she said, her heart breaking. "I miss her, and that's why my sister used her. I needed closure with Aleks, so she summoned him, too. It put up the facade that the restaurant was real. I bet if we go back now, it's either gone or rundown."

"But…" He paused. "That was a lot of energy for a facade."

"I know, but she uses anything she can to get what she wants. It took a lot of effort, and snowed me. I truly believed they were there and I got closure."

"Viv helped to rescue me."

"I'm sure she did." Tears burned at the corners of her eyes. "Her spirit must've truly shone through when Runa put up the spell. She was good to me when she was alive, and she must've seen something special about you."

"I'm glad. She brought other elves to get me out of the way."

She grasped his hand, needing his strength. "I'm glad."

"Just glad?"

"No. I love you, Hunter. That's not something I say lightly." She rested her forehead on his chin. "I don't give my heart away easily."

"And I treasure it." He held her tight. "I love you, too. I'd have come back from the dead to haunt and protect you. I've never felt like this before, and I love it. I'm nuts for you."

Her spirits soared. Her worries weren't gone, but she could deal with them. She had what she'd always wanted -- to love and be loved.

"You make me happy." He rested his forehead

against her temple. "Will you take me to the Hall? The faster we go there, the faster we can come home and I can hold you."

"Yes." She sighed. Things were going her way. "Let's see how you do on the way, and if you can handle it, we'll seal the mating tonight." If he still wished to, after whatever he'd find out when he went to the Hall.

"Deal." He grinned. "You're driving a hard bargain, though. My cock isn't interested in going down any time soon."

She stared at him for a moment. "It's got a mind of its own?"

"Yes. You keep being so adorable and sexy. I can't focus." He grasped her hands. "So yeah, it's going to be embarrassing, but I'll survive."

She swore her cheeks burned. He'd be the death of her one of these days. "You will."

"Let's get dressed."

"Okay." She let go and watched him as he fumbled into a pair of jeans. He had a nice ass. She longed to swat it and feel the taut flesh under her fingers, but she refrained so he wouldn't lose his balance and get hurt.

"You're staring at me," he said, speaking over his shoulder. "Is it up to par?"

"Yeah." She swore she was drooling. "Sorry."

"Don't be. If you were getting dressed in front of me, I'd be drooling."

"Or grabbing me."

"Both." He donned the jeans, then a shirt. "I'm not complaining, but I do still hurt."

"Where?" She wanted to put him back to bed.

"No." He held up his hands. "I'm not arguing this. Just saying, I do hurt."

"I'm sure. She broke your limbs." Which was why she wondered if they should be attempting this trip.

"She did. I'm in one piece, but still. I'm not at full capacity."

"Which is why I didn't want you to overexert yourself." She dressed in seconds, happy to be wearing something that wasn't gauzy and white. She liked the dresses, but preferred some variety.

"Slacks and a blouse. Sexy." He bobbed his eyebrows, then sobered. "Are you scared?"

"Yes. What about?"

"I should ask you that. What about?"

"You'll find out you're an angel or something and decide to experience that for a while, then forget about me." She hated to admit that.

"I get it, but I said I'm showing up and I am."

"I remember."

"You're scared I'll leave or that we won't get to be together?"

"Yes." It was the truth.

"Then we keep figuring this out together," Hunter said. "We've got each other."

"We do." She should be concerned, but carrying those worries around got tiresome. Time to let go and find out where the future would lead. Past time.

Chapter Thirteen

Hunter finished dressing, and he wondered what went through her mind. He needed years to get used to her, so he could read her thoughts. The fear made sense to him. To be honest, he worried about what he'd learn at the Hall. For all he knew, he wasn't truly paranormal and he'd only gained entry into Eerie by mistake.

"Ready?" She pulled her hair back into a clip and stepped into a pair of shoes. "I'm ready."

"Yes." Even if he wasn't, he'd follow her anywhere. He donned his socks and shoes before joining her at the door.

She hesitated. "I know she's got a lock on the box, but I'm worried about going outside. I don't want to leave her alone, either. I don't trust her. Don't trust that when we go out, she won't appear. I shouldn't be afraid of the outside world."

"You've been penned up for a long time," he replied. "It makes sense. I'm with you and I'm sure that if Piper wasn't sure the magic would hold, she wouldn't have used that lock. It's okay. We'll go at your pace."

"You're the one who is healing."

He shrugged again. "We're both healing, if you want to be honest. You from your past and me from her."

"True."

"But we've got each other, and we'll be fine." He had no doubt. "Let's go. The sooner we find out, the quicker we can make more exciting plans."

She nodded. "I'm with you."

He walked with her to the door. "I'm ready." One step at a time, leading toward the changes that would happen. Was he prepared?

"I am, too." She grasped his hand and laced their fingers together. As he opened the door, she held his hand tighter and didn't let go.

He refused to ask her once again if she was scared. This was a big step, and he had her. He had to be strong for her, too.

He walked with her through the woods to the edge. "You didn't use your super speed."

"No." She bumped shoulders with him. "I'm not trying to run away from anyone."

"I suppose you're not." He kept up with her as they made their way to the Hall. When they weren't trying to run and hide, the building was much bigger and more foreboding. The stone facade and large gargoyles cast an intimidating shadow against the sky. He nearly wanted to turn around, but why? They'd come this far, and it was too late to turn around.

He opened the door, needing to take charge of this part of their journey. The darkness was a stark contrast to the bright light of the day outside.

"Are you hurting?" she asked. "Want to take a break?"

"No, sweetheart. I'm a bit overwhelmed. It's like night and day. Inside, it's quiet and dark. Outside, it's vibrant and active."

"You're right." She inched closer to him. "I bet Tasia and Thaddeus already know we're here."

"I'll bet." He didn't hear them, but he hadn't detected them the first time they'd been here. Should he say something?

"Tasia? Thaddeus?" Annika called. "We're here. Do we shout to you or to the Historian?"

Thaddeus rushed up to them. "Sorry." He tucked his shirt into his jeans and fiddled with his zipper.

"Did we interrupt you?" Hunter asked. "Looks like we did." He chuckled. There had to be something about the Hall that encouraged and elicited such sexy behaviors.

"Maybe." Thaddeus blushed. "I don't embarrass easily, but you've managed to catch me in one of those moments."

"It happens," Annika said. "We're here to find out what his story is. Do we have to ask or make a sacrifice or something? A donation?"

Thaddeus frowned. "I forgot you're of an ancient line and have a much larger set of experiences. No, you don't have to make a sacrifice. I'm not even sure where you'd do it if you did. As for a donation, it's welcome, but not expected."

"Oh." She ducked behind Hunter. "Sorry."

"Why?" Hunter asked. "I might have asked the same things if given the chance. You don't know until you ask."

"Very true," Thaddeus said. "So, you're asking."

"I am." He squeezed Annika's hand. "Can you help me?"

"I can, but Tasia knows where the scrolls are and which ones would give us the information. Hold on," Thaddeus said. "Tasia?"

"Yes?" She strode over to them with a scroll in her hand. "I wondered when you'd be back."

"We fought off a bully," Hunter said. "It took time to heal."

"Is she stopped?" Thaddeus asked. "Or not?"

"She sleeps," Annika said. "She won't hurt anyone for now, and I've got her locked up. It's fine."

"Sure." Thaddeus nodded. "As long as you know what you're doing."

"It was Piper's doing. She... contained her."

Annika shrugged. "It's fine."

Tasia eyed him but said nothing.

"She won't hurt anyone," Hunter said. "But we're not worried about her. Can you help me?"

Thaddeus nodded, as if he snapped his attention back to the present again. "Yes. Tasia, we have a request for help. Hunter would like to know his legacy. We should aid him."

She shrugged. "Fine." Tasia waved the scroll. "We have the information."

Annika frowned. "Why do you seem so reluctant to help, and why are you angry? Just say it."

"You brought a danger here and could've gotten the place destroyed and didn't seem to care. You desecrated the joint by having sex here," Tasia said. "It irks me."

Thaddeus clicked his tongue. "You need to relax. I'm supposed to be the grump, but you're doing a great job of being a brat. We were just caught in the midst of... having a good time, so stop. They didn't break too many rules that we haven't already broken."

Tasia curled her lip in a pout, then sighed. "Sure."

"You have the scroll," Thaddeus said. "Will you read it?"

His heart pounded. The scroll? Hunter leaned into Annika, trying not to collapse. Holy shit. He had the chance to find out where he'd come from... and what magic he possessed. "Wow. Thank you."

"I haven't done anything yet," Tasia said. She unrolled the document, then placed the scroll on the table. "Well, it wasn't easy to sort this out because you've been adopted and so was your mother, so I had to parse out where you landed and what happened to her. It wasn't easy, but I figured it out."

"And?" Annika asked. She clutched Hunter's arm. "Is it bad?"

"Not necessarily bad," Tasia said. "Just complicated. Are you ready?"

"I suppose I am." He had no choice. He needed to know the truth. "Please, go on."

"So…" Tasia hesitated. "We should get the Princess here."

"Why? Annika asked. "Should we be arrested?"

"No." Tasia snapped her fingers. "I didn't see this coming, and we need her here."

"On the way. She's bringing Diesel," Thaddeus replied. "Won't be long."

Hunter shook his head. Hades, this was so fucked up. He didn't want to know now. Nope, not if the Princess was involved. If she needed to be involved, then this couldn't be good. "This is ridiculous. If I'm being charged with something, then I should know so I can prepare." He was spiraling and scared.

"Who said you were being arrested?" Thaddeus asked. "You're not, because you haven't done anything wrong."

"Did my family?"

"Not directly," Tasia said. "Please."

He wasn't sure he could calm down now. Fear overwhelmed him. Someone had done something shitty, and he'd have to pay for it. Not good. Pretty fucking terrible, really. He couldn't control his family or what they'd done, but he'd certainly pay for it.

"You called me?" Piper walked into the room. Diesel followed her. Despite the darkness in the building, he wore his customary sunglasses. He said nothing as he stood beside Piper. She hooked her fingers into her front pockets on her jeans. "What's wrong?" she asked.

"Well, I think you need to hear this," Tasia said. "I've uncovered information about Hunter."

"And that means I need to be here, why?" Piper asked. "I mean, I'm glad, but you needed me?"

Hunter wondered the same thing.

Annika tucked against Hunter. She said nothing, but trembled. He wished he could reassure her, but he wasn't entirely sure himself.

"Well?" Piper asked. "I hate suspense."

"Get on with it," Thaddeus said.

"Fine." Tasia flattened the scroll. "Hunter, you've been told you're a shifter and that's not entirely wrong. You're the son of a woman who was part shifter, and a human father. Your mother was a wolf shifter, but her father was a shifter and your grandmother was a witch."

"Full?" he asked. It made little sense.

"She was," Tasia continued. "But here's where it gets sticky. They couldn't care for your mother, so her abilities never developed. They gave her to an orphanage just outside of Cleveland. No, not they. He did. Your mother was raised by humans, but told she had a gift. She knew because she'd been left a note from her father."

"Wait, you said 'he'. So she knew them? Her grandfather was the one who dropped her off?" Piper asked. "Why did they give her up?"

"Her mother had died and her father felt he couldn't handle a three-year-old." Tasia flattened the scroll again. "But I said it gets sticky. Her mother, the witch, worked for the court. She was the seer of the court and had a relationship with the King."

Hunter wobbled. "Wait. What?" His grandmother got around? Geez.

"She had a relationship with the King?" Piper asked. "Hunter could be my cousin?"

"Yes." Tasia snapped her attention to Piper. "He has no claim to the crown as he isn't legitimate, but he has a bit of royal blood. Tiny bit."

Annika whimpered. "Oh, no."

Piper stared at Hunter. "Well, who'd have guessed? Welcome to the family."

"Hi," he mumbled. He wasn't anyone who should be part of the court for real or the royal family, even if he was a distant relative. He was just a guy... right?

"I like it," Piper said. "I have no other blood family, so I'm good with it."

Nice to know.

"There's more," Tasia said. "Because he's mixed with magic and human qualities, he's not exactly a shifter or a witch."

"What am I, then?" Hunter asked. Besides a holy fucking mess.

"You're magic, simply put. You can't shift, but you have the heightened senses and notice what others might not -- now that you know, that's what that is. You also aren't a witch, but you can handle magic. That's how you were able to withstand the spell from Piper and see the visions. You can't do magic, but you're more open to spells and can detect them when used."

He had so much to understand. "So that means?"

Piper folded her arms. "It means my spell worked, but Runa could see through it because you're more open to all kinds of magic. Hers, mine, everyone's, which is not a bad thing. You'll be able to see through lies and bullshit, once you get your mental compass tuned. That'll make you doubly good for the court. You already have a place, and now that you've got that bit of royal blood, you're doubly good. Go you."

"Wait." He needed a breath and time to think. This was all too much. "Wait. I have royal blood? You're sure?"

"You do," Tasia said. "I was trying to soften the blow. Your grandfather didn't know about the indiscretions, but he had an inkling. I'm sure that's what made it harder for him to care for your mother."

His head hurt. His grandmother had dabbled with a man she had no business being with, his grandfather didn't know, and to hide what was done, his grandfather had given the child up... his mother. He doubted his grandmother and grandfather were even in love. Sad. He paused. "Wait. You said my grandmother died. How?"

Tasia bowed her head. "She... took her own life."

"Fuck," Annika whispered.

His knees buckled. "I need to sit down. I can't process all of this. My brain aches." He'd never met these people, but his heart went out to them. How could beings have such cruelty toward each other?

"I'm sure you've got a whopper of a headache." Piper pushed a chair over to him. "I'll get you something."

"No." He simply needed a moment. "I'm not sure I can handle much more information."

"How... witches can't..." Annika shook her head. "I mean... I thought they were immortal."

"Not all witches are," Piper said. "There are major and minor witches. Sounds like she was a minor one, which isn't bad, but they aren't as powerful."

"How'd she do it? My grandfather must've loved her, right?" Hunter asked.

"That's one more sticky part. It was a marriage of convenience. He wanted a wife, and she agreed. I'm not sure how they felt about each other. I can guess your grandmother had some feelings for the King and some for her husband, or she wouldn't have done what she did at the end."

Annika sighed. "She loved the King and he wasn't available, so she married a man who was available, even if there wasn't any love, so she wouldn't be alone."

"Pretty much." Tasia closed the scrolls. "I can tell you more if you want, but you seem overwhelmed. Suffice it to say, you are immortal and have magic, but you can't cast spells. Your talent is seeing through lies. You're not versed in it yet, but you will be."

"I see." Hunter stared at Annika. "What does that mean for us?"

"You're immortal and found a place on the court," Annika said, her words hardly above a whisper. "You've found where you belong, and it sounds like you've sorted out who you are. You're important." Sadness filled her eyes, and she smiled -- feebly, but she did.

"We've let you know, and have other work to do," Tasia said. She nudged Thaddeus and the two of them left.

"Welcome to the family and court. Get yourselves sorted out," Piper said. "We expect you *both* at the castle this weekend." She winked, then opened a portal and exited with Diesel hot on her heels.

When the portal closed, Hunter exhaled. He and Annika were alone, finally. Good. He needed to speak to her. He refused to let her go -- court and royal blood be damned. "Annika."

"So, you're important." She inched away from

him. "You'll have a title."

"Don't want it." Didn't need it.

"You've got your story."

"I do, but it doesn't change ours."

"It does."

"No." He wasn't going to allow it.

"You'll want someone more befitting of you."

"Nah. I found the one who fits me just fine."

She picked at the hem of her shirt. "You're human."

"I am."

"You can leave."

"I could."

"When will you head to the castle? I'm sure you could live there."

"I won't." She could try like hell to get rid of him, but it wasn't going to work. He didn't give up that easily.

"Why not?"

"I haven't been invited to live there, and I don't want to. It's too stuffy for me." He knew where he wanted to be. "I'm more of an open air, living among the trees kind of guy."

"Hunter."

"I'm a simple man and I don't need a castle or anything else. I don't need money or a title. I need the love of a woman who understands me. One who has saved my ass and seems to like me. I love her and can't see being with anyone else. Can't imagine it."

"But what you learned --"

"I learned that I come from a complicated past, but it doesn't have to complicate my future. I know my heart and it belongs to you."

Annika froze. "Even after all that you've learned, you still want me?" She wrapped her tail around her waist. "All of it?"

"Yes." He toyed with the fuzzy end of her tail. "I love all of you and treasure the fact that we have eternity to fall more in love with each other. I'm nuts for you."

"You're silly from the injuries and the blood loss," she said. "You should be resting."

"Don't stall. I can tell that's what you're doing." He tugged her onto his lap. "I picked you because the magic knew we were supposed to be together. I fell for you before I knew about the mating thing, and while I was pissed you didn't tell me, it felt right when you did. The pieces clicked into place. I want you. I love you. I can't do this without you."

She threaded her arms around his neck. "I swore I'd never give love another chance, but here I go again, getting caught up with someone."

"Just someone?" he asked. "You'd call me just someone?"

"With my mate." She finally smiled and the expression lit in her eyes. "I'm sorry I've been difficult."

"You've had to be protected. It's fine." He kissed the tip of her nose. "I love you and I want you to take me home. Can't say I'm much good right now, because you were right. I've overdone it, but that doesn't mean we can't cuddle."

"Means we should hole up in the tree house while you recuperate." She rested her forehead on his. "I love you, too, Hunter."

"Then that's all I need to know." He'd been taken by and taken with the Huldra. What a way to go and what a life to have. He'd found his heart.

Hell-fucking-yeah.

Chapter Fourteen

Annika couldn't believe her luck. Not that she'd landed royalty; that didn't matter. Not the admittance to the court because that meant little. But having a second chance at forever with Hunter -- now *that* was the prize. She'd been on her own for so long.

No sister to spoil her chances now. Just time with Hunter.

Her mate.

It sounded so strange yet right. Her mate. The one being her soul had been searching for was there beside her. The impossible had become possible.

"What are you thinking?" Hunter walked with her through town. "Something good?"

"Yes, and no." She paused at the crossroads. "We should've taken a taxi home. This walk has to be hard on you. After the day you've had, it can't be easy."

"It's not."

Then she'd find a taxi.

"Do the ride shares go all the way to the tree house?" he asked. "Seems a bit dense to get that far."

"True." No real roads ran by her house. But that was part of the point of hiding in plain sight.

"We can walk. It's good exercise," he said. "I like the feel of the sunshine on my face."

"Yeah?" It was comfortably warm.

"I love having my girl beside me."

"It pleases you?"

"Very much so," he said. "I want everyone to know I found the most exciting, beautiful girl and she even likes me back."

"Loves," she corrected.

"Yes, loves. Like I love her."

"Guilty as charged." She held onto his fingers.

"Are you ever going back to your old life? I could get you a car to take you."

"Can you come with me?"

"Leave Eerie?" She'd done it long ago but hadn't considered doing it since. "I could."

"Do you want to?"

"If I go with you, I might." The idea scared her, but she'd give it a try.

"Not today or anytime soon. My old life doesn't want or miss me."

"No? Not even your adoptive parents?" Surely, they did.

"Dead."

"They're dead?" she asked, not sure she'd heard him right. "I'm sorry."

"Cancer."

She wanted to ask what had happened, but it wasn't her business.

"It was better that way. They smoked like chimneys and chewed tobacco. It wasn't good, but it made them happy. I can't imagine that much nicotine in my body, but oh well."

"So they're gone?"

"Yeah. I was rudderless through college. I couldn't decide what I wanted to do or get out of my own way."

"What's college like? I've never been." She'd wondered about it every so often.

He shrugged. "Expensive, exciting, but difficult. It's like being in a big group of people who don't care about you, trying to find what makes sense and spending too much money."

"Sounds so fun."

"It could be a good time. I learned a lot about sales and merchandising, which I used at my job."

"What did you do?"

"I sold clothes. I worked at a high-end clothing store and created window displays," he said, and stopped at a bench. "Mind if we sit?"

"Sure." She settled beside him. "I could use a rest."

"Me, too." He sighed and crossed his ankles. "I sold clothes to wealthy people and caught hell when what they chose didn't look right or didn't fit properly -- which usually meant it didn't fit the way they wanted. I had a good eye for what would fit and what would look right on their particular body shape, but some didn't listen to me. I should've told them otherwise, but I wanted to keep my job. Then Sally happened and I spent too many days getting berated for things out of my hands. That's why I quit."

"It happens." She'd never quit anything like that, but she understood giving up. "You have to do what makes you happy."

"Agreed, but I gave up on me and everything else. I quit what I did because someone treated me terribly. So silly. I gave Sally so much weight in my life and ignored my own desires."

She could understand that. She'd made a lot of wrong turns in her life. One day, she'd forgive Runa. One day, she might forgive herself, too. "Did you like your job?" She knew a couple of people who detested theirs.

"I did. I liked helping someone find just the right garment for their event. Making them look good made me happy."

"You seem to shine when you talk about it." A true glow.

"I did love it. Then Sally kept coming in. On top of the cranky customers, she'd show up and expect free stuff. I should've known she'd do me wrong."

"You thought you'd found love. It's understandable."

"Maybe." He slid his arm around her. "I knew I liked clothes and dressing people, but I didn't know why. I guess it was the artistic side of me."

"Possible." She leaned into him. "We have a theatre troupe here in Eerie. Maybe you can use your talents there."

"I'd like that." He smiled and rubbed her shoulder. "I'd like to be useful again."

"You are." He was -- to her.

A man rushed up to them. She noticed his short stature and dress suit. Norm Slone, the divorce attorney gnome. "Norm?" She'd known him since she'd arrived in Eerie. "You're flushed. Are you okay?"

"I'm fine." Norm bent over and puffed. "I remember why I stopped running. It sucks."

If he was nothing else, Norm was blunt. "What do you need? Besides exercise and a diet? I'm not trying to get a divorce." She'd have to be married first.

"I need him." Norm pointed to Hunter. "You're a challenge to find."

"I am?" Hunter shock his head. "I'm beat up and haven't gone too far."

"Maybe not, but I do have cases," Norm said. "Anyway, I have something for you."

"You do? I'm not sure I understand," Hunter asked. "What?"

"Your phone."

"What about it?" Hunter asked.

"The scavengers didn't want it since they couldn't use it. I guess they could only answer it." Norm shrugged. "Score one for security working. Anyway, I guess they had a conversation with someone."

She snorted and rolled her eyes. The fact the scavengers hadn't destroyed the device to steal the parts amazed her. She wondered who'd called him -- not that it was hers to know.

"Who called me?" Hunter accepted the device and tapped in his code. The screen lit up with a photo of a blonde woman.

Her heart ached. Yes, they were meant to be together, but that didn't mean they were completely solid or that she didn't have a twinge of jealousy. The woman was gorgeous.

"Annika? Smile." Hunter held up the phone. "Please?"

She did as he asked and watched him. He held the phone up a moment, then fiddled with the screen. "Much better."

She didn't dare look. She hated her appearance in photos. No matter how hard she tried, she always managed to make an odd face.

"So the caller... I should've guessed." Hunter shook his head. "Always. Would've been nice if she'd have deviated."

"Huh?" Annika didn't want to ask questions, but it'd tumbled out. "Sorry."

"Don't be. It's sad." Hunter tapped the phone.

"Hello? Hunter? Where are you? You always get sad and need an hour, then you come around. I need you," the caller said. "Jesus, Hunter. You're being pouty and cruel. You know I need access to your accounts. You owe me."

He put the phone on his lap. "See? Same thing every time. She wants to sound sweet, then gets cranky when I don't cooperate. This message is mean, and in the next one she'll be sweet-ish. She'll call me names."

"Why? She's upset, but there's no need to be like that," Annika said. "Always?"

"Always. To her, it's being blunt and telling me how it is," Hunter replied. "Is it cool? No."

"It's terrible," Norm said. "Sounds like the start of so many of the divorce cases I handle. People can't treat each other with dignity."

"No, they can't." Hunter darkened the phone. "I need a couple of the contacts, but otherwise, I'll get another one. This one is bad mojo."

"But…" She swore she should talk him out of it. He needed the device, right?

"No, I don't want it." Hunter flipped the phone in his hands. "Not worth it."

"You don't want to contact Sally to tell her you're okay?" It was foolish. Why was she pushing him toward his ex? Because she worried still. That human side and his connection to Sally had her fearful.

"I could." Hunter fiddled with the phone. "Would you stick around? I want another witness."

"Me?" Norm asked.

"Yes." Hunter snorted. "I'm sorry. I never got your name."

Her ears burned. She should've introduced them. "I'm sorry. This is Norm Slone, divorce attorney gnome. He's quite famous around here. If you want a divorce, then you go to him. Norm Slone, this is Hunter."

"Hunter Hallahan," Hunter said. "Although, I suppose that might not be my name any longer." He shrugged and stuck out his hand.

"Nice to meet you," Norm said. "I knew you were the one who bested Runa and that's good enough for me."

"Annika helped. I never could've done it without

her." Hunter grinned and patted her thigh. "She's my rock and my saving grace."

He was too kind.

"Annika's a good scout. I'd want her on my side in a fight," Norm said. "I'd argue against calling your ex-girlfriend, but that's me. Cut her loose and run."

Hunter kept his hand on Annika's thigh. He patted her as he stared at Norm. "I'll do it because I need the closure. I need to hear her and know I tried to tell her I'm no longer interested."

Norm sat on the opposite side of him. "Suit yourself. I'll listen if you need another witness."

"Thank you." Hunter swiped the phone to the numbers. Within seconds, he'd dialed Sally's number.

Annika wanted to stop him but didn't. If he had to do this, then she'd stick by him. She didn't agree with his choice, but she'd been given a chance for closure with Aleksandr. Maybe that's what Hunter needed -- to close the book so he could move forward. She didn't have to like it, but she refused to deny him.

Hunter tapped the call button. "Here goes nothing."

She held her breath as she waited for Sally to answer. Time seemed to move at half-speed. Her hands trembled.

After three rings, the call connected. "Hello? Hunter?"

"Hi, Sally," Hunter said. "How are you?"

"I'm fine, but I thought you'd fallen off the face of the planet. Where are you?" she asked. "I needed you and you haven't been around."

"I haven't." He met Annika's gaze. He squeezed her fingers and smiled.

She should feel reassurance, but her stomach clenched. She didn't trust Sally.

"Well? What do you have to say for yourself?" Sally asked. "Did you hear me? I said I needed you and you let me down."

"I heard you. How could I have let you down?" he asked, his voice even.

Norm shook his head. He remained seated, but didn't appear thrilled.

Annika wasn't terribly happy. Something felt off about the situation and how Sally kept pushing.

"You let me down because you disappeared. You didn't tell me where you were or how long you'd be gone. You changed the locks on the apartment, and I couldn't get in to use the safe."

"What would you need with it?" Hunter asked. "It's empty."

"It isn't. You left me money."

"Nope. I took it with me."

Annika pressed her lips together to keep from speaking. Gods, the woman wanted a lot.

"What? You took it? That belonged to me," Sally snapped. "You made the money, but you promised you'd take care of me. If you died, then that money became mine."

"I haven't planned on dying," Hunter replied.

What a sweet woman. She wanted him to die -- a lot like Runa. No wonder he'd run away from her.

"Well, you were gone and I thought you had. You've always been so flighty. You're always running from something," Sally said.

"I had a good reason," Hunter replied. "I wasn't happy. I had --"

"Oh, stop," Sally interrupted. "You love me."

"I do?" Hunter asked.

Norm grunted and shook his head.

She had to agree. Sally wasn't a kind person.

"You do. We were close once and you said what you had was mine," Sally said. "I thought you'd be honest with me."

"I was." This time, Hunter grunted. "I didn't tell you I loved you. I believe I said I'd give everything to keep you, but it didn't matter. You insisted on cheating on me. You weren't even repentant when I caught you."

Ouch. He should've run so fast from her. He deserved better.

"You used me," Hunter said. "And you expect a lot from me."

"Of course, I do," Sally said. "What else should I want?"

"Did you ever love me?" Hunter asked.

The sadness in his voice broke something in Annika. She hated to see him upset and even more hated that she knew why.

"I did," Sally replied. "But you never loved me. You should've loved me. If you'd have loved me as much as I did you, then you wouldn't have made me cheat on you. It's your fault I slept around."

Annika nearly swallowed her tongue. His fault? Not at all. She'd cheated, not Hunter. What a crock of shit to blame him.

"You don't need to try to gaslight me," Hunter said, his voice even again. "I'm not buying it. I know what I did and didn't do. I know what effect I had on you, and none of it involved cheating."

"You're blind."

"Maybe," he said. "But I figured out something. I left the apartment, ended the lease, sold my stuff, plus I had my deposit box information changed because I knew in my soul that you'd do me dirty, and you did. You only love yourself."

"I have healthy self-esteem," Sally said.

"You have a narcissistic streak," Annika muttered.

"Who said that?" Sally snapped. "I heard another woman. How dare you replace me so quickly and callously? How dare you?"

"I dare quite easily. I came to the woods here and thought my life was over. It was just starting," Hunter said. "A whole new start."

Annika balled up her free hand. All the things he'd told Sally, and her biggest worry was money. She hadn't worried if he was okay or where he really was or how she could help him. Nope. She'd worried about herself.

"You were going to kill yourself over me?" Sally asked. "Because our true and nurturing love had faded and you couldn't love me?"

"Not in the least," Hunter said. "I hated my life."

"What?" Sally asked, her tone flat.

"We never had a nurturing love. It wasn't going to sustain either one of us, and you know it," he replied. "But I realize that coming to the woods was for my spiritual rebirth. I found me again."

"Without me," Sally said, her tone dramatic.

"Yes, absolutely without you. Best decision I've ever made. We were toxic for each other and you deserve better." He held up his hand, as if to silence Annika. "I'm grateful for the time we had together, and I'm glad you moved on."

"You owe me money," Sally snapped. "At least that. You ruined my life."

"And we're done," Hunter said. He hung up the call. "I remembered five seconds in why that wasn't a good idea. She showed every inch of her ass to doubly remind me."

"She did." Annika wanted to leave. The fact that Norm had to witness it made the situation worse. Yes, she didn't like Sally, but that didn't mean she had to have bystanders. Then again, this wasn't her issue.

"So, I'll get a new phone, but Norm Slone, you're an attorney, so why don't you keep this until then? I've got bigger things to worry about, like being with my mate."

Norm's eyes lit up. "So you've chosen one?"

"And chosen to stay," Hunter said. "I know she's still not trusting that I will, but I'm home and happy. Can't beat that."

She nearly fell off the bench. No way. She'd hoped it was true and wished for it to actually happen, but now that it had? Hot dog. He was serious.

"Well, I'll lock this up until you're ready for it -- if you ever are," Norm said. "Good idea to get rid of it. You deserve better."

"You're right. I do and I've got better, too." He squeezed Annika's thigh. "I'm glad she encouraged me to come here."

"Annika?" Norm asked.

"Sally. If she hadn't been so... Sally... I'd have stayed and never would've found my heart."

Norm beamed. "I love going to court and kicking ass in a divorce hearing, but I love it so much more when I get to witness a couple I know I'll never see as clients. You're going to make it."

"Never doubted it," Hunter said.

Good thing they were sure. Until the mating ceremony happened, she'd be leery. Hunter was everything she wanted and never thought she'd find. He was the closest thing to a dream man, and he wanted her.

But until they cemented the mating, she'd be

concerned. It was silly, really. He kept telling her he loved her, but she'd been burned so many times before.

"I need to go." Norm held onto the phone. "If you need this, let me know and we'll get it sorted out."

"I'd love that," Hunter said.

"Thank you," Annika said. "Appreciate it."

"Yes, we do." Hunter waved as Norm left them alone.

"You're still scared, aren't you?" Hunter asked. He massaged her thigh. "Convinced I'm not sticking around?"

"Yes." She'd learned not to bother to lie to him. He'd see through it, even if she tried.

"Why? What have I done to make you think I'm that shady?"

She picked at her shirt hem. She hadn't realized how much she needed to stall. It was so silly, really. She didn't need to stall or anything else. "You haven't."

It wasn't a great answer, but it was the truth.

"Okay, so if I hadn't, then why don't you trust me?"

"The call." She shook her head. "I refuse to keep stalling. I'm scared still because I'm afraid to end up alone. I've been on my own for so long and I don't want to again, but I know I will. You have the power to change that, but I'm not sure you will."

He chuckled. "Aren't we a pair?"

"How so?" She didn't understand and hoped he wasn't making fun of her.

"Because we've both been damaged by life and loves. We're both not sure about so much because of our damage and it sucks because we second-guess. We question everyone around us. I let the worst in my life run it. I've let those bad actors go. Now, will you let go of yours? I'm on this journey with you all the way."

She stared at him. All she had to do was trust him, believe in their union and let go. It seemed so easy, but impossible. She slid her hand into his. If she was going to leap, then it was time. "You'll go on the journey with me?"

"Yes, I will." He nuzzled her cheek. "I'll keep showing up, just like I said I would."

She stared into his eyes. The honesty spoke to her, and she finally allowed herself to let go. "You will and I'm ready to go with you on it."

"Good." He kissed the tip of her nose. "Let's go home. I want to stay with my mate and claim her, so she can claim me, too."

"Yes." She wanted, no *needed*, that. "Claim me."

"And you claim me." He toyed with a loose lock of her hair. "Let's go home."

"Let's." She helped him to his feet. She couldn't wait to get back to the tree house. He should have more rest, but before much longer, she wanted her mate.

Chapter Fifteen

Hunter didn't care how long it took to get home. Wherever Annika was, that was home to him. He'd follow her anywhere. Kind of already had.

He allowed her to set the pace as they went back to the tree house. The more time he spent with her, the more he knew he wanted to be there. How could he not? Because his heart and soul belonged to her.

He'd thought it belonged to Sally, but had he really believed it? No. Somewhere in his gut, he knew they'd never have worked out. Sally expected and demanded too much. He'd never be able to live up to her desires.

Would he be able to live up to Annika's? He had no doubts he could.

He followed her into the tree house and sighed with relief. They were home. "Good. Where we belong."

"Yes." She let go of his hand, then locked the door.

"What?" He slid his gaze over her body. His mouth watered. He longed to kiss every inch of her and taste her everywhere. He kicked out of his shoes and unbuttoned his shirtsleeves. "I need you."

"You do?" She grinned and her eyes glinted. "Then catch me." She turned on her heel and raced to the bedroom.

He'd chase her anywhere. He hobbled into the bedroom. When he finally reached the room, he noticed her on the bed. She wore nothing but a smile. She'd even let her hair down.

"Holy shit," he muttered. He fumbled to get undressed. He tripped over his own feet trying to get out of his jeans.

She giggled and broke the tension in the room. He managed to untangle himself from his jeans, then stood tall. Blood rushed to his dick. For once, he didn't care if she saw he was excited. He had nothing to hide.

"Look at you." Her eyes glittered. "Sexy and confused."

"You're that alluring." He wrestled free from his shirt, then crawled onto the bed with her. "Hi."

"Hi." She tangled up with him. "So this is what it's like to be with you when we're both naked, you're well-ish, and we're about to have sex for real."

"Yes." He couldn't wait. He rubbed the head of his cock between her legs. As much as he wanted this to be slow and sweet, he knew better. He doubted any time with her would be slow. Just looking at her made him want to combust. He couldn't be inside her fast enough.

"You look odd." She giggled again and rubbed his arm. "Like you're thinking too hard about something."

"I am hard." He wasn't really thinking, either. He rolled to his back and tugged her onto his chest. She straddled him. A grin not only shimmered on her lips, but in her eyes.

"You didn't answer me." She situated his dick between her legs. "I won't go any further until you talk."

She had a point. "I'm not thinking -- not about anything except being with you, loving you, holding you, and having this time with you. I want everything with you. I want time, love, and forever."

"Yeah?" she whispered. "Forever?"

"Yes." Without a doubt. "Will you accept me as your mate? I can't imagine my life without you and want you to be my mate forever." He eased her onto his cock. As she slid down onto his shaft, he considered what he'd said. He hadn't known what words to say and hadn't planned any of it. The words tumbled out, but he had no regrets. None. He'd spoken them from his heart.

A single tear slid down her cheek. "Yes. I take you as my mate and accept you with my whole heart that I'm yours. I love you, Hunter."

"I love you, Annika." He pulled her fully onto his erection, wholly inside her. His world righted in a second. He was home because he had her.

He grasped her hips and began to thrust. Nothing else mattered except this moment and being with her. He marveled at every ripple and nuance of her body. He loved the way she hugged him within her. How she fit him and made him whole -- in the bedroom and out.

Her breasts jiggled and she gasped. "Hunter."

"Yes, babe. Cry out for me. Let go and enjoy this." He held on tighter. He moved faster, building into the best rhythm -- theirs. He lost himself in the thrill of being with her. He'd found his mate. Found his heart.

She met him thrust for thrust. Her cries filled the room. She clutched his shoulders and her nails bit into his skin, but he welcomed the pain. He welcomed everything she could give him. He groaned with delight.

The beginning of the orgasm rushed through his veins. Magic filled the air. The noises in the room changed. Crackles and sizzles joined their groans. When he opened his eyes, he saw sparkles.

"Are those...?" He didn't finish the question. He couldn't. Not when every cell in his body switched into high gear. The sparkles increased, blanketing them in silver and gold flecks.

Annika slid her hands over her body, rubbing her breasts, then tweaking her nipples before running her fingers through her hair.

The move pushed him right over the edge into oblivion. He tumbled headlong into orgasm. He cried out and surged into her body. His thoughts completely blanked. All he could do was ride the wave of ecstasy. He drove his cock into her, filling her with his seed.

The climax happened far too quickly, but he had the feeling that every time with her would be this quick and explosive. But now it was time for her to come.

He did his best to focus, despite his orgasm still racing through his body. He situated one hand between their bodies and rubbed her clit. Slow circles at first, then pinching a bit.

"Come for me, baby. Come for me and let go." He used her cream to slicken his finger over her sensitive skin. "Let go."

She shivered and flexed the walls of her pussy around his dick. She writhed on him. When she closed her eyes, she crumpled forward but continued to ride him. "My gods."

"Yes." He dug his fingers into her hips. He couldn't let go. Couldn't miss this moment. The sparkles increased in a fresh wave. The sensations overwhelmed him. The scent of her perfume, as well as the pine of the trees surrounding them, filled his nose. The memory of the taste of her kiss cemented in his mind. The vision of her covered in sparkles and riding him rooted in his brain. The sound of the crackles and her groans echoed around him. She was a vision. Pure, sweet love in his arms.

She'd changed him for the better. Not only that

but changed him for good.

Annika cried out and tensed before collapsing against him. Her breath tickled his chest, and her hair tickled his nose.

He held her, never wanting this moment to end. Ever.

"Mate," he said. It wasn't a question, but a declaration. He'd found her and he couldn't ever let her go.

"Mate," she replied. She rested her head on his shoulder. "I've never made glitter."

"Me, either." Just as quickly as the sparkles appeared, they vanished. He paused. "Was that part of the mating ceremony?" He wasn't sure. He'd never had a mate before, but it stood to reason there would be some fantastic magic involved. Not that he knew for sure.

"Must be." She kept her head down. "I've never had it happen, but until I met you, I didn't have a mate, either. So I guess it must be the way to know this was a true mating."

"Makes sense." He petted her hair as his cock slipped from her pussy. He didn't want to move. This moment needed to last much longer because he'd found bliss.

"So, we're mates," she said and smiled. "I can't believe it, but I love it."

"I can believe it." He knew when he looked into her eyes he'd found his forever. "We're going to have the best future trying to navigate this thing called love. We've got each other and that's more than a lot of people or beings could ask for. If I were picking someone to have for a mate, I'd choose you."

She met his gaze and grinned. "Despite my loony sister, the fact you were assaulted a bunch of times, and the long-shot odds against us, you still want to do this?"

"No question." He had no doubts. "You might have absconded with me, but you've also captured my heart. I love you, Annika."

"I love you, too," she replied. She closed her eyes and stretched out on top of him. "My mate."

He'd been taken by the Huldra and found himself in the process. Best ending ever.

Megan Slayer

Megan Slayer, aka Wendi Zwaduk, is a multi-published, award-winning author of more than one-hundred short stories and novels. She's been writing since 2008 and published since 2009. Her stories range from the contemporary and paranormal to LGBTQ and white hot themes. No matter what the length, her works are always hot, but with a lot of heart. She enjoys giving her characters a second chance at love, no matter what the form. She's been nominated at the LRC for Best Author, Best Contemporary, Best Ménage, Best BDSM and Best Anthology. Her books have made it to the bestseller lists on various e-tailer sites.

When she's not writing, Megan enjoys art, music and racing, but football is her sport of choice. She's an active member of the Friends of the Keystone-LaGrange Public library.

Megan at Changeling: changelingpress.com/megan-slayer-a-161

Changeling Press LLC

Contemporary Action Adventure, Sci-Fi, Steampunk, Dark Fantasy, Urban Fantasy, Paranormal, and BDSM Romance available in e-book, audio, and print format at ChangelingPress.com -- MC Romance, Werewolves, Vampires, Dragons, Shapeshifters and Horror -- Tales from the edge of your imagination.

Where can I get Changeling Press Books?

Changeling Press e-books are available at ChangelingPress.com, Amazon, Apple Books, Barnes & Noble, Kobo, Smashwords, and other online retailers, including Everand Subscription and Kobo Subscription Services. Print books are available at Amazon, Barnes and Noble, and by ISBN special order through your local bookstores.

ChangelingPress.com

www.ingramcontent.com/pod-product-compliance
Lightning Source LLC
Chambersburg PA
CBHW051244260626
47162CB00002B/603